GRUMPY AS HELL

Hellman Brothers #1

MARIKA RAY

Grumpy As Hell

INTRODUCTION

The town's hottest firefighter just put out the fire in my pants. Literally.

Ace Hellman. Star quarterback. Grumpy-as-hell firefighter. Chief pain in my ass.

He's beyond arrogant, inducing women to fake emergencies just to see his sexy swagger as he comes to save them. Not me though. That fire was a total accident. I swear. He and I actually have a long history of hating each other, starting with him ruining my live performance of the Nutcracker in kindergarten and ending with me being the only woman in town under forty whom he hasn't dated. I wear that title with pride.

Now that we've been roped into teaching a first aid class together, things can't get more awkward. He's determined to prove me wrong at every turn, and I'm determined to stop picturing him without his coveralls. I refuse to hide who I am, and Ace stands for everything I'm against.

He's so wrong for me the whole town knows it. So why do I feel like we start a fire every time we're together?

CHAPTER ONE

$\mathcal{A}$ddy

THERE WAS an ant about to get intimate with parts of me that didn't want to fully connect with nature.

"Let your spine melt into the ground. Becoming one with the dirt, like a tree root seeking stability and growth." I sucked in an audible breath and swiped at the offending insect that had crawled up inside my pant leg. "Deep breath in. Fill those lungs and then let it out, releasing all thoughts except for how your body feels in this exact moment."

This was the part of the outdoor class that made me feel high as a kite. How anyone could refuse to do yoga was beyond me. When I got done contorting my body, it felt like every single cell in my body hummed with pleasure. "Cellular orgasm guaranteed" was the tagline on my business cards, and I stood by it firmly.

"Now continue to focus on that breath and let everything go. Five minutes of perfect peace, my friends."

I could hear the class taking deep nasal inhales, some a bit more wheezy than others. I had a few elderly clients mixed in with the harried moms, the executives that had been told to get ahold of their stress or get ready for an early grave, and a few hardcore naturalists like myself. Yoga was for everyone.

The sun had set gently into the pine trees as we'd wound down our class. The namaste at the very end was for both my students and the universe providing another perfect day in Auburn Hill, aka Hell. I'd lived here my whole life, this forest my backyard and those pine trees my first friends.

"Thanks, Addy." Yedda clapped me on my shoulder and gave me a toothless grin. She didn't like to wear her dentures while doing yoga. They'd fallen into the dirt one too many times when she did her downward dog. "Jus' what I needed to fix my hip."

"What happened to your hip?" This was the first I was hearing about it. If she injured herself, she should have told me. I had a salve that was pure magic for fascia injuries.

"Oh, nothing serious. Just got a little too frisky with Tomás the other day." Yedda waggled her painted-on eyebrows, and I couldn't help the giggle. Nothing better than knowing sexual energy didn't deplete even when our bodies had aged to eighty.

"Well, let me know if it flares up again. I have a potion for that."

Yedda cackled. "I'm sure you do! But speaking of potions, any word on when Cornelius will be back in town?"

My heart dipped, losing that post-yoga glow. "I'm not sure. You know my parents. They go where the heart leads them."

Yedda's eyebrows drew together, forming a straight line. "Well, I'm on the last of the good stuff. I could really use a restock."

"I'll let him know," I responded dryly.

Yedda and the rest of the class wandered down the long gravel driveway to their cars. The last bit of light helped them pick their way safely across the land I rarely tended to. I preferred to let nature tend to herself as she intended. I rolled my eyes as I rolled up the mats we'd used for the harder poses. Yedda only wanted to see my father to buy more of his weed.

The man had a seemingly infinite supply. Sure, it was legal now, but back when I was growing up, it wasn't.

I stuck out like a sore thumb in Hell for many reasons, but the main one was my stoner of a father. Everyone loved him, and Chief Waldo hadn't arrested him too many times, but having the local weed dealer for a parent wasn't the easiest thing for a girl. And despite all that, I missed my parents dearly. They'd been gone for close to eight months now, not even returning home for my birthday this year.

My chest squeezed and I thanked my heart for her message by patting my sternum and stoking the fire I had burning in the ring of gray rocks worn smooth by the tides. I sat down on the pine needle floor and stared at the flames, processing all that I was feeling. The moon rose high in the dark sky, pulling me from my musings. It had taken me a long time to learn to sit with my feelings instead of trying to outrun them. Daily practice was the only way for me to stay grounded.

All alone now on my property, I tilted my head back and let the moon shine its healing rays on my cheeks. A sense of gratitude washed away all the feelings of abandonment I felt earlier. With a yip and holler at the moon, I whipped off my shirt and sports bra, leaving me only in the wide-legged pants I loved for yoga. I knew most of the town would call me crazy, but I could literally feel my heart chakra receiving energy from the moon and healing all the little cracks of doubt.

I stayed just like that for what could have been an hour or only ten minutes. Time didn't seem to matter when nature was healing what ailed you. I drifted into that state of meditation that felt a bit like sleepwalking when the wind began to pick up. My skin prickled with goose bumps. Blinking away the fog I'd found myself in, I was surprised to see the flames dancing higher than they had when I'd started meditating. The rev of an engine nearby had my head whipping behind me.

The form of a man appeared in the shadows. Heat spilled across my skin as my awareness grew. The man stepped forward, and I jumped to my feet. The moon cast a beam of light across his features.

Ace Hellman.

Local firefighter hero.

My nemesis.

I gasped, the heat turning to an inferno. Ace's dark gaze darted down my body and then he was a blur of motion. He charged forward, his shoulder clipping me in the stomach as he barreled into me. The next thing I knew, my back lay on the cold ground as Ace repeatedly hit my legs, a man out of control. I blinked again, my mouth open to scold him within an inch of his life, only to stop short when I saw the flames from the fire dancing along my ankles. I shrieked and Ace moved faster, whipping his T-shirt over his head and blotting out the flames.

Blessed relief flooded through my stunned veins as he put it out, and I lay back down, staring up at the moon with a prayer of thanks. I'd caught on fire, for goddess's sake.

"What. The. Fuck. Were. You. Thinking?" Ace ground out, the rumble of his voice ruining the moment of gratitude.

My head popped up and the first thing I saw was that jawline that could cut glass. And then it was the vein pulsing in his forehead. And the way his eyes snapped far hotter than the fire that had tried to ruin my pants.

And then. Dear goddess.

I saw my bare nipples.

Just out there. In the open. Rock hard and pointed to the east and west constellations.

The second my gaze fell to my naked chest, so did Ace's. The man jumped up faster than my father when Mary Jane came calling. I sat up and threw an arm over my chest, a ridiculous fix when I was blessed with breasts far too large to be covered by a forearm. Flesh drooped below and even more pressed above, but thank the stars, my nipples were hidden. I scrambled to my feet and wished for a sudden meteor to strike me down.

Normally, being naked didn't faze me. But in front of Ace? The guy who'd crushed my heart in kindergarten? The boy who'd humiliated me in front of the whole town? The grown man who shot me glares from across the street whenever our paths should cross?

Intolerable.

"Jesus, Adelia," Ace snapped, his head down and his hand shielding his eyes. Like the sight of my naked breasts might blind him for life. Most men had the opposite reaction when faced with my bare breasts, but of course Ace would find them offensive. "What the hell were you thinking?"

I swallowed hard and tried to find enough saliva to answer him. The problem was, no matter how much I might dislike— and that was my kind way of saying I experienced the emotion commonly known as *hate*—Ace Hellman, he was a fine specimen. A gift from the universe for women everywhere. His muscles bulged and jumped as he kicked dirt on the fire still inside the ring and put it out. As much as I'd disliked him over the years, I was also hyperaware of his level of attraction.

Ace with a uniform on was magnificent. Ace without a shirt on was in another category entirely.

"I—I was charging my heart chakra," I managed to say.

His head popped up and he clenched his jaw so hard I worried for his future TMJ diagnosis. The jaws of life must have worked for his concentration though because his gaze stayed firmly above my neck. "I don't know what the fuck that even means. I'll rephrase. Why did you set yourself on fire?"

It was the tone that had me focusing on something other than his beautiful bare chest. The tone that clearly stated I was stupid.

"I didn't intend to set myself on fire. An ember must have landed on my pants. If I hadn't been distracted by *someone* trespassing on my land, I would have put it out before it got out of hand."

Ace folded his arms across his chest and my stupid heart got a little excited. He lifted a dark eyebrow and other things got excited too. "Did the embers also burn your shirt?"

Ugh! This infuriating man. I marched up to him, sure to keep my forearms strategically in place lest I flash him the best breasts he ever had the privilege of seeing. "Last I checked, this is private property. I can run around buck naked if I wanted to."

"It's butt naked." Ace had the audacity to ignore my point while also starting an argument. It was a special skill of his.

"No, it's buck."

"I don't care what it is when you're burning on a no-burn day. Keep the fires out, Adelia." Ace leaned a little closer, and I could see he needed to shave.

"I didn't realize you got paid to drive around and harass citizens."

Ace released his arms and reached one hand out. I didn't flinch back, even though I wanted to. Never give your enemy an inch. Besides, I wanted to know what he'd do. I had zero doubts he'd hurt me, but I also craved to know what his hands felt like on my skin. Sure, he'd tackled me earlier, but the little situation with the fire on my legs had distracted me. I needed a do-over.

He flicked a long strand of hair behind my shoulder. "Got a call from Lucy. Said she saw smoke and was worried. It's my job to protect Hell citizens." He paused, and I could have sworn I saw something flicker through his eyes I'd never seen before. But just as quickly, it was gone, making me think it was a trick of the moonlight. "Even if they're a pain in the ass."

My nervous system slipped into overdrive, most likely from narrowly missing a fiery death, and a shiver ran up my spine. Ace smirked, not the smoldering look I'd seen him give every single female in Hell over eighteen years old, but rather a look that barely concealed what he truly thought of me. I was a speck of ash on this firefighter's timeline. I'd put a black mark on his evening. Here stood a ridiculous woman with her hands too full of her own breasts to properly argue.

He stood up tall and looked like he'd rather be anywhere but here. "You all right?" He glanced away when he said it, like it physically pained him to ask about my well-being.

And I was most certainly not all right. My chakras had been rearranged and torched by just one look from my nemesis. My discombobulation must have shown on my face because he sighed.

"Any burns on your legs?"

I looked down at said legs, dismayed to find my favorite yoga pants hanging in tatters around my shins, the ends singed beyond repair. Ace's AHFD T-shirt lay on the ground in a smoking heap. "I don't think I'm burned. I have a salve I can put on just in case."

Ace let out a noise that was one degree shy of a snort. "Call Callan if you need first aid."

And then he spun on his heel and left, his boots crunching on the gravel, the darkness swallowing his broad shoulders and tight ass bit by bit. When I heard the engine of his truck fire up, and he was well and truly gone, I let out the breath I didn't know I'd been holding. I let the girls go too and even they drooped in the absence of a fine male specimen.

Call Callan. What an egotistical asshole. I didn't need Ace or his EMT brother to help me. I could run circles around them both when it came to healing the human body. Half the town came to me for advice and herbs and tinctures and teas. The fact Ace didn't believe in me was not a surprise, but it hurt just the same.

Once upon a time, a long, long time ago, I'd actually liked him.

An owl hooted, pulling me from my thoughts. It was far too cold to stay out here half-dressed without the fire pit going. My heart might have been racing as I collected his shirt from the ground and gave it a tiny sniff, but I knew it was only from the adrenaline of the fire.

It was definitely not because of Ace Hellman.

Or his ridiculous pile of muscles.

CHAPTER TWO

ce

I WASN'T one to think with my pipe, but not even a four-alarm fire in an empty warehouse at the edge of the county line during the last few hours of my shift could take my mind off the sight of Adelia Bammingford and those gorgeous—

"Enjoy your forty-eight!" called Ronnie, one of the new hires that hadn't been on the job long enough to settle down. Everything he said came with a goddamn exclamation mark at the end of it. Plus, his made-up slang had me cringing inside.

Schooling my facial expression, I gave him a polite head nod and exited the station. As one of the senior guys on the crew, I was careful to keep us a cohesive team, which did not include ridiculing the new guy. Ronnie would come around eventually or he'd wash out on his own. They always did.

The fire station was my happy place usually, which meant I was even more annoyed with Adelia for disrupting my shift. I'd wanted to be a firefighter my whole life, ever since that day when I was seven and my seat belt got stuck and a firefighter had to cut me loose. They'd let me climb on the fire truck after and even honk the horn. I was a goner. That dream of one day being a firefighter was what had pulled me through a rocky childhood.

"'Night, Ace," called Joe, one of the guys I actually liked.

I gave him a smile and an elaborate bow at the waist. "The pots are all yours."

"Shut the fuck up," he grumbled in response, swiping his hand through the air.

I snorted and he shook his head, walking into the station. I normally cooked for the guys when I was on duty. It had taken a kitchen fire in our own firehouse before we banned Joe from the kitchen. That guy could burn boiled water.

I threw my bag in the back seat of my extended-cab truck, ready to go work out before I headed home. Maybe a tough workout could rid my memory of Adelia's breasts. Jesus. I swiped a hand over my forehead, wishing I could physically swipe that vision from my brain. I opened the door to climb in and nearly clipped myself in the face like a dumbass.

"Fuck!" I mumbled under my breath.

This is why I needed those perfect, lush breasts exorcised out of my head. They'd had dusty-rose nipples, pebbled tight like they were expecting my touch. And then Adelia had tried to cover up, but no matter what she did, she couldn't contain them. My hands had literally ached to help her, as if knowing their weight was information I had to know to keep living. How could a woman I despise have the most perfect rack of anyone I'd ever seen? Was life really that unfair?

A ping had me pulling my phone out of my back pocket before I climbed in the truck. I pulled up the text message and saw it was on the string I had going with my brothers. With five of us, there was always plenty of messages pinging back and forth. They'd been busy this afternoon while I worked a fire.

Callan: Bros. North Valley Festival is in a few weeks. Who we taking?

Daxon: Ah yeah...it's my favorite time of year. The margarita truck pulls up, the country band starts playing, and all the ladies eat out of my hand.

Ethan: Jesus, Dax. Save a few for the rest of us.

Daxon: Not my fault you friend them all and then never seal the deal.

Callan: Guys. It's a night for romance, not being sleezy.

Daxon: Speak for yourself, Mr. Nice Guy.

Callan: I'm just saying we need to call dibs ahead of time or we'll have an issue like last year.

That was the problem with a small town. Five Hellman brothers all on the prowl and only so many women. After the fight over a girl last year between Daxon and Ethan, we'd made up a new rule. You had to officially call dibs or the woman was fair game. Sounded like we were a bunch of douche-bros who didn't respect women, but this was the only way to make sure we didn't step on each other's toes. Or dicks, as it were. I swear it was for the best for all involved.

I also noticed Blaze hadn't participated in the text string. No surprise there. That dude had been ghosting us pretty much since he'd moved away. As the oldest brother, I was going to have to have a word with him soon. You don't ghost your own brothers.

Me: I agree with Callan. If you have your eye on someone, you need to call dibs before the damn concert starts. Agree?

Ethan: Hell, yeah.

Daxon: Oh please, E. You're gonna ask some girl to ride the Ferris wheel and then just hold hands.

Ethan: What's wrong with that? Some of us believe in a long romance. A slow burn. Wooing a girl. You should try it sometime.

Daxon: I believe in both the woman and me having some fun. If that includes a little D-to-V action in a dark corner, then so be it.

Callan: Dude. Did you literally say D to V?? What the actual fuck?

Daxon: I was trying to be sensitive to little Ethan.

Ethan: Fuck you.

Daxon: That's the only fucking you're getting...

I belted out a laugh and put the phone down in the

cupholder. Leave it to my stupid brothers to pull me out of my funk. I started up the truck and pulled out of the lot, headed for the park. Mayor Rip had allocated funds a few years ago to add exercise equipment around the sprawling park. I'd rather get some pull-ups and push-ups in under the fading sun than go to a gym.

I was on my second lap of the park, a healthy sweat layering my skin, when a female voice called out. Swiveling my head, but not slowing down, I saw Jenny waving to me. Her dog was trying to squat on the grass to do his business, but she was pulling him on the leash to catch up with me. I winced and took pity on the poor animal. Every creature deserved a little peace to take a crap.

"Hey, Jenny." I swiped at my forehead to keep the sweat from dripping in my eyes.

"Are you going to the festival?" she asked with an overly bright smile.

Jesus. Everyone was harping about this damn festival. I'd taken Jenny out on a date a few months back, deciding that while she was pretty and seemed very kind, there was no spark between us. Not even a tiny little flutter that could be fanned into a pinprick of heat. I hadn't tried for a goodnight kiss when I dropped her off. That was happening more and more lately. It was like the older I got, the more discerning I was becoming with the women I dated. If I didn't watch it, I'd become a permanent bachelor with a layer of dust an inch thick on my dick from no use. That would certainly give my brothers fodder for ridicule.

"Not sure, to be honest. I'll probably be working that weekend." I didn't actually know that yet, and I could get it off if I wanted. I made the schedule most of the time anyway with Captain Murray taking a lot of sick time recently.

Her face immediately drooped, but I wasn't going to lead her on. The fact I hadn't called for a second date since the first should have been the first sign I wasn't interested. Besides, I wasn't exactly known for dating a girl beyond the first date. Hadn't done that since high school, actually. I wasn't generally opposed to second dates. I just hadn't ever felt the need to ask a woman out again.

"Oh, sure. Well, that makes sense."

I looked down at her dog, who'd left a little something for her to pick up. He was now sitting in the grass and looking up at me with a look of gratitude in his brown eyes. I gave him and Jenny a head nod and went back to my workout.

When every muscle in my body was burning and exhausted, I headed for my truck. All I wanted was some heated-up leftovers and to face-plant in my bed. Unfortunately, the road to my house took me right by the road that leads to Adelia's.

Just the sight of her mailbox with "Bammingford" in small letters at the fork in the road, made me tap the brakes. A niggle of something that felt like guilt made me grip the steering wheel harder. The last ray of sun had sunk behind the ocean and left only the light of the moon. Exactly how I'd found her last night. Last night when she'd nearly burned herself to death if I hadn't stopped by when I did.

"Fucking hell," I muttered, turning the wheel left and bouncing down her potholed road. Had it been anyone else, I would have already followed up this morning to make sure the person didn't have any burns. I hadn't done that with Adelia because the idea of seeing her again so soon had messed with my head. Then the warehouse fire happened. For all I knew, she'd had burns on her legs and been in pain all day.

I could hate her all I wanted, but falling down on the job was not acceptable.

Her tiny house came into view with the addition of my head-lights. Not one light was on inside. She probably wasn't even home. I could knock on her door and then turn right back around and go home, knowing I'd done my duty. I climbed out of the truck, the cool night air giving me a bit of a chill with my sweat-soaked clothes. I looked at the pine needles lying right up next to the foundation of her house. Safety violation. I shook my head at her negligence and knocked on the door.

Who lives in five hundred square feet anyway? And who lets debris build up around the perimeter of their home? Didn't she know that was a burn hazard so close to the structure?

As I expected, she didn't answer the door. I spun right around and headed for my truck again. I stopped mid-stride when I heard a giggle. I frowned and turned back around to scan the tree line behind her house. There it was again.

I huffed and headed in that direction, resigned to seeing Adelia again. She was probably outdoors with another fire, ready to set herself ablaze with her carelessness. The pine needles on the ground softened my footfalls. An owl hooted hello from somewhere in the tall trees above me. I could have sworn I heard the creek that ran through this part of town too. I frowned into the dark, thinking this wasn't the safest place for a single woman to be living.

Hopefully this time Adelia had all her damn clothes on. My brain warred with itself, half of me wanting her to be so covered up she looked like it was mid-winter in Alaska. The other part of me very much wanted to see her tits again. Why were boobs so fascinating to men? I didn't have the answer to that, but I did find Adelia.

Fully clothed.

Sitting inside a circle of some sort with her hands on her knees, head tilted back to the moon.

All by herself in the middle of the forest.

What the fuck was wrong with this woman?

CHAPTER THREE

$\mathcal{A}$ddy

EVERY SENSE I possessed flooded with nature the way our ancestors experienced her hundreds of years ago. I was in my happy place, butt on the ground, moonlight on my face, the smell of pine trees all around me, and a twig from a neem tree clutched in my teeth. When the moon was full, I particularly felt the call to be outside. Some called it forest bathing. I just called it a Tuesday night.

Ever since my encounter with Ace, I'd been off-balance. I could feel it in the way my brain would veer from the task at hand and focus in on the way his tan skin had filled my vision after he tackled me to the ground. I'd hear a noise and wonder if he was coming to rescue me again. The shiver that swept across my limbs told me I'd welcome that invasion no matter how much I logically knew I didn't need saving.

Which was so wrong it made me angry at myself. Ace was not a good guy. And I sure as hell could not be attracted to him.

Besides, in yoga class today, Yedda told me another rumor

about me was swirling through the town. Apparently, word of a fire on my property got out and people were saying my practices weren't safe. I understood how the rumor got started and why rumors about me kept spreading. When people didn't understand something, they typically opposed it vehemently without bothering to investigate or question their ingrained narrative.

I was the weird girl who talked to the moon and meditated and walked barefoot through town. I got it. It was easier to tell people I was crazy than to ask me why I did what I did. I understood it, but I didn't like it.

I knew my practices were right for me. I felt it in my bones the way your body inherently senses danger. My methods weren't madness, no matter how contrary to modern life they seemed. I wouldn't forsake my calling to simply fit in, but I also hated knowing I was being gossiped about.

Like they always did, the trickle of the stream and the scented breeze were doing more for me than anything ever could. Sure, I could try to be more normal—whatever that meant—when I was around other people, but why? Why hide my true self when those friendships would only be based on a lie?

"You realize your fucking back door is wide open, right?"

Ace's angry voice cut through my meditation. That familiar shiver swept over me, and for a second there, I wondered if I manifested him showing up by envisioning this moment all day.

I really needed to get a better handle on my daydreams.

I quickly pulled the twig from my mouth, but I didn't bother turning around. I could handle him better if I didn't have to see his gorgeous face. Or those broad shoulders.

"You realize you're on private property, right?"

The scoff behind me had my lips tilting up. There was joy to be found in ruffling his pretty feathers.

"I just came by to make sure you weren't having any issues after the fire last night."

That got my head tilting. "Ahh, were you worried about me?"

The scoff came again, more forceful this time. I heard his boots crunch across the ground before coming to a stop to my right. I sucked in a breath to fortify myself before arching my neck and looking up at him.

Yep, just as I suspected. He was frowning, that perpetual pinch of his face that set my nerves on edge. And oh dear heavens above, he had gray sweatpants on. Why would a man do that unless he specifically wanted all the women in town to be staring at his crotch? I averted my gaze quickly. Ace's dick print was not something I needed in my memory bank. His bare chest was harmful enough.

"Why are you outside, sitting in a rock circle?" He glanced around at my crystals, scorn now mixing with the frown when I snuck a glimpse upward.

"They're crystals. Recharging in the moonlight. And it's called meditating. You should try it sometime. Might help with that constipated look you always have."

The answer was immediate. "No, fucking thank you. Too busy putting out negligent people's fires."

The aim was obvious, but I kept my breathing even and refused to let his barb hurt me. After all, I'd lobbed my own fair share of barbs. "Why are you here again?"

With a huff, Ace reached down and scooted a few of my crystals out of the way. He sat down next to me and looked out at the trees instead of at me. His knee was just inches from mine, his built thighs stretching the limits of the cotton workout pants. Of course, Ace Hellman wouldn't have forgotten leg day.

"It's standard to check in after a small fire and make sure there weren't further damages." He turned his head, his brown eyes basically daring me to look away first. "So, how are the ankles, Adelia?"

I narrowed my eyes, ignoring the heat I felt across my cheeks and neck. I could smell him from this close. Some kind of manly scent that probably emanated from his charmed pores, combined with a healthy sweat. That second part wouldn't make most women swoon, but for a girl who valued healthy sweating without the toxic deodorants, I liked his smell. Damn him and his stupid sweat glands for making my body react.

"My ankles are fine. A bit of pain last night, so I put oils on it. Just some lingering redness this morning. Another round of oils tonight and I should be all healed." I gritted my teeth and made myself say it. "Thank you for asking."

One dark eyebrow lifted, his brown eyes twinkling, but not in a fun way. In a make-fun-of-Addy way. Trust me, I'd seen that look plenty enough over the years to know what it looked like.

"Oils? Please tell me you aren't talking about essential oils."

Here we go. "Yes, I do mean essential oils. A combination of lavender and frankincense, followed by a chamomile bath."

His eyes didn't even blink, but I could have sworn they heated the second I said bath. My scalp crawled with embarrassment. I shouldn't have said bath. Now he was thinking of my breasts. The very same breasts he got a close-up view of last night.

"See?" I stuck my leg out, feeling the need to move on from the bath comment before he spent too long picturing my boobs. My bare foot landed in his lap, the slightly pink ankle there for him to peruse below my second favorite pair of wide-legged cotton pants. Unfortunately, my aim was not good in my haste and the second I hit flesh, he doubled over with a groan.

"Jesus, Adelia."

I winced, maybe from realizing I'd just dealt him a blow to the dick, or maybe it was from being incredibly regretful that it had been my foot to cop a feel. I tried to snatch my foot back, but he grabbed it, his huge hands holding my foot hostage. He took a few deep breaths and then straightened his back, all the while the feel of his hands on my foot felt like we'd created another fire.

He let go with one hand to rearrange things in his gray sweatpants. I looked away quickly, feeling all kinds of conflicting things I shouldn't be feeling. I should be high-fiving myself for literally kicking my enemy in the crotch. The stirring in my gut was not celebratory in nature. It was a bolt of nervous lust that I needed to shut down. ASAP.

Perhaps I needed to put up a fence around my property after all. I couldn't keep having these encounters with Ace and live to tell about them. Could acute embarrassment actually kill a person?

Then his finger was sliding across my ankle and I sucked in an audible breath, looking down at my foot in his lap. Nothing could have dragged my gaze away from the wonder of Ace Hellman touching me with what felt like the utmost of care. And, oh fuck me, he had nice hands. The kind of strong male hands that a woman could daydream about caressing her skin. I swallowed hard and tried to ignore the way his touch seemed to set off electrical signals throughout my body.

"Looks good." His voice was rough. Intimate even in the stillness of the night around us.

And then he was letting go of my ankle and standing so quickly I could see why he was good at his job. The man moved like a big cat, swift and purposeful.

"Doubt it was the oils though. You're lucky you didn't get burned worse."

Now it was my turn to scoff. I'd provided evidence of how well the oils had worked and he still couldn't open his mind to them. "Fine. We'll have to agree to disagree." I stood and wiped the back of my pants, sending pine needles fluttering to the ground.

Ace was back to frowning. "Fine."

I nodded, folding my arms across my chest to hide the fact that my nipples very much liked him touching my foot. There was nothing exciting about a foot caress, but tell that to my nipples. Damn traitors. "Fine."

The moonlight was playing tricks tonight, making it seem like his gaze fluttered down to my chest for a split second before he spun and walked off the way he'd come.

He was all the way to the corner of my house before he called over his shoulder. "Might want to close your door though. Lots of animals out here."

I rolled my eyes and prayed for the goddesses to give me strength. He couldn't leave well enough alone. Always had to get the last word in. He'd been like that since we were kids. Well, whenever he deemed me worthy of conversation, that is.

I gathered my shoes and stomped to the house, knowing I'd never be able to get back into my meditation now. Might as well head to bed and hope for a better day tomorrow. I heard his truck roar away. I hated the way my ears strained until the sound completely faded.

I guessed we weren't going to talk about how he'd seen me topless.

Or how my foot had made contact with his dick.

Fine by me. I could handle the arguing and the insults. The rest would get swept to the back of my brain where I'd one day forget about it. One day far, far in the future.

CHAPTER FOUR

ce

THE COUNTRY MUSIC pulsing out of Hell's Tavern and across the gravel parking lot had me sighing with relief. Friday night. I'd made it to the second-best part of my week. The first was when we got the upper hand on a tough fire. That moment when all the hard work and adrenaline turned the tides made me feel like a goddamn superhero. Taming nature wasn't for the shy.

But this was good too. A night to shoot the shit with my boys and finally relax. My brothers and I were close. A little thing like adulthood wasn't going to separate us. Not if I could help it.

The tavern door swung open before I could grab the heavy iron handle shaped like a tree branch. A couple came barreling out, laughing at something. The woman raised her head and I saw it was Kim, a girl I'd dated once a few years ago.

"Hey, Ace!" Her face lit up even more, her brown eyes reflecting the neon lights from the beer signs in the windows.

Her date, a guy who'd been a couple years older than me in

school, gave me a death stare, but I didn't care. I shot Kim a wink. "Hey, Kim. Granger." I made the move to enter the bar, with Kim turning back to her date. I shot Granger a shrug and a cocky smile. He pulled Kim away, but flipped me the bird behind his back.

I couldn't help but chuckle as I entered the Tavern, my eyes adjusting to the dim lights. Granger was a good guy, and I had no interest in stealing Kim away. I wasn't a threat and he knew it.

"There he is! Our local hero!" I heard Dax shout above the music. I scanned the bar to find him holding his longneck bottle of beer in the air, a devilish smirk on his face. The triplets were already here, occupying the table in the back corner of the bar.

Heads swiveled and several people shouted hello or slapped me on the back as I made my way to the table. I gave a good-natured head nod and smile as I went, giving people the friendly, confident swagger they'd come to expect from me. Honestly, I hated it when anyone brought undue attention to me, but it came with the job. The better I got at protecting my community on the job, the more they started to look to me as a leader in all things.

Callan kicked a wooden chair out for me and I sunk into it gratefully. There was a frosted glass of beer waiting for me. These little brothers of mine drove me crazy most of the time, but they sometimes did things that made me proud. Knowing when a man needed an immediate slug of beer was one of them.

I chugged half the glass down before I came up for air. "Damn, that's fucking good."

Ethan cracked up, the patchy beard he'd started growing twitching. "Had a hard week or something?"

Or something. I wasn't going to get into the real reason for my tough week: it started with an A and ended with a permanent snapshot of boobs in my brain. If I even mentioned Adelia's name, they'd launch into a blistering string of teasing that might last until my hair turned gray.

"Yeah, us gainfully employed people who save lives on the daily carry a lot of stress. Isn't that right, Callan?"

Callan's ready smile lit up. "Hey, leave me out of this."

"I've got a job, dumbass," Ethan said with a frown, taking the bait. "It's called independent contracting. I may not save lives, but I pay the bills."

The guy hadn't had a steady career since graduating high school. He'd dabbled at college, mostly working odd jobs, and never finding his groove. We teased him, but every town needs a handyman or two and he had plenty of business to keep him in the black.

"You know, Roxanne was in here earlier looking for you." Callan took a swig of beer, a look in his eyes that spelled trouble for me. "Had to buy her a drink and talk her down from a crying fit."

I cringed and rubbed my thumb across the condensation on the glass, watching the water drip down. "I was very clear about only being friends."

I'd taken her out on a date last week after she'd spent months flirting with me every chance she got. I realized my mistake right away. A serial bachelor like myself recognized a stage-four clinger. I'd done my best to make sure she understood where I was coming from and what could be expected from me, but it sounded like she hadn't gotten the message loud enough.

Callan tilted his head. "I'm just saying...you're breaking hearts, Ace. I have to keep cleaning up the mess of your panty parade. Maybe we should figure out your problem."

I nearly pulled a muscle in my neck as I reared back. "My *problem*? I don't have a fucking problem."

Ethan snorted, and I had to grip my beer to keep from smacking him. "You've dated every girl south of sixty years old in this town and found fault with them all. There's only one common denominator. You."

I took a heavy drink of beer to keep from saying something that would sound like I was getting defensive. Fuck them and their "problem" bullshit. As the cold beer slid down my throat and cooled my temper, I remembered that teasing was our love language. The guys were just giving me shit to rile me up and it had almost worked.

Until Daxon opened his mouth, sounding far too serious. "I think Dad messed you up."

I put my beer down carefully and pinned him with a look that had always made my little brothers fall in line when we were growing up. "Don't you fucking bring up that bastard's name. Me not wanting to take a girl out on a second date has nothing to do with our sperm donor."

Daxon's eyebrow lifted and he just stared at me, daring me to examine his claim. The fucker.

Callan covered the charged silence. "How about we not go there. It's Friday night at the Tavern, not psych hour, okay?"

"I, for one, love taking women out on dates. The more dates you go on, the more they loosen up and show you the real woman behind the mask, you know? Maybe you just need to try it sometime and you'll realize the joy in bonding with a woman on a deeper level." Ethan had a look on his face that reminded me of Adelia when she was staring up at the moon. Shit, maybe *he* should date her.

Fuck. What was I thinking? I didn't want that woman around me or my brothers.

"Lookin' a little serious for a Friday night." Ben's voice came from behind me. The tension drained away as we all shouted our hellos. I moved over so he could drag a chair next to me.

Ben was my brother Blaze's best friend, but with Blaze living elsewhere, Ben had started to hang out with us instead. He was tall with dark auburn hair that we used to tease him about when we were kids. It had been a whole lot redder back then. He'd dyed it black one time in middle school just to see how we'd react. Joke was on him though as it was a permanent dye and didn't wash out. He'd had to just grow it out, becoming even more of a source of entertainment for us brothers in its various stages of grow out. He was a good guy though, and I trusted him with my life, just like my brothers.

"We're just trying to find dates to the festival," Callan interjected, turning the conversation away from me, which I appreciated. Callan was the best peacekeeper of the group.

"Oh, well, in that case, I saw a woman by the other side of the bar that Ace hasn't dated yet. Who wants dibs?" Ben pointed over Callan's shoulder. All our heads swiveled in that direction, but I couldn't see who this mystery woman was.

Daxon pushed back from the table and pretended to smooth his hair back even though not one strand was currently out of place. "I think I'll grab the next round, boys."

"Bullshit! You're gonna snag her, aren't you?" Ethan hooted.

Daxon shrugged. "When you got the looks, you gotta use 'em."

Daxon used to model when he was a teenager. A famous jeans brand used him as a model online for a couple years, which not only gave him a nice paycheck, but made him famous in our small town. I think our mother still had some of those branded store bags they'd made with his bare-chested self in low-slung jeans. Embarrassing, if you ask me. Dax had the ego to go with the notoriety, but most of it was bluster. As a guy who could put the swagger on command, I recognized bluster when I saw it. He left the table to suss out the new woman.

"Thankfully, I don't need any help in the ladies' department. I have no problem finding dates." I shot Callan a look, daring him to label me a problem again.

Ben pushed his glasses further up his nose. "Not your fault your mama named you so appropriately."

I frowned. "What's that?"

Ben's lips tugged upward. "Ace. Means 'one,' right? One-date Ace."

"Fuck you." I gave him a deadpanned stare while Callan and Ethan cracked up, nearly spitting out their beer. Like I hadn't heard that nickname before. Just most people didn't have the balls to say it to my face.

My phone vibrated in my pocket and I took it out, mostly so I could take a break from the teasing that seemed to be pointed at my chest tonight. There was a text from our fire chief. Which was odd. I couldn't think of a single time he'd ever texted me before, preferring to communicate with Captain Murray as the next in command.

Chief: Have time to meet with me tomorrow morning at nine?

My gut clenched, wondering what this could be about. I wracked my brain but couldn't come up with anything that I'd fucked up recently. I blew out a heavy breath and typed out a quick response. Nothing to do but show up and find out.

Me: Sure thing. Auburn Hill station?

Chief: Excellent. See you there.

I sat there staring at my blank screen for several minutes, trying to calm myself down. Being a firefighter was everything to me. It had been my dream for years. It was my identity. An identity I felt extremely confident about when I was in public. It was those rare moments alone at home that I began to doubt myself. Did I really have what it took to be a success? Was I just one fuckup away from losing everything I'd worked so hard for?

"Ace. You okay there, man?" Ben's elbow hit me in the ribs. "I was just teasing. Maybe went a little too far."

I slid the phone back in my pocket and slapped the swagger back on my face with ease. It was a routine I'd been doing forever. If you didn't feel confident, just act overly confident until it didn't feel fake.

"Actually, I think I saw a girl over by the door that I haven't dated yet. Thought I might ask her to the festival."

"Really? Where?" Ben craned his neck to see her. So did Ethan and Callan.

I waited for dramatic effect. "Yeah, right there."

They followed my pointing finger to the cluster of girls who'd just walked into the bar. Right to Annie. Ben's little sister.

Ben jumped up so fast his chair scraped behind him. He leaned into my face and opened his mouth to give me hell. He snapped it shut again when he saw the shit-eating grin on my face.

"You little shit," he muttered, sitting down again and grabbing his beer.

"I was just teasing," I parroted back to him. Ethan and Callan snickered. We all knew Annie was off-limits. "In all seriousness, I would never. I hope you know that."

Ben managed a smile. "Yeah, I know. Had me going there for a second though."

We all took a sip of our beers and looked around the ever-increasing crowd. The Tavern was the place to be on a Friday night. Women came up to our table and flirted. My brothers took turns asking girls to dance. And throughout it all I had zero interest in joining in.

Maybe it was the meeting with the chief tomorrow.

Maybe it was the thoughts of Adelia I couldn't get out of my head.

Maybe it was the topic my brothers had teased me about.

Whatever it was, there wasn't enough beer in the world to drown out the thoughts swirling around my brain, each more depressing than the other.

Maybe I needed to take a little trip out of town to fish in a new fishing hole. Yeah. That was it. Barring any bad news from the chief tomorrow, I was going to take a trip to Blueball and see if a fresh set of beautiful women could restart my fickle heart. Besides, I hadn't taken a vacation in years. Maybe some time away was just the thing I needed.

Maybe one-date Ace needed to leave Hell to find happiness.

CHAPTER FIVE

ddy

"IT'S SERIOUSLY the cutest thing ever, but my ears just can't take another recital right now." Meadow practically threw herself onto my supersized beanbag, the huge puffy bubble encasing her in a fabric embrace. "Twenty-nine kids puffing away on their recorders is enough to send a woman into a full-blown migraine attack."

I sat down gingerly next to her and handed her a bowl of mint chocolate chip ice cream. I didn't normally do dairy, but Meadow knew me well enough to bring over my favorite. Jeez. One time I give her oat milk ice cream flavored with hemp and she brings her own now.

"I can't imagine," I mutter, thinking a recital would be kind of cute.

With noise-cancelling earplugs, of course.

"I love that Judd's a teacher. He's going to make such a good dad one day." Meadow got that faraway look she got whenever she talked about her boyfriend. I'd seen her through some bad relationships over the years, and then through the dry years. The ones when she'd given up on men altogether. I was seriously happy for her and her newfound love with her kindergarten crush, but it also highlighted my loneliness.

I'd grown up feeling like a third wheel as an only child. My parents had been sickeningly in love, sometimes forgetting they'd spawned a love child. Meadow had been my best friend since first grade, filling that void. She was the only person who made me feel like I belonged. And now she belonged with Judd, leaving me feeling adrift.

"You know what we need?" I asked, setting down my bowl on the woven carpet in front of us. The ice cream needed time to melt a bit. I liked my ice cream on its way to soupy. "Kombrewcha!"

Meadow nearly spit out her huge bite of ice cream. "Ohh, it's one of those nights, huh?"

Leave it to a Hell citizen to put alcohol into a product meant to improve your health. The combination of beer and kombucha was straight genius. I pulled open my tiny fridge and grabbed two bottles from the stock I rarely broke into. Two steps to the right and I was at my beanbag again, handing one of the bottles to Meadow.

"How about you tell me why we're drinking alcohol and eating ice cream. That's quite a departure from your wheatgrass and tofu, BamBam."

I rolled my eyes at the use of the nickname Meadow had given me when we were barely old enough to write our own names. Thing was, I kept nothing from Meadow. She knew all my dreams, my problems with my parents, and my deep-seated hate for Ace Hellman.

"You know how I burned myself earlier this week?" I took the first long drink of the kombrewcha. It bubbled against my tongue, the sweet and sour mixing together perfectly. Like nectar from the gods.

Meadow put her bottle down to finish off her ice cream. She

didn't care for it once it started to melt. "Yeah, I heard about that. Told Poppy to shut her fucking mouth when she tried to spread that little rumor right in front of me in the line at Coffee."

I nearly choked. "You said that to her?"

Meadow shrugged. "Yeah. The woman has a big mouth. Even bigger now that she's retired and has nothing to do. Somebody needs to make her rein it in."

I took another sip. "Um, well, thank you." I preferred to keep the peace with softly spoken words, but Meadow was my opposite, not afraid to tell it like it is with zero filter. "But what I didn't tell you was that Ace put out the fire by tackling me and then whipping off his shirt to put out the flames."

Meadow sat up so fast I nearly rolled right off the beanbag as everything shifted inside. As it was, I spilled a bit of the kombrewcha on my pajama pants. "Ace Hellman without a shirt?" She whooped and I cringed, wondering why I felt compelled to tell her everything. "Every woman in Hell would have paid for a front-row seat to that little display. Did you cop a feel?"

I grimaced. "I was on fire, Meadow."

She sat there, unmoving. "So?"

"So, I was a little busy not burning to death! I didn't feel him up!"

She leaned back, and I lifted my kombrewcha in the air to prevent another spill. "Opportunity lost right there, BamBam."

I blew out a frustrated breath and leaned my head back to look at the wood beams that held up the roof of my tiny house. The beams swayed for a second, reminding me of the high alcohol content of the kombrewcha.

"You know I can't stand him."

Meadow set her bowl of ice cream down on the floor and grabbed her bottle of kombrewcha. "Again I ask...so? You don't have to like him to appreciate the genetics that made the statue of David come alive." She frowned. "Though I hope he's hung better than the famous statue."

I did choke then, the sting of the brew sliding down my throat. "Oh, he is. Trust me."

The millisecond the words were out of my mouth, I regretted them. Meadow twisted around and slapped her hand down on my arm, as if worried I'd run away without answering her burning questions.

"And just how do you know that, Adelia Bammingford?"

My cheeks went hot and I cursed myself for opening that door. It was like waving a juicy steak in front of a starving, rabid dog. Meadow was not going to let the subject drop. I think I liked her better when she was on the no-men-allowed self-pleasure wagon with me. Well, not with me. You know what I mean. She started getting good dick on the regular now that she had Judd. She was dick-obsessed.

I sighed and resigned myself to finishing my tale. "Well, you see. I was topless when I caught on fire."

Meadow's mouth dropped open. Her dad had clearly spent some money on her orthodontia. Her teeth were perfectly straight, unlike mine.

"So, he tackled me, put out the fire, and then, well, we had an awkward moment."

Meadow blinked and snapped her jaw shut. "Had an awkward moment? You mean when he tackled you and his mouth was mere inches away from suckling your naked boobs?"

I shook my head, sending my long hair flying out of the messy topknot that would never stay. "Suckling? Who says that? No. He scrambled off of me the second he realized I was topless, and then wouldn't look at me. We argued. He left."

Meadow stared at me like I'd grown a horn. "So, where in there did you see his pleasure stick?"

I went to take another drink just to give myself time to breathe, but there was nothing left in the bottle. I put it down with a harsh clink on the wood floor. "He came by the next night

—uninvited again, I might add—and asked if I'd been burned. I showed him my foot when we were sitting next to each other, and I accidentally beaned him in the junk."

Meadow's mouth dropped open again. I rolled my eyes, feeling highly uncomfortable. She was seriously overreacting.

"Oh man, this is so much better than a recorder recital..."

I shoved her with my elbow. Not hard. Just hard enough to make her shift on the beanbag. While she was trying to right herself, I hopped up and ran to my bed shoved in the corner of my house. I grabbed the photo album from under it and came back to her side.

I had a seat and flipped it open to one of the first pictures from school. I'd begged my parents for weeks to let me go to a real school for kindergarten. My mom had it in her head to homeschool me forever, like she'd been doing while all my peers got to finger-paint in preschool. My mom's idea of homeschool was to let me run wild all day by myself in the forest. She called it "unschooling." All I wanted was to be around other kids. She'd finally relented and kindergarten had been like a dream come true. Until the holiday recital.

"Look at this!" I shoved the book on Meadow's lap, ignoring the way she sighed. I'd shown her this photo and told this story many times over the years, but it was clear she needed a refresher.

"See that shiny happy face of mine?" I pointed to the image of myself in the back row on stage, a bleached-blonde girl in a frilly dress with a smile from ear to ear. A beautiful homemade flower crown sat on my head. I truly thought I was a princess that night with such a thing of beauty as my crown. My parents and I had made it together earlier that day, a rare event when they included me in their activities.

I slid my finger down to the row in front of me and there was Ace Hellman, age six, with a scowl that could make the devil tremble in his boots. "That asshole tore up my crown."

"He probably—"

"My parents had been talking about his dad leaving town and it made me sad for him. He looked like he was about to cry right there on stage. I gave it to him to cheer him up, and he ruined it in front of everyone right before the concert started!" I cut off Meadow, not wanting to hear her excuse for the town's pretty-boy-turned-hero. He'd humiliated me that night, and I'd never forgiven him. That night had started a twenty-year feud that was alive and well today. Small towns were good places to hold a life-time grudge.

Meadow tried out a smile. "So, you say he's hung like a horse?"

I huffed and lifted my hand in the air, proceeding to number off the ways the guy was a certifiable asshole of epic proportions. I spent the rest of the evening expounding upon the many ways I hated Ace Hellman. Meadow got so sick of me she fell asleep right there on the beanbag just to shut me up.

Ranting isn't nearly as fun when there was no one to listen to the rant, so I finally wound down, put our empty bowls in the sink, and took a quick stroll around my backyard to clear my head. The crystals where I'd been sitting when Ace showed up the other night were still in a heap from him pushing them out of the way. I put them back in a circle and then tipped my head back to check out the moon.

"Could use some life guidance right now. I'm feeling a bit off-center."

Yes, I was talking to the moon. Or the universe in general. Tonight, neither offered direction, but there was one thought floating through my brain as I stared up into the starlit sky.

I hoped to never, ever have to see Ace Hellman again.

Sure, it was a small town, but I liked to keep to myself. I'd just never light a bonfire again and hopefully stay off his radar. My heart chakra would settle down and then I could live happily ever after...Ace-free.

And with that pleasant thought, I headed inside, draped a blanket over Meadow, and fell right to sleep in my bed.

CHAPTER SIX

ce

"THANKS FOR MEETING WITH ME, ACE." Chief held out his hand as I stepped through the door of the tiny office at the fire station, making sure to close it behind me. Normally, Captain Murray was in here, but with him out sick so often, I guessed Chief felt comfortable using it as a meeting spot. Then again, he was the fire chief for the whole county. He could use any damn room he wanted to in quite a few fire stations.

I shook his hand and had a seat in the metal chair after he sat down behind the cluttered desk. "Happy to, sir."

Chief laced his fingers together and rested them on the desk, his big belly taking up a battle with the edge of the metal desk. He leaned forward to study my face. I wasn't sure what he was seeing there, but I was hoping he couldn't see the slight sheen of sweat on my brow. I'd barely slept last night, wondering what he wanted to talk to me about. I'd even left the bar last night after two beers, not wanting the smell of hops coming out my pores for this meeting.

"As you know, Captain Murray has been experiencing some health issues recently." I nodded and he kept going. "In fact, he's decided to take early retirement at the advice of his doctor."

My spine froze. I didn't even dare breathe. Retire? Captain Murray had been my mentor since I stepped foot in the fire station at eighteen years old looking for a job. I figured I had many more years to develop under his tutelage.

"I'll cut right to the chase. I'd like to promote you to captain. You have an exemplary history with the fire department, and I think you'll be just what this place needs."

A stiff wind blew past my ears, but not one paper on the desk stirred. I swallowed hard, not sure if what I was hearing was simply what I wanted to hear or what he'd actually said out loud. Chief paused and I knew this was my time to say something, but words were having a hard time forming on my tongue. I'd worked the last ten years to one day have this opportunity given to me, but I figured it would take at least ten more before I got so lucky.

"Thank you. Thank you, sir," I managed to spit out.

He dipped his head a fraction and carried on. "Now this position comes with many more responsibilities. More stress. More hours. More management of firefighters than you've had to do previously. Just ask Captain Murray. That heart attack didn't come from too many trips to the spa."

I cringed. "I didn't realize he'd had a heart attack." We'd only been told he'd been sick. I thought of his poor wife. The woman must be beside herself with worry.

Chief nodded again. "Like I said, more stress. But you're young, and I'm confident you can hack it. If you accept the position, I'll have human resources send over your new employment contract today. I'd like to have you transition immediately into the new role."

I nodded vigorously. "I accept."

Chief stood and extended his hand again. I stood and we shook on it. All the while I was having a bit of an out-of-body experience. This had been my dream since I was a kid. And now here it was, handed to me at twenty-eight years old. A part of me felt badly about it taking a heart attack for Captain Murray to step down and give me this opportunity, but I didn't feel so bad that I'd turn it down.

"All right, then. It's a done deal. We'll be talking quite a bit more in the future, so make sure you memorize my phone number." He chuckled, but his eyes told me he was dead serious.

"Yes, sir."

He walked out to probably shake hands and talk to the guys just coming on shift. Whenever he visited the station, we took notice, putting our best foot forward. I stayed where I was, looking around the office that would soon be mine.

"Holy shit," I muttered.

"Just realized it's your turn to make dinner tonight?" John said with a smile, his head stuck in the doorway, his bag at his feet.

I smirked. As captain, I would never have to cook again if I didn't want to. Though I didn't really mind. I kind of liked being part of the team and I didn't intend to let something like a job title separate me from the guys.

"That's right," I drawled. "I'm making eggplant lasagna."

John's face puckered immediately. "Dude, seriously? Replacing noodles with veggies is just wrong."

I clapped him on the shoulder and we headed to dump our stuff off in our cubbies. "You should really get more fiber in your diet, John. I've had to use the bathroom right after you. Something ain't right about your bowels."

John guffawed. "Shut the fuck up. My bowels are just fine. Never seen bowels prettier than mine."

"What the hell are you guys talking about?" Joe asked, his face a mask of revulsion as he stood by his bed staring at us.

John and I both cracked up and got busy storing the things we'd need for the next forty-eight hours. I left the two of them to debate the merits of vegetables while I went back to help get

things organized. If I was to become captain, I'd need to frater-
nize less and do more behind the scenes to keep this fire station
running smoothly.

Chief found me a bit later as I was checking over the equipment that had been used by the prior shift.

"One more thing, Ace." Chief ran a hand through his hair
and then checked the black watch on his wrist. "Murray was set
to co-host a community first aid class here in Auburn Hill. It's
six weeks long, Tuesday nights. I need you to take that over. I'll
make sure to rearrange your schedule so you're off duty."

He spun around in a hurry. "Sure thing, Chief," I called after
him, as if refusing was even a possibility. As he left, the buzz of
conversation among the guys crept back in.

I frowned, setting down the hose regulator. Why didn't they
have a nurse or an EMT like my brother host the damn class? I
mean, I knew basic first aid like any other firefighter since I'd
been through an EMT class, but having the captain teach the
class seemed a little odd. Then again, maybe I needed to get
used to doing more administrative tasks.

My phone buzzed in my back pocket. Since nothing was
happening right now that needed my focus, I took it out to see
some texts from my brothers.

*Daxon: Totally scored a date to the festival. The girl at the bar was
from out of town. Don't be jealous, boys.*

*Ethan: Good move. Get to her before she hears about the Hellman
reputation.*

*Callan: Dude. What are you talking about? I'm straight up book
boyfriend material!*

I choked back a laugh.

Me: what the actual fuck is book boyfriend material??

Callan: You'd know if you ever talked to a girl beyond the first date.

Daxon: I call bullshit. Cricket told you that, right?

I hooted out loud. I freaking loved my brothers. Cricket was
Callan's best friend, a girl we teased him about constantly. He
swore they were only friends, but Cricket was hot in a girl-next-

door kind of way. We didn't believe for one second that Callan didn't recognize her hotness.

Me: Before this devolves into a pissing match...I've got news.

Ethan: You really asked out Annie???

Daxon: WHAT

Callan: Holy shit, I gotta see this

They were firing off texts before I could even respond.

Me: Jesus. No to Annie. I would never do that to Ben. This isn't about a girl.

Ethan: Then is it really news?

I sighed and thumbed out my announcement before they could launch into a new line of teasing that would last the next half hour. Didn't these assholes have jobs?

Me: I just got promoted to captain.

Three bubbles popped up on the screen at once. A grin grew on my face, waiting for what I knew their responses would be. I sucked in a huge breath and felt the pride take hold of my chest. I'd been in a state of shock since Chief offered it to me, but now the emotions were starting to rush in.

Callan: CONGRATS! You deserve it.

Daxon: Super proud of you, big bro!

Ethan: Does this mean we can finally ride on the fire truck during the Christmas parade this year?

I burst out laughing. Several heads turned my way, but I didn't care. I was too happy to worry about how I was being perceived. It didn't happen often when I let myself just be happy, so I was going to milk it for all it was worth.

Callan: Seriously, Ethan?

Daxon: That's what you respond with? Are you eight?

Ethan: I'm not ashamed to say I will never lose touch with my inner little boy.

Me: Thanks, guys. I'll see what I can do, Ethan. Though I'm a bit concerned about knowing there's a little boy inside of you.

Callan: I'm done. I'm putting my phone down now.

Daxon: bahahaha

I shut my own phone screen off, only to pull it right out of my pocket again when it vibrated.

Mom: I hear congratulations are in order, my darling boy.

Jesus. Apparently the boys already managed to tell Mom about my good news. There was only four years between us, but I sometimes felt like an old man compared to them. I couldn't even text as fast as they could.

Me: You heard right. Although I prefer you call me Captain Hellman.

Mom: I wiped your butt, young man. I'll call you whatever I please. Come over for dinner and we'll celebrate. Maybe even get that silent brother of yours to come home for once.

A pang of sadness broke through the pride and excitement. I knew Blaze practically abandoning our family the last few years hurt Mom the worst. I doubted my promotion would be enough to get him back in Hell. He seemed to be avoiding us like the plague. I made a mental note to reach out to him soon. Enough was enough.

Me: I'm off tomorrow at six. I can come straight over. But only if you make your famous tacos.

That was the only meal she could seem to make that didn't come out burned or inedible. I shivered just thinking about the cinnamon rolls she tried making one Christmas morning. She'd accidentally put in salt instead of sugar. Instead of opening presents, we'd spent the morning each drinking a gallon of water.

Mom: I have always had the best taco in Hell.

I wanted to clean my eyeballs out with bleach.

Me: Jesus, Mom.

Mom: What? We're all adults now, right?

Me: I have to work now.

Mom: Uh-huh. Sure. You just can't handle talking about how your mother still has it going on.

Me: Bye. See you tomorrow.

I shut the phone all the way off and shoved it in my back pocket. Why did family have to be so weird? If the triplets weren't enough, I had another brother who was trying to divorce himself from us entirely. And then there was Mom. The former beauty queen who had the confidence level of a Roman emperor. Or maybe the queen of the Amazons would be more appropriate. She was a character with a capital C.

I motioned for John to back the truck out of the station so we could give it a wash. As I looked around at everyone doing what they needed to do without direction by me, I felt that sense of pride surge back. I had two families essentially: my blood relatives and my brothers here at the station.

Like father, like son.

The thought danced through my brain before I could push it back out. I was nothing like my father. I wondered for a moment if he'd be proud of what I'd accomplished in life, and then sneered. That motherfucker was off living with his other family, pretending we never existed. I couldn't care less what he thought of me, if he ever did.

I'd never abandon either of my families, unlike him.

I'd double down on this job promotion and work even harder. I'd be so damn responsible no one would ever feel like I wasn't giving them one hundred percent of me.

That little trip out of town I'd been thinking about last night? No way was I doing that now. I was staying right here in Hell. I didn't need to find a woman to date. Nor did I need distraction to get Adelia out of my brain. My time and attention would be filled with work.

And that was just fine by me.

CHAPTER SEVEN

$\mathcal{A}$ddy

"Do you have an oil for increased libido?" Nikki asked, fluttering her lashes, though I didn't buy the innocent act for one freaking second.

This was a prime example of why small towns could be challenging. I'd known Nikki my whole life. From afar of course. Growing up, I could never come near her after Ace and I became unspoken enemies. She'd been kind to me when our paths crossed though, despite all the curveballs life handed her over the years. I may not have liked Ace, but I loved his mother. She'd not only aged gracefully, she'd embraced it with a feminine fire I could only hope to emulate one day.

"There are definitely some oils that can help in that department. Should I add a few of those to your order?"

Nikki patted my arm, giving me a wink that echoed the beauty queen she'd been decades ago. She might be older and heavier, but she still had a way about her that spoke of elegance and confidence.

"Most definitely. I've found most men my age have issues keeping up with me. I didn't bust my gorgeous butt to retire early just to have all the men needing naps before they can come back for round two. You know what I mean?" She clutched her expansive bosom in a shiver of horror. "If I can sneak some oils into the massage oil, maybe I can rev 'em up a bit."

I pasted on a smile and added two essential oils to her order that might help. I really, really hoped she wouldn't come back and tell me the gory details after she tried them out. Though, knowing Nikki, she would.

Her cell phone began making a horrific high-pitched noise. She jumped to her feet and snatched it off the table where we'd been sitting going over how to use the oils I sold for a living.

"Sorry about that. I have to set alarms or I lose all track of time. You stay right there and keep educating me. I just have to pull some ground beef out of the freezer. My boys are coming over for dinner."

Her expressive brown eyes sparkled as they always did when she talked about her sons. The thought of those boys—or one in particular—didn't have the same effect on me. I tried for a believable smile, but she was already off, her bright turquoise caftan fluttering as she breezed into the kitchen.

"Okay, so next step would be to talk about diffusing oils." I carried on with my practiced sales pitch. I knew some people looked down on multi-level marketing products, but it was no different than a company hiring an in-house marketing team to promote their products. This way, the marketing team was mostly women like myself who could use the income.

"Sign me up!" Nikki hollered from somewhere in the kitchen.

"Do you need help?" I asked, craning my head from the dining room table to see if she had things under control.

Nikki cooked with enthusiasm—like she did all things in life —but she wasn't known for being the best chef. She typically forgot she had something on the stove. It always gave me a bit of a chuckle when the Hell newspaper had a short paragraph about the firefighters putting out another kitchen fire at her house. I shouldn't laugh. Kitchen fires weren't funny, but it kind of was when it was Ace's mother. All that lecturing from him about my bonfire, and his own mother used his services more than me.

Nikki twirled around the corner, posing with one hand up on the doorway like there was a photographer from Vogue in the room. "No, darling. I've got it defrosting and I'm pretty sure one can't start a fire by defrosting meat in the microwave." Her beautiful face screwed up into a frown. "Actually, I don't know that. I'll have to ask Ace."

Nikki sashayed—she never just walked like a normal human —into the room and sat back down at the table. "Oh! You should stay for dinner, darling. My sons could probably use some oils too."

I was shaking my head before she finished her sentence. "I wouldn't dream of it, Nikki. Enjoy an evening with them without disruption." I'd rather burn in the fires of Hell before sitting at a table with Ace Hellman. He'd probably scowl so hard I'd lose my appetite anyway.

I looked at the grandfather clock against the wall. I needed to get out of here before the oldest son swooped in like the devil on a mission to humiliate me. "In fact, I should probably get going so you can prepare. Maybe we can meet up tomorrow and finish your order?"

"What order?" The grumpy voice that interrupted sent shivers down my spine.

Nikki twirled in her chair with a gasp. "Ace, my baby! You're early!" She stood up and spread her arms wide, waiting for Ace to enter the room and give her a hug.

His scent wafted over as he came near. I scrambled to my feet and tried to collect my things for a hasty retreat. I did not care for the way my hands shook. Ace looked damn good in jeans that molded to his ass and a T-shirt that highlighted his muscles. His dark hair was wet as if he'd just taken a shower. Ace hugged his mother and then gave her a kiss on her cheek before stepping back and shooting daggers in my direction.

"What order?" he barked again.

Nikki slapped the back of her hand on his chest. "Jesus, Joseph, and Mary, Ace! Did I not teach you any manners? How about a hello first?"

I may have just been imagining it, but the tips of Ace's ears looked a bit red. His frown morphed into a smile that was even more terrifying. He opened his mouth to speak, and I had to practice my "breath of fire" Kundalini breathing to strengthen my wobbly knees. It made me sound a bit like a bull, but I needed all the help I could get. Why did this man irritate me on a cellular level?

"Hello, Adelia. To what do we owe the great pleasure of seeing you today?" Every single word was dripping with sarcasm.

I sniffed, lifting my nose in the air. "Nikki invited me over, but I was just leaving."

Ace folded his arms across his chest and I begged my eyes not to drop to take in the expanse of muscles that had haunted my dreams. "Oh good. Let me get the door for you so it doesn't hit you on the way out."

"Oh! But don't forget to call me tomorrow, Addy." Nikki called after me as I made my way out of the dining room to the front door. "I want to buy all the oils!"

Ace came to a screeching halt with one hand on the door-knob. His whole body tightened up and it was a sight to see. "Oils?"

Oh, great. Here we go. I'd learned there were two responses to hearing I sold essential oils: excited interest or scoffing disbelief that one could believe in something so ridiculous. Based on his disbelief that they'd helped my burns, I could guess which way Ace would go.

I tossed my long hair behind my shoulder. "Yes, that's right. Your mother is interested in essential oils to improve her health naturally."

Ace rolled his eyes. "You gotta be shitting me."

Yep, just as I figured. "I definitely am not shitting you."

"Is he giving you trouble?" came Nikki's voice from behind Ace. She shoved him aside with a practiced hip check I admired. "Forgive him. He's got a gorgeous outer shell, but he's misled."

"Mom!" Ace responded, turning to glare incredulously at his mom.

The corners of my lips tugged upward. "It's not his fault really," I told Nikki, ignoring how I could literally feel the daggers from Ace's stare. "He's been fawned over all his life."

Nikki nodded, her bob of caramel highlights swinging. "It's true. A pretty face can ruin a man. But I have hope for him yet." She snapped her fingers, already on to another subject. "Wait, doesn't your class start tomorrow?"

I nodded. "It does. Are you coming?"

Nikki smiled and pulled me into a hug. I glanced up and saw Ace's eyes narrowed at me as I hugged his mother. I quickly pulled back, wanting to be out of there before he exploded. I didn't need his negative energy dampening my happy aura.

"I wouldn't miss it for the world. Why don't we meet the day after and finish my order then?"

"Perfect." I shot Nikki a smile and stepped out onto her porch. She had flowers in pots everywhere, leaving just enough room for two wooden rocking chairs. I drifted my fingertips over the begonia petals nearest me. This looked like just the type of porch I'd love. Though nothing beat sitting out in the dirt in the middle of the forest.

Nikki went back in the house, but Ace slipped out and stopped me from descending the three steps to the walkway. For such a large man, he sure did tread softly. "What class are you talking about?"

I looked down at his hand on my elbow. He snatched it back and rubbed his fingers on his jeans like I'd infected him.

"My first aid class." I spun to walk away but he grabbed me

again, this time leaving his hand on my arm, his warmth practically scorching my skin.

"The first aid class down at the community center? Tuesday nights for six weeks?"

I frowned back at him. "Yes. Glad you read the flyer. Hope you won't be there."

He huffed through his nose before throwing a smirk at me that had me wanting to lick the dimple to the right of his mouth, followed by a hard slap to the face.

"Oh, I'll be there, hippie girl." He stepped in closer, dipping his head to not break eye contact. "I'm teaching it."

"What?" I reared my head back, aware I was giving him at least three chins in this position, but too horrified at his announcement to care. This was my class. My brain child. I'd asked Captain Murray to help me teach it just to involve more of the community and he'd agreed, stating he'd let me set the curriculum.

He grinned and the devil danced in his eyes. "Captain Murray retired. I'm the new captain."

My eyes darted back and forth across his face, thinking he might be just messing with me. "But Captain Murray said he'd do it."

Ace shrugged and let go of my arm. "Now he can't. I'm the substitute."

I snapped my mouth shut and tried to remember how I'd been taught to breathe to relieve stress. It wasn't working.

"Well, don't bother. I already have the curriculum outlined and don't really need a partner."

Ace looked down at me with a look I couldn't decipher. "It's not up to you, now is it? I'll be there to teach my half. You know, real first aid. Not rubbing lavender oil on a broken arm."

My spine locked up and I felt the fire of fury lighting up my nerve endings. I could kill him. Me, the girl who wouldn't kill a spider, was ready to end this man's life. Happily. I might even dance on his motionless body when I was done.

"It's an hour class. You can take the first thirty and I'll take the second. That's the best I'll do for you."

A dark smile grew on Ace's face. I itched so badly to reach out and smack him I had to dig my nails into my palms as I made a fist. His brothers would be here soon and I wanted to be long gone before all that testosterone descended on this place. Ace was bad enough.

He finally dipped his head, accepting the agreement to how we'd teach the class. Then he reached up and flicked a lock of my hair, the section that had a feather hanging from it, ruining our tentative truce when he opened his mouth.

"Get in a fight with an owl?"

"Gah!" I spun around and flounced down the steps. I didn't slow down until I'd reached the end of the street and found myself berating Ace under my breath with each stomping step. My chi was absolutely ruined, squashed and darkened by that asshole of a man.

Darkness fell around me, the streetlights flipping on and illuminating my path home. A little fresh air and wind on my cheeks finally had me calming down. How could one person get under my skin like that? And when would I quit giving him power over me? All these years of yoga, meditation, and retreats to heal my spirit, and all of it went out the window when Ace Hellman opened his disturbingly beautiful mouth.

Somehow, someway, I'd have to teach this class with him and not lose my cool.

Maybe there was an oil for that...

CHAPTER EIGHT

*A*ce

I TRIED TURNING AROUND and walking back in the house like Adelia leaving in a huff didn't affect me, but at the last minute I felt compelled to watch. That feather I'd flicked fluttered in the breeze, a sexy-as-hell addition to a woman who was already hotter than anyone needed to be. Her long blonde hair wasn't curled perfectly like most of the women did these days. You could tell it was naturally wavy and she didn't do a damn thing to tame it. My hands wanted to though. They wanted to dig right into those strands and wrap them around my fists just to see how thick her hair was.

I couldn't even describe what she was wearing. It looked like a skirt, but there were so many colors and layers to it, I wasn't sure where the material ended and Adelia began. She should have looked homeless in her mismatched clothes and strappy shoes that Jesus probably wore back in the day. Bracelets lined her arm, and I could have bet not one swipe of makeup had been on her face.

And yet...she was stunning.

There was no warning of impending assault, just a heavy slap to the back of the head and then pain blossoming across my skull.

"Ouch!" I grabbed my head and turned to see my mother in the doorway, her hands on her hips.

"I could have sworn I didn't raise you to be a dumbass, but I'm having some serious concerns right now." And then for the second time in the last minute, a woman flounced away from me.

"What is with everybody today?" I mumbled, following her back in the house and shutting the door. I was contemplating what to say to smooth things over with Mom, but quite frankly, I thought she was the one to owe me an apology. I'd saved her from buying snake oil and she thanked me by smacking me?

The front door banged open behind me and I abandoned helping Mom cook in the kitchen. At least if she caught something on fire, I'd be on hand to put it out quickly.

"The good-looking brother has arrived." Daxon shot a wink and a smile to the mostly empty room as if there were invisible fans waiting for him when it was just me. Sometimes I wondered where he got his ego, and then I spent time with Mom and it all made sense again.

"Oh, thank God. I was worried we wouldn't have a pretty boy at the table," I deadpanned.

Daxon opened his mouth to retort something snarky, but got bumped aside when Callan and Ethan came in. Soon, the volume of voices increased until we were shouting over each other. Our house had always been a loud one. I wasn't sure how Mom handled five rowdy boys without losing her mind.

"Why is this one so damn grouchy?" Ethan pointed at my face.

I reared back. "I'm not grouchy."

Callan clapped me on the back. "It's okay. We're used to that frown. Did Mom already start a fire?"

I smirked. "Nah. She hasn't started the meat yet. I got a fire extinguisher under the sink now though, so we should be good."

"Then why the frown?" Ethan didn't know when to let things go, always wanting to get to the bottom of the problem. He should think about being a goddamn therapist instead of a handyman.

I sighed, remembering the bad news. "I have to teach a first aid class that Captain Murray was supposed to do."

Callan matched my frown. "You don't know shit about first aid."

"Dude. I so do. Remember when I sewed your knee when you were ten?" We didn't have a ton of money growing up and I wasn't going to stick Mom with an emergency room bill. For not having done it before, and with all the crying Callan was doing, I thought I'd done a stand-up job.

"Yeah, still got the scar. Thanks for that."

"But did you die?"

Ethan stepped between us. "Why are you so mad about teaching a class? Just use it as a way to meet women."

All heads looked to me for an answer. A flash of blonde hair and gorgeous breasts swept through my brain. I couldn't hide the growl in my voice as I spit out her name. "I'm teaching the class with Adelia Bammingford."

Silence ensued. My brothers all knew how much I despised her.

"I'm just gonna put this out there. Addy's kind of hot now," Daxon said with a grin that made hot lava flow through my veins.

Ethan scratched his beard. "Yeah, she is. None of us have dated her, right? She's fair game?"

I stepped into the middle of the circle and addressed them all. "So help me God, if any of you go near her, I will disfigure your pretty faces and then make your life a living hell."

Callan seemed unruffled by my very real threat. "Don't you think it's time to let that petty childhood stuff go?"

I knew I was being ridiculous, but I couldn't help myself. I was their big brother and they were going to listen. "She's still nuttier than a squirrel. I don't want any of my brothers near her. Understood?"

They all eventually nodded and then the fire alarm in the kitchen went off and the subject was dropped. We got the fire out quickly and even managed to salvage dinner. Thankfully, Adelia's name didn't come up the rest of the night. Not thankfully, I couldn't get her beautiful face out of my head the rest of the night.

THE LAST THING I wanted to be doing was standing in front of the whole town and teaching a class when I had so many other things I needed to do. Chief had already emailed over all the files that Captain Murray had kept up over the years with expectations that I'd jump right in. I had a to-do list a mile long. But here I was, standing at the front of the largest room in the community center, nodding hello as people entered the room and had a seat on the chairs I'd set up without the help of my co-host who wasn't even here yet.

Thirty pairs or so of expectant eyes stared back at me when the clock hit seven o'clock. I knew everyone there, including Annie, Ben's little sister, and my own mother. The retired posse of ladies that terrorized Hell were also there, devious smiles on their faces that set my teeth on edge. I put on a practiced smile and began to teach without my co-host.

Anger simmered low in my gut. Adelia'd made such a big deal of telling me exactly how I was allowed to teach "her" fucking class and then didn't show up on time. I should have expected such an unprofessional display from her. A twinge of disappointment joined in, if I was being honest with myself.

"Welcome to the first night of first aid basics training. I hope you'll never need to use what we learn here tonight, but I've always believed in being fully prepared for whatever life hands you. I commend you for being here and learning the skills that could one day save a life. I'd like to start with the easier skills and work our way into more in-depth first aid response." I put my hand up. "Who here has ever fallen down?"

Just as I expected, everyone raised their hand.

As I did not expect, Yedda cackled out what she probably thought was a whisper from the front row next to her partners in crime, Poppy and Penelope. "I'd fall down every damn day if Ace came to rescue me!"

The crowd tittered with laughter, a few of the ladies agreeing with Yedda. I also saw a couple husbands elbow their wives when they agreed a bit too enthusiastically.

I cleared my throat and continued on as if that kind of thing happened every day and I just took it in stride when it actually made me super uncomfortable. "As I was saying, falls are super common and also one of the—"

The door to the private room banged open and Adelia walked in, cutting me off as all heads swiveled in her direction. I didn't blame them. She was a sight to see. Her hair blew around her like a goddamn shampoo commercial as she walked. A little tinkling bell sounded with every step, like she was floating on music. The breasts I'd been seeing in my dreams every night were bouncing around in a brown shirt that shouldn't have been attractive and yet was. Simply because it was on Adelia. I didn't want to, but I did. My gaze dipped and I realized very quickly she wasn't wearing a bra. Why the fuck wasn't she wearing a bra?

My hand swiped through my hair and I felt like a deer in headlights. Adelia's headlights. How the fuck was I going to teach a class with her when every move sent them jiggling? Lust and anger—of equal portions—swept through my system, leaving me without a single thought in my head as to how to finish the sentence I'd started.

"Sorry I'm late!" Adelia trilled, tossing a brilliant smile to everyone while sounding out of breath. She hopped up to have a seat on the table where I was talking, her skirt sweeping several of my hastily made notes onto the floor. "Please carry on, Ace." The smile turned brittle when she glanced at me. The fire in her eyes told me two things: one, she'd purposely come late to mess with me, and two, she had more things up her sleeve.

The lust fell into the background and anger took over. Turning back to the crowd, I kept right on going, refusing to give more time and attention to someone who didn't deserve it. There was no way you could convince me she should be teaching this class with her snake oil and crystal circles.

I got through most of the basic first aid for scratches, cuts, and burns before Adelia finally cut in. She tapped her wrist subtly, letting me know I'd reached my thirty minutes and she was taking over whether I was at a good stopping point or not.

"Now I understand some of you prefer a more natural way of healing the body, which is why I'm here. Not every first aid situation requires a trip to the hospital that'll leave you with a hefty bill or a round of antibiotics that'll wipe out all your good gut bacteria."

Adelia hopped off the table and began to pace as she went over all the same injury scenarios I had, but introduced natural ways to heal. Some of them made some sense, but most were so outrageous I had a hard time holding back the bark of laughter. A coffee enema to heal a headache? Yeah, no. I'll take my coffee the regular way, thank you very much.

There were quite a few questions and Adelia answered them easily, her ready smile and soft voice creating almost a trancelike experience. I had to blink and pull myself back from smiling at her myself.

"Okay, that's all we have for you tonight. We can't wait to see you next week, right, Ace?" She finally looked over at me, a glow about her that made me pause. She looked like she was in her element and something about darkening her sunshine felt wrong.

Yet some of her suggestions had made me uneasy. Manuka honey for a wound? That was a recipe for infection if I ever heard one.

"That's right. Thanks for coming, everyone." I turned my smile on the crowd, like I knew they expected, resolving to talk to Adelia after everyone had left.

Townsfolk came up to say thank you and ask lingering questions. Adelia and I took up residence on opposite ends of the room and answered all the questions until the last person exited the community center. The door swung shut and it was just us.

The silence that remained was deadly. I looked at Adelia. She looked back at me. I moved to straighten the chairs and pick up leftover trash. Adelia joined me until we met somewhere in the middle, our hands full of forgotten cups and candy wrappers. There was also a suspicious miniature vodka bottle that you can find at a convenient store that I could have sworn was stashed under Poppy's chair. I wondered how she'd snuck that in.

"Coffee enemas for headaches? Really, Adelia?" I lifted an eyebrow, waiting for that blush to hit her cheeks. Every time we fought, I waited for it, always immensely pleased when I could make it appear like magic.

She lifted her nose in the air. "I know it's hard to imagine, but it really does work."

Part of me admired her for sticking to her guns so fiercely. And then she continued.

"Not for you though. Your asshole's puckered so tight you couldn't get the enema tube in there."

The anger flared hot and bright. "I can promise you my asshole, or any other part of my body, has no problems."

Adelia didn't look smug, she just looked confident. And it was fucking sexy. "I highly doubt that. Your aura is strangled from being strung so tight all the time. You should try meditation. I think it would really help you."

I took a step closer, enjoying the way I could look down at her. "No, thanks."

She simply shrugged, the scent of lemons and lavender

wafting up. "You probably can't meditate. Most type-A people can't. Too much energetic constipation."

I frowned. She had no place telling me what I could and could not do. And seriously? She thought I was constipated? I could shit just fine, thank you very much. Not that that topic was up for conversation.

"I can meditate." I didn't like how my voice sounded like a petulant teenager, but I couldn't seem to help it.

"No, you can't."

"Yes. I. Can." I was so close now, the tips of her unbound breasts brushed against my torso when she inhaled sharply. It was heaven.

No. Shit. It was hell. Being anywhere near her was hell.

"Prove it."

I narrowed my eyes, trying to remember what the fuck we were even arguing about. "Fine."

She grinned up at me and my heart stopped. "Fine. Tomorrow night, then."

With that settled, she spun around and walked out with her hair all aflutter, leaving me to collect my notes and shut off the lights.

And wonder what the fuck I'd just gotten myself into.

CHAPTER NINE

*A*ddy

"SHIITAKE MUSHROOMS!" I hopped around on one foot, holding my other throbbing one in my hands. My pinkie toe had met the side of my bed frame as I rushed around cleaning my tiny home. Normally I loved living in five hundred square feet. Less to clean, less to maintain, and the mortgage had been low enough to allow me to buy more land. Who needed a big house when you had a few acres of forest to call home?

But on days like today, when I was rushing around and in my head with thoughts I couldn't control, it ended up feeling like the walls were closing in on me. I threw down the shawl I'd been attempting to fold and headed outside. The sun was just setting, that golden light filtering through the trees as though the sun itself was reaching out to say goodnight. I walked out into the trees, letting my pounding pinkie toe squish into the dirt. There was healing in being grounded to the earth.

I tossed my head back and sucked in a deep breath, holding it at the top before blowing it out, along with the thoughts that had plagued me through two yoga classes today. A little wood-pecker drilled against one of the pine trees, snagging my atten-tion. It stopped and turned to look right at me. As if to ask why I'd interrupted him.

"Sorry, Mr. Woodpecker. Just needed to get some perspective."

He didn't move, his little beady eyes staring me down.

"Why did I invite Ace to meditate with me?" I asked him, knowing this was why some people thought I was crazy. I knew the woodpecker couldn't answer, but sometimes a girl just needed someone—human or avian—to talk to. "I don't want him over here and yet that's exactly what I invited him to do. What was I thinking?"

I began to pace in front of the tree. I know what I'd been thinking. I'd been thinking he looked ridiculously handsome in his dress attire. I was used to seeing him in work pants and a AHFD T-shirt. Put him in a collared uniform shirt and he fried my brain cells. "And why does he have to be so hot? I mean, shouldn't nasty people be nasty on the outside too?"

This time, the woodpecker rotated his head away from me and began to pound away at the tree trunk. His rhythmic pecking reminded me of how these questions had pecked away at my brain all day, leaving me irritable.

"Why was he so nice to everyone at that class except for me? I know why I don't care for him, but why does he hate *me*? What did I ever do?"

This time the woodpecker stopped banging his beak against the tree and took flight. He swooped down and made a beeline for my head. I ducked and he kept right on going, probably looking for a quieter forest.

"Sorry!" I called after him.

"Apologizing already?" a voice said from my left. Heart in my throat, I spun around to see Ace walking toward me in his casual uniform of blue pants, black T-shirt, and heavy boots. The last rays of the sun lit up behind him, making him look like an angel stepping from the heavens into the forest.

I blinked and his face shifted from the snarky smirk to a frown. There. That was more normal. *Nothing to get excited about, Addy.*

"How come every time I can't find you, you're outside just staring off into space?" Ace's gaze took a trip down my body, a glance I could have sworn I felt on my skin. "At least this time you're fully clothed."

My body heated under his scrutiny, a reaction I did not appreciate but had come to accept was just what happened when I was around him. "Well, when people are invited to my property, I tend to make sure I'm clothed. Trespassers...? Well, they come at their own risk."

The side of Ace's mouth twitched, a dimple flashing and then disappearing like a star winking out in the night sky. Could grumpy Ace Hellman have been on the verge of directing a smile in my direction?

"Also, I'm not just staring out into space, I'm communing with nature." I pointed to the ground at our feet. "Have a seat and I'll show you how."

Ace huffed out a breath. "I have a feeling I'll regret this. If nothing else though, maybe I'll get in a good nap."

I sat down, ignoring his insult, crossing my legs, and waiting for him to do the same. He didn't know it yet, but he was in for a treat. Meditation virgins were my catnip. As he sat, Ace's knee brushed against mine, so close I could smell his usual scent. Sweat and soap. And maybe a little bit of smoke this time.

"Had a hard day?" Not that I cared. I only invited him to make him eat his own words.

Ace nodded, looking out into the forest. "Yeah. Two fires outside of town, one of which started just after our class last night."

I reached over and positioned his hands on his knees, palms up. Heat emanated off his chest. I glanced up and saw him watching me closely, his nostrils flared. He blinked and batted away my hands.

"I got it."

"Okay, okay." I sat back and placed my own hands on my knees. "Now close your eyes and follow my lead. Relax your shoulders. Roll them back and let them drop away from your ears."

I heard Ace follow along, his breath already evening out as I went through the normal ritual of relaxing the body. It was surprisingly peaceful. Maybe because he wasn't opening his annoying mouth to put me down. He surprised me by sitting there in silence for ten minutes or so, actually meditating. I honestly didn't think he had it in him to sit still for that long. Especially around me.

"Now take another deep breath," I whispered, ready to walk him through the end of one of my most favorite meditations. Based on all the frowns he put his face through, I thought he might find it useful too. "Think of your earliest childhood memory of being angry. The one that sticks out the most in your mind. See it all play out from afar, like a spectator at a movie."

For me, I pictured Ace on that stage at Christmas, ripping apart my flower crown and shouting something about me being a stupid girl. I felt the humiliation. The hurt. The confusion.

"Take all those emotions and put them in a box. Thank the emotions for the lessons, but let them know they're not needed any longer. Close the lid and push it away from you."

Silence stretched out and I gave him space to picture it in his head.

"My dad left us," Ace whispered next to me, his voice sounding like rusty metal scraping together.

I swallowed hard, my heart rate picking up. My eyelids blinked open to find darkness all around us. I snuck a peek over at Ace to see his eyes screwed shut and his jaw as hard as granite.

I knew his dad left their family. It had been the talk of the town for months. That was why I gave him my flower crown. He needed it more than me. I opened my mouth to continue the meditation when he cut me off, the words flowing from him like they'd been bottled up under pressure for centuries.

"I hated him. He left my mom with five kids so he could go out and live his life free of responsibilities. What kind of monster would do that?" He sucked in a lungful of air. "I still hate him."

Under normal circumstances, I would place my hands on a person in so much emotional pain to offer support. But with Ace? I was afraid. Afraid he'd reject me. Afraid I'd touch him and never want to stop.

With a gasp, he lurched back, his eyes flying open. He looked over at me, his dark eyes shifting with each second that passed. I couldn't seem to look away. Emotions I couldn't possibly keep up with passed over his face: anger, surprise, hurt, embarrassment. And then rage.

Ace jumped to his feet, his knee bumping me hard as he did so. I scrambled to my feet also, slower than him and unsure what to say. This was new territory for us. We didn't talk about emotions. We traded insults, barbed words meant to hurt, not heal.

"What the fuck did you just do?" He towered over me. "Did you drug me or something?"

My limbs began to shake. His emotions crashed into my chest, seeping inside as if they were mine. Empaths like me get really good at pushing away others' emotions, not allowing them to affect us. If we didn't do that, we'd be caught up in a shifting sea of everyone else's emotions all day long. But with Ace, I couldn't seem to keep up that barrier.

"I didn't—" I licked my lips. "I didn't do anything, Ace. That was just what came up when you stilled your mind."

I put my hand out, sliding my fingers down his arm to his clenched fist. I squeezed his fingers, trying to provide comfort when I should have been scared he'd turn those fists on me. His eyes were glassy. Scared. I could practically see the frightened little boy he'd been long ago. The same boy who'd touched my heart in kindergarten. I'd seen that same look of anger and fear in his eyes that day I'd given him my flower crown. I didn't have one to give him now, but I had something more powerful: compassion. Connection. A safe space to acknowledge all that he'd felt.

"Meditation gives us a chance to examine old wounds. Tap into emotions. It's a good thing, Ace," I assured him.

He didn't flick my hand away. He simply stared into my eyes for several long minutes. I could give him all the time he needed if he let me. The moon reflected off his dark hair. Little critters in the night began to move about the longer we stood there in complete silence.

His eyes began to change, the fear leaving and something I couldn't describe taking its place. His fist finally opened up and he slid his fingers between mine. How the brush of fingers could make my knees quake was a force not yet catalogued here on planet earth. Ace finally moved, but not in the direction I was expecting. With every inhale as we stood there in silence, I thought he'd turn and leave. During all our teasing over the years, both of us left when the button-pushing turned too fierce. The back of his head was more etched into my brain than the front.

But not this time.

No, Ace didn't tuck and run this time.

He stepped closer. His boots took up residence on either side of my bare toes.

I swallowed hard, my head tipping back to hold his heated gaze. His free hand came up. I felt his thumb trace from my chin to my ear and then his work-roughened palm cupped my jaw. My eyes fluttered closed and then opened again. He was closer now, so close I could see each tiny black hair that made up his five o'clock shadow. I felt his breath on my lips. My heart beat wildly, or maybe it was his.

"What is happening?" Ace whispered right before his lips landed on mine.

I had no answer for him. No thought. No idea of time and space now that he touched me so intimately. His warm tongue flicked against my bottom lip. His teeth nipped and then his lips soothed. I gasped at the heat that tore through my body, and he took advantage, stealing inside to duel with my tongue. The kiss changed, turning hard and rough, the pent-up anger from his confession now inflicted upon me. I knew without even a moment's hesitation I would take it. I would take it all from him and beg him for more.

His hand slid from my jaw to my hair, those strong fingers clenching around the strands. He pulled and I felt every single hair follicle lighting up a pattern on my scalp. An Ace-shaped pattern of want and need so desperate I didn't recognize myself. Nor the pants and moans that escaped between us. This was the kiss to end all kisses. The most intense I'd ever experienced.

So. Fucking. Good.

Ace ripped his mouth from mine with a groan from deep in his throat, both of our eyes blinking open to stare at one another. I was breathing hard and so was he. His hand didn't leave my hair, only gripping tighter until I mewled against the pain. His eyes heated and then he dipped his head again.

I'd never fought a forest fire before, but I felt singed by one just the same.

CHAPTER TEN

*A*ce

FUCKING HELL.

How did a mouth that spoke such acerbic comments have such soft lips? I hadn't expected Adelia to be so soft. So malleable. So sweet in my arms. In the past, when I thought of her, I pictured a porcupine, its barbs a visible barrier that threatened without even trying. But now? Holy shit. The woman could kiss.

I tightened my grip on her hair just trying to get ahold of myself, but the little sound she made acted like an accelerant to my need. I had to have more or I actually believed I might die on the spot. My lips were on hers before I even completed the thought. She opened immediately, the elemental taste of her now imprinted in my brain. Her hand slid up my chest to grip behind my neck, holding me to her in a death grip. The epiphany felt like lighting hitting me.

Little Adelia Bammingford wanted me as much as I wanted her.

My hips, having a mind of their own and a lust as ancient as time itself, thrust against her belly, finding a soft warmth that felt as close to perfection as I could imagine. Something danced across my boot. I flicked it away and thrust my tongue inside her mouth like I wished to do with my cock. It was back again, that patter of feet against the toe of my boot.

Feet?

I broke off the kiss and looked down, seeing a squirrel sitting on its hindquarters on my boot, staring up at me.

"Jesus!" I hopped back, regretfully letting go of Adelia.

The squirrel scampered over to Adelia, looking up at her and then back at me, as if to say, "do I need to get rid of this guy for you?" I blinked and scrubbed a hand across my eyes.

Great. I was envisioning squirrels talking now.

The cool night breeze slapped some sense into me. I looked over at Adelia to see her cheeks heated, her eyes fuzzy, and the most delicious wetness on her lips. Fuck me. She looked like she'd been kissed within an inch of her life, and I wanted back in on that action.

"Don't worry. That's just Chuck." Adelia pointed to the squirrel.

I felt my eyebrows lifting. "You name the squirrels?"

The fuzziness in her eyes left immediately, the usual sharpness I saw there locked in place just like old times. "I do when I feed them daily."

"You shouldn't feed wild animals." It was out before I thought about it. I'd seen plenty of wildlife in my job, and you could never predict what they'd do. She shouldn't be feeding them. It just wasn't safe.

"Thank you, Ace. I'm not sure how I've lived twenty-eight years without your sage advice."

I clenched my jaw, seeing porcupine quills instead of the soft woman I'd just devoured a second ago. "Let's get you inside, huh?" I stepped forward and put my hand on her back, ridiculously looking down to make sure the squirrel didn't have an army of his friends waiting to take me down. I wouldn't put it past her. Why did craziness follow Adelia wherever she went?

She didn't fight me as we walked to the back of her house like I thought she would. I opened her back door while giving her a raised eyebrow over it being unlocked. Adelia lifted her nose in the air and sailed right by me, about to close the door in my face.

"Will you do me a favor?"

She sighed, but stayed her hand.

"Please lock your doors tonight?"

Her gaze snapped to mine. She paused and then gave a slight head nod before closing the door. I waited until I heard the lock snap into place. The walk back to my truck felt like emerging from one universe and stepping into another. By the time I got back to my house, I'd convinced myself that I'd had a momentary brain lapse. That meditation shit must have messed me up.

I climbed out of the truck and headed inside my house, the one I'd bought two years ago and still hadn't renovated like I planned. "Meditation is not for me," I mumbled, heading inside to take a shower. Maybe if I used all the hot water in the tank, I could get the scent of Adelia off me. And maybe, just maybe, I could get this erection to go down.

"Okay, today we're delving into burns, head trauma, and broken bones." I scanned the crowd, smiling for all I was worth. I'd successfully avoided Adelia all week. This class, however, had hung over my head. I knew I couldn't avoid her here, but I could act like the professional I was and get the job done.

It was ten minutes after the hour, and as usual, Adelia was late. I heard a loud squeaking noise coming from outside which cut off my first lesson on first aid for burns, something I was intimately familiar with.

"Excuse me, folks. Just one second." I hustled out the door of the classroom and then the community center, arriving outside just in time to see Adelia pulling up in the parking lot on a rusted-out old bike that was letting out a racket.

She hopped off smoothly and tried to lug it up the stairs. I stepped down and took the bike from her, carrying it up to the front porch and waited while she locked it up. As if someone was going to steal that hunk of junk. They'd probably get tetanus from the damn thing before they could sell it on the black market.

"What the hell is that thing?" I asked as she straightened up and sent me a smile that looked about as fake as mine. She smoothed down her tank top, a tangle of varying lengths of necklaces sparkling from her chest. She looked fucking hot in a weird wood-nymph-playboy-centerfold kind of way. A tiny braid peeked out from her hair where the feather had been last week. Her skirt was all one color this time, but—unfortunately for my control over my dick—hugged her hips more than before.

"My trusty transportation," she said proudly.

I grimaced. "More like rusty."

She snorted and spun on her heel, leaving me there to wonder why she'd ride a bike all the way to the community center in a skirt. Why not just drive?

I followed after her and continued the class. This time, Adelia jumped in and gave her two cents as I talked rather than waiting for the end of my half hour.

"Burns are a serious matter and should always be looked at by a doctor," I was saying.

Adelia leaned across me. "But if there's no bubbling, you can use a layer of lavender and frankincense essential oil for a natural approach to healing that won't put you out the cost of a copay." She put her hand on my arm and lifted her leg in the air to show off her ankle. Thank God she was wearing shoes this time. "I had a burn right here, and as you can see, there's just the slightest bit of pink left. In a few days, it should be totally gone with zero scarring."

"Ohh, I have that same ankle bracelet," Yedda cooed from the second row. "It makes that little bell noise just like my cats."

"I think I'd look good in one of those too," my mother chimed in from the second-to-last row.

"I can make you one!" Adelia offered, smiling brightly. "In fact, I can make one for all of you."

"Even me?" groused Lenny, one of the oldest citizens here in Hell. Funny, he didn't strike me as a man who wore ankle bracelets, but he was staring at Adelia like she'd hung the moon just for him.

What was happening here? I clapped my hands. "Okay, let's get back to first aid. How about we talk concussions?"

Adelia rolled her eyes comically and the class tittered. I leaned down to whisper in her ear. "Got an oil to help a concussion?"

She glared at me, but let me get through my talk on what to do if someone hit their head. The rest of the class went well. Better than I thought it would, actually. Adelia jumped in with suggestions that didn't seem so crazy, even managing to make the class laugh as the two of us sparred. Her barbs didn't seem so sharp this time. She aimed them at my suggestions and not at me personally. I followed suit, feeling a lot better about teasing her when it didn't snuff out the light shining in her eyes.

Class ended and we stayed to clean up. It could have been my imagination, but it felt like the silence this time was friendly. Like maybe we'd struck some sort of silent truce.

"Well, I think that's it." Adelia surveyed the room and then at my head nod of agreement, we walked out together and I locked the door with the city key I was given with my promotion to captain.

"Dang, they give those keys to just anybody these days," Adelia said in a teasing voice next to me.

I smirked at her and shoved it back in my pocket. I put my hand on her back and steered us outside where the moon had climbed high in the dark sky as we'd taught the class. Adelia moved to unlock her bike. I scratched the side of my head and prepared for her to put up a fight with what I did next.

When she had it unlocked, I lifted the bike and walked it down the steps, not stopping until I got to my truck. With a grunt, I got it over the side and laid it down in the back of the truck bed.

"Hey!" I could hear Adelia running after me, that tiny bell on her ankle clanging away.

"I'm taking you home, woman. You shouldn't be riding in the dark." I opened the passenger door to my truck and matched her glare. Her hands were on her hips, defiance in every line of her body. She was thinking though, that much I could see. It was like the wheels of her brain were going through all the arguments and realizing not a single damn one of them would change my mind.

"Fine," she huffed, climbing up into my truck and tucking her skirt in so I could shut the door.

I went around the hood and got behind the wheel, starting the truck and turning down the music. I'd rather talk the whole way home. I chuckled out loud.

"What's so funny?"

I tapped my thumb against the steering wheel, wondering if there was some essential oil Adelia wore that turned my brain inside out every time I was around her.

"I was thinking I wanted to chat on the way home and it hit me that I don't think I've ever wanted to sit and chat with you before."

"Ouch. That's a hurtful thing to say, Ace." Her gaze stayed trained out the windshield, but I could see my comment had actually hurt her in the way her shoulders rounded. Like she was tucking into herself for protection.

Against me.

Fuck. I was an asshole.

"I—I didn't mean it that way. I just meant..." Fuck. I was seriously screwing this up, and for some reason, it actually mattered to me that she understand me. I reached over and put my hand on her thigh. She stiffened, but didn't flick my hand off of her.

"I meant I like how we are with each other right now. Civil. Maybe even friendly."

I glanced over to see Adelia fighting a smile. "Is that what you call that kiss? Friendly?"

Instead of answering her, I turned down the long road to her house. We bounced through the potholes in charged silence. Someone should fix those potholes for her. I'd have to see if this was a city road or private.

When I pulled to a stop outside her house and cut the engine, I pulled my hand back and got out of the truck. The air was thick with tension between us now that she'd brought up the kiss. The very same one I'd spent all week thinking about and trying to forget. The one that woke me up with the taste of her still on my lips and a raging boner that even a daily solo session in the shower couldn't tame.

I pulled the bike out and set it against the back of her house. When I turned around, she'd exited my truck and stood next to the huge pine tree that was the closest to her house. Suddenly I was thinking about how unsafe it was to have that thing so close to her house. A bad storm could send a branch down on her roof.

"You shouldn't—"

"I swear to all the goddesses, if you tell me one more thing I shouldn't do, Ace Hellman, I'll sneak into the fire station and put itch powder in your uniforms."

I shut my mouth and tried not to smile at her ridiculous threat. Itch powder? How old was she? Eight?

I walked right up to her, watching the way her eyes seemed to soak in my every move. Her necklaces sparkled in the moonlight. Even her blonde hair seemed to glow like a golden aura around her. It was like watching a wild animal in their natural habitat. Glorious. Beautiful.

And then that wild animal pounced and she was in my arms, her mouth on mine, and her scent all around me. Lust so strong I didn't know what to do with it all, surged through me. I pushed her backward and followed her, pinning her against the rough pine tree. Her tongue flicked against mine, teasing me like she'd teased me all night.

My hand trailed down her waist, over her hip, and down her thigh. I gathered her skirt in my fist and found naked flesh beneath all those layers of clothes. My head was spinning, my heart was hammering inside every cell, and my blood had turned to hot lava.

"You're a goddamn wood nymph," I muttered against her lips in between kisses.

I felt Adelia giggle and then she jumped, wrapping her legs around my waist. Fuck, I loved how aggressive she was. I pushed her harder into the tree, my groin nearly crying with relief when she ground her hot center against me.

She gasped and broke the kiss, tossing her arms out to the side and shouted at the moon. "Nuh-uh." Her face broke into a smile and then she was back to kissing me.

"Definitely...a witch," I managed to say. Even while she was seducing me with her mouth, she was arguing with me. Typical Adelia.

She kept shaking her head and denying it as we made out against the tree. But one thing was crystal clear: I couldn't deny her. Couldn't deny how much I wanted her. And definitely couldn't deny how good we were together there in the cover of darkness in the woods.

CHAPTER ELEVEN

$\mathcal{A}$ddy

I WAS a go-with-the-flow kind of girl. I didn't question where the universe was taking me, or think too hard about consequences beyond what my spirit was telling me to do. So when Ace kissed me like he could put aside twenty years of hatred for just another second worshipping my mouth, I was going to go for it. All the way.

The bark of the tree bit into my back, but my front was in heaven plastered against Ace. His hand had slid back under my skirt, his fingers crawling up my thigh, dangerously close to where he'd nestled his hard cock. I'd have to report to Meadow that Ace was, thank the goddesses, not hung like the statue of David.

I broke away from his lips just long enough to ask for what I wanted. "Have you ever had sex outside with only the moonlight and the occasional squirrel watching?"

The right side of Ace's mouth hitched up in a lopsided smile I'd never seen directed at me before. It was adorable. His hips thrust against me and my eyes rolled back in my head. Forget adorable. Ace was hot. Five-alarm-fire hot. I thoroughly understood now why women all over town tripped over themselves to get his attention.

"Can't say that I have." Ace waited until I locked eyes with him again. "Are you offering?"

The pulsing between my thighs traveled up into my heart chakra, pounding away in a message I couldn't ignore, no matter how badly I wanted to rip Ace's uniform shirt off and have my way with him. Stupid heart chakra. I'd been working on it for weeks now and still it reared its ugly head at the most inopportune times.

"I offered you my flower crown before the Nutcracker and you tore it up. I'm not sure if I should offer you anything else."

Ace's eyes shuttered and then squeezed shut. He rested his forehead against mine, his breath slowing down. I could practically hear the crickets filling the silence in the wake of my horrible timing. *Way to kill the sex frenzy, Addy.* Meadow would have my head for turning down eager dick like that.

His eyes finally opened again, and he pulled his head back. He lowered my feet to the ground, and my heart sank right with them. This rejection stung worse than it had in kindergarten.

Ace squeezed my waist and that was when I realized he hadn't stepped away from me. "Look at me, Addy."

My gaze swept up to his face, shock making me comply. He called me Addy.

"I'm sorry for destroying your flower crown. If I recall correctly, that was just after my father left town."

That didn't explain destroying my flowers, but it was more than he'd ever said on the topic. "I know. That's why I gave it to you. To help you not be sad."

His head dropped and suddenly I was looking at the top of his hair. "Ace?"

He heaved a sigh and looked up again, no trace of the signature frown on his face. In its place, I only saw sadness. "I'm sorry, Addy. I'm sorry for not accepting your gift. I'm sorry for hurting you. I'm sorry for all these years of being so hard on you. Teasing you just became a habit I fell into, I guess."

That still didn't explain why, but an apology was an apology. Besides, I'd teased him back just as much. Both of us were to blame for keeping the hatred going. "Forgiven," I whispered, really and truly meaning it.

The thing was, Ace somehow had a way about him that could destroy a girl. When we hated each other, it was easy to keep him at a distance. If Ace had just changed the game and became a friend, I wasn't sure how well my heart could withstand his charm.

"Thank you," he whispered, leaning back in to kiss my cheek, his hands sliding around and pulling me from the tree. Suddenly I was pressed against his warm chest, his arms holding me in the nicest hug I'd ever received.

Ace Hellman and I were standing in the forest late at night... hugging. Shock didn't even begin to describe it.

We stayed that way for a few minutes. Long enough for my body to relax. Long enough for awareness to return regarding the steel pipe pressed against my stomach. Long enough for Ace to begin to rub his hands along my back, massaging my muscles and turning me to putty.

"I don't suppose that offer still stands?" Ace whispered in my ear.

I snorted against his chest, and I could feel the rumble of his laughter. Part of me wanted to snap something back, the same part that had run the show the last twenty years. But we'd entered new territory. The type of place that required honesty.

"I have an itch that needs scratching, Ace."

Ace's hands froze on my back. "I think there's an essential oil for that."

I pulled back and burst into laughter. He joined me, the two of us laughing with our arms still around each other. It was nice. Too nice.

"No, I mean the tension between us. I think we need to fuck it out."

Ace looked like he'd swallowed his tongue. "Jesus, Addy," he mumbled.

I let go of him, sliding my hands up his chest, over the name patch sewn into his dress shirt, and up to grab the open collar. "Promise me that if I offer you my body tonight, you won't try to destroy my heart?"

That teasing light was back in his eyes, the one that pulled me in like a gnat to a flame. "Tell you what. You let me inside that pretty pussy, and I promise to never tear apart anything of yours again."

Holy hot flush. Ace Hellman was a dirty talker. Sit back, heart chakra. The sacral chakra and I got it from here.

"How do you know it's pretty? You haven't seen it," I replied coyly, leaning into him further.

He dipped his head, his lips just a fraction of an inch away from mine. His eyes went hooded and time stood still. "Everything about you is pretty, Addy."

If grumpy Ace got me fired up, sweet Ace melted me right down into a puddle of pulsing need. His lips drifted over mine, light as a feather. He took his time, changing the pressure and the speed of his kisses. His hand came up to cup my jaw and tilt my head the other direction. His lips trailed across my jaw and down my throat. He found a spot that made me gasp and stayed there, tormenting me in the very best way.

"Do you have a blanket handy, my little wood nymph?" His lips tickled my neck as he spoke.

My heart pounded, and I knew he could feel my pulse. I couldn't help it. He'd called me his, and even though I knew that was completely false—one-date Ace didn't stick around long enough to have a woman become his—I still liked hearing it. I'd been waiting for my other half to appear like a gift from the universe, and while I knew Ace wasn't him, I ached to feel a man's weight on top of me. A heavy human blanket to give me some sense of connection. Temporary though it may be.

"In the house," I murmured, my hands already trailing down his shirt and freeing his buttons.

He pulled away from me. "Don't move." And then he was running like the forest was on fire and the only fire extinguisher was in my tiny house. I swayed on my feet, looking around at the familiar woods and wondering if this was really happening.

Ace came back out in record time with a heavy blanket I'd had for years and frequently used outdoors. He laid it out at my feet and toed off his boots before stepping on it. He held out his hand and I slid my palm across his. A quick tug and I was back in his arms, laughing because the universe was a strange beast. I mean, really. Sending me Ace Hellman to scratch the itch?

"What's so funny?" he asked me with a smile that made him look younger. He slid his hands under my shirt and pulled it over my head with one quick tug. Hair went every which way. He smoothed the strands away from my face and then trailed a finger down my chest and between my lace-covered breasts. "Fuck, Addy. I've been dreaming about these breasts."

I cringed at the reminder of flashing him. He barked out a laugh. "That seriously made my day."

He reached around and had the bra unsnapped before I could say something snarky about him tackling me by the fire pit. He slid the straps down my arms and let the bra fall to the ground. His inhale was sharp, almost like he was in pain.

"You okay?" I teased.

His hands came up to gently cup my breasts, his gaze trained on them like he was hypnotized. "I could have killed you for coming to class without a bra on."

"Oh, you noticed?" I bit my lip.

His gaze flew up to my face. "Fuck, Addy. I'd have to be blind not to notice that. You have the most incredible rack I've ever seen, and I don't mean that in a demeaning way. I could worship these things. Make a citywide holiday for them. Bronze them and put the statue up in the roundabout so everyone could appreciate perfection. Then I'd have to take it down in the middle of the night so no one else could gaze upon them."

I didn't know how to respond to that. I thought my boobs were pretty awesome too, but to hear the possessiveness from Ace's lips was not something I ever thought would happen.

"Can I see yours again too?"

Ace's lopsided grin was back. With a flick of his thumbs over my nipples that had me gasping, he let go and spread his arms wide. The dimples flashed. "I'm all yours."

The local celebrity hero I'd seen be jovial and magnanimous with people in town was now aimed at me. I could see why everyone fawned over him. I could see why girls fell for him.

I knew he meant he was mine just for right now, but again, my stupid heart wanted to read more into it. This was just a physical release, I reminded myself. Nothing more to it. I pulled his shirt over his shoulders and let him drop it to the ground. I pulled his white undershirt from his pants and pulled that over his head though I had to go on tippy-toes to make it happen.

His broad chest filled my vision, an expansive playground I intended to explore. A tiny trail of dark hair sprinkled across his chest before arrowing down into his pants. I slid the belt out of the pant loops and threw it down on the ground. The button came undone and the sound of the zipper echoed off the trees.

"Like unwrapping a present," I murmured.

I hooked my thumbs in the waistband of his pants and underwear and yanked them down, careful not to assault the erection I'd felt against me all evening. Ace yelped, but I was too intrigued with the perfect cock that sprang forth like a jack-in-the-box. I dropped to my knees, to worship it or to get a closer look. Either would have worked for me.

"I knew it," I whispered, thinking about when my foot had accidentally kicked him and I got a distinct impression of this firefighter's hose.

Like a woman possessed, all ten fingers wrapped around it

and still the leaking tip was exposed. My tongue darted out and swiped across, the bloom of musk and salt bursting in my mouth. Of course, Ace had a perfect cock. The universe had granted him the perfect face, body, and penis. She'd maybe messed up a bit in the personality department, but I was just here for the packaging anyway.

I hummed my appreciation and Ace growled. I wrapped my lips around the straining head and sucked. My hands tugged on his velvety length and suddenly I was being lifted away from my new favorite toy, my back hitting the blanketed ground and Ace hovering above me.

"Jesus, Addy. Give a guy a break, huh?"

I smiled up at him, out of breath from anticipating what was going to happen next. Who needed cardio when they had sex? "Too much for you to handle?"

Yes, that was it. Sparring was familiar. I could remember what we were if we sparred. Those sweet comments were for lovers, not for what Ace and I would be doing here tonight.

Ace's left eyebrow lifted on his forehead. "Oh, I'm just getting started." He climbed over me, his thighs bracketing my body. "Hold your breasts, gorgeous." I did, pressing my boobs together like an offering. With a smirk, he thrust his hips and slid his dick between them.

"Hold my head," I demanded, not one for letting him call all the shots. He paused for a moment, but complied, placing one fist in the blanket by my face and the other cupping the back of my head. I licked my lips and he growled. He thrust again, and this time, my mouth was there waiting for his length to appear from between the mounds of my breasts. The tip of him slid right inside my mouth, my tongue swiping across before he pulled back out.

"Fuck, I like that," he hissed between clenched teeth.

"Then keep going," I urged, wetting my lips again. I tensed my thighs to stave off the need that already had me dripping wet.

Ace thrust one more time and then pulled away, climbing

back down my body. "As much as I could do that all night, I have a pretty pussy waiting for me and that's even better."

I tossed my head back and smiled up at the tree tops reaching for the moon like a total goof. There was nothing quite like a man who liked to go down on a girl to make her feel like she hit the jackpot. Ace's calloused hands slid my skirt down and off my legs, leaving me completely naked and free as a bird.

"Spread your legs, Addy."

CHAPTER TWELVE

ce

FUCKING HELL.

I'd never thought of Adelia Bammingford in a sexual way before a few weeks ago. I mean, I'd known her most of my life and the sight or thought of her always made me grimace.

And then I'd seen her boobs.

I'd like to think I wasn't like other basic men, mesmerized by a nice set of tits, but fuck. Addy's were magical. One look and it had changed everything. I was suddenly seeing other sides of her that I'd either ignored or perceived as a defect before. I just made a joke about essential oils for God's sake!

Addy stacked her hands behind her head like she was perfectly comfortable naked in the middle of the forest—which she probably was, knowing her—and began to spread her legs slowly for me. The moon gave off just enough light for me to confirm what I'd already guessed.

"Yep, a pussy pretty enough to eat," I told her with a grin. She grinned back and I had a split second there where my entire body seemed to say the exact same thing at the same time: this is fucking nice. And it wasn't the sex—or the gorgeous boobs I was now intimately familiar with. It was just sharing a smile with Addy without all the history and nasty comments coming between us.

I grabbed her knees and bent them, slinging her legs over my shoulders and hunkering down to get a closer look. I planned to stay awhile.

"Don't mind the forest." I looked up to see a flicker of doubt cross her face. At my blank expression, she explained. "I'm sure you can guess I'm an all-natural sort of girl."

I looked back down at the light-brown curls that covered her sex. If she'd ever seen a razor, it hadn't been in the last few years. I'd never been with a woman who let her hair grow naturally down there, but based on the erection that was trying to drill a hole in the ground, I found there was something highly erotic about it. Seeing a woman in exactly the way nature intended her stirred something primal in my chest.

"Does it look like it bothers me?" I didn't wait for her to answer. I drifted a finger right through the curls and spread her open for my tongue. The taste of her hit like a wall of heat to the face. I was drawn to her for more, my tongue lapping her up in a frenzy as she made noises above me. But there was also a level of caution there. A bell ringing in the back of my brain. I didn't know why it decided to clang away now.

"Ace!" Addy cried out, her legs trembling on my shoulders.

I didn't care if there was a whole fire truck of sirens going off in my brain, I'd push them away and focus on the task at hand. I never let a woman leave my bed without at least two orgasms, but with Addy, I wanted to rock her entire universe. I wanted her to cry out to the moon she loved so much. I needed to hear her say my name with desperation lacing her voice.

I slid two fingers into her tight heat, curling the tips up to hit her front wall. My tongue found her clit and gave it hell. Her

thighs tightened around my head, threatening to cut off circula-
tion. Thankfully, I excelled in dangerous situations.

"Ace, Ace, Ace," Addy chanted. Her hands left the back of
her head to dig into my hair. She didn't need to hold me there. I
didn't plan to go anywhere until she was limp on the ground.

Fuck, I loved eating pussy. Especially hers. It was being
surrounded by her that did it for me. Legs around my head, heels
beating against my back, scent clinging to my face, my fingers
inside of her, and her hands clawing desperately at my scalp. She
cried out again and I felt her tense on my fingers before shaking
like a leaf and relaxing her hold on me.

I kept stroking my fingers and lapping softly at her flesh until
she laughed into the night sky and pulled on my ears. "Dammit,
Ace. You're trying to kill me."

I grinned against her pussy, then lifted away from her with a
final kiss that made her jump. "I wouldn't dream of it."

"Mhm." Addy's eyes looked like she was half-asleep. Pride
surged through my chest for having gotten the first orgasm out
of her. I had all fucking night to get a few more. Challenge
accepted.

I held my weight on my elbows, ignoring the rock digging
into my skin through the blanket. I just hoped to God that
squirrel friend of hers, Chuck, didn't swing by for a visit. I was
enjoying having her naked skin against me too much to stop and
take her inside. Though a squirrel anywhere near my balls would
be the kind of motivation I needed to haul ass.

Addy blinked up at me, a soft smile directed my way that set
those warning bells clanking again. I ignored them and leaned
down for a kiss instead.

"You taste like heaven," I murmured against her lips.

She nipped at my bottom lip. "I didn't get a chance to really
taste you."

I pulled back, my dick nestling between her legs like a heat-
seeking missile. "Are you pouting?"

She gave me a look that reminded me of Addy from years ago. "Not pouting, just stating facts."

"Maybe next time, sweetheart. Right now though? I want to be inside of that sweet pussy more than I want to breathe."

Addy answered by spreading her thighs and letting my body settle into her curves. My hips acted on their own accord, thrusting just the tip inside her heat. My eyes nearly rolled back in my head.

"Fuck." I pulled back with a shiver and gave her a warning look. "You're a witch, woman." My pants were somewhere around here. I found them, hands fumbling for my wallet where I kept a condom, while I listened to Addy's tinkling laugh.

"Which is it? Witch or wood nymph?"

I ripped that fucker open and rolled it down my cock, swallowing hard to keep from exploding in my own hand. It had been awhile for me. My dates recently hadn't left me feeling inspired enough to bother with sex. I was sure that was the only reason I could barely control myself with Addy. That energetic constipation she'd accused me of having.

I climbed back between her legs and didn't waste a second sliding into her in one forceful thrust. Addy let out the kind of moaning gasp that made my balls tighten.

I stayed still, my forehead leaning against hers as we both caught our breath. "Fuck, Addy. You feel so good." I slowly pulled almost all the way out and then pushed back in. Her soft heat was like catnip to my hard cock.

Addy scrambled to hook her legs around my back. Her hands slid up my arms and around my shoulders, her nails grazing my back. Goose bumps lit up my skin. I kept thrusting, my balls becoming almost painful with how badly they wanted to explode. Her tits bounced in rhythmic circles, an erotic sight that just added to the pleasure pinging me from all angles. I reached a hand between us and grabbed one, holding it steady for my mouth. My tongue laved her tight nipple before sucking it inside my mouth and flicking it.

"Yes, Ace. More." Addy's nails bit into my back.

I thrust harder and faster. Dear God, if she didn't come in the next ten seconds, I might embarrass myself. Addy let go of my back and grabbed my ass, one hand per butt cheek and pulled me into her even harder, surprising me.

Oh, she liked it hard? I could certainly test that theory. I slammed into her for all I was worth, probably harder than I should have. Definitely harder than a first time on the damn ground called for, but she only gasped louder, calling out to all kinds of goddesses I'd never heard of, but I didn't care. Her head was almost off the blanket and still I didn't stop, giving her exactly what she wanted.

Her eyes popped open wide and her mouth froze on an inhale. I felt her walls pulse around me and spots of black filled my vision. Something hit my balls—a lightning rod or a clawed swipe from a squirrel, I wasn't sure which—and suddenly I was shooting hot ropes inside of her, every muscle in my body straining under the pressure. At some point I lost the ability to hold myself up and instead just pinned her to the ground.

Addy gasped air into her lungs, her breasts trembling against my chest. "Holy shit, Ace."

I used my last bit of energy and lifted my head, blinking slowly to clear my vision. Addy's face was flushed, the redness traveling down to her breasts. Her hair made for a tangled halo around her head. I didn't think I'd ever seen a prettier woman.

"You can check forest sex off my list," I said absentmindedly before dropping my forehead to her chest. Pretty sure the blood was not back to my brain yet.

I felt Addy look at me and then burst into laughter. Her body shook underneath me, the vibration like jumper cables to my dick. I thrust my hips and the laughter cut off. She looked up at me with wide eyes.

"Again?"

I pulled all the way out of her and stood up, my cock already at half-mast again. I held my hand out, thinking I'd never get the picture of her naked there on the blanket out of my head. But seriously, I couldn't take my chances with the squirrel. Besides, my knees were probably bruised from the hard-packed dirt. "I'll give you a three-second head start to get inside."

Addy sat up and took my hand. "If I lose?"

I pulled her upright and couldn't help but reach out to tweak her nipple. Fuck, I really was obsessed with them. "Have you ever been spanked, Adelia?"

Her eyes warmed as the grin spread across her face.

And then she took off running.

CHAPTER THIRTEEN

ce

MY WHOLE BODY jolted me awake, pain blooming in my toe. I blinked to clear my vision, seeing that my leg had fallen off the tiny double bed in Addy's house for the tenth time. I would have bitched about it, but a naked Addy was currently lying half across my chest, her long blonde hair like a scarf over my neck, her gorgeous boobs pressed against my chest. When we took it inside last night, it had felt a lot like my youth, trying to get busy in the back seat of a vehicle. Only this was a house. Well, I guess you could call it a house, though the square footage wasn't much bigger than a vehicle.

I pulled my arm away from where it had been wrapped around her and checked the time on my watch. Unfortunately, I had to get going. No work today, but I had a long list of errands I had to get done. I'd been putting so much time into my new position at the station, plus the first aid class, I was behind on absolutely everything in my home life. I wasn't even sure if I had a clean pair of work pants for tomorrow's shift.

"Goodbye, boobs," I whispered to the mounds I'd had my hands and mouth on a lot last night.

Moving as slowly as I could, I slid out from under Addy and stood, glancing around for my clothes. My brain warred with itself. I wanted to slide right back into bed and into her body. The other half of me wondered why the hell I'd even stayed the night.

I stared down at her, taking advantage of her being asleep to really look at her. I'd spent the last twenty years being so rude to her I didn't ever really look at the beautiful woman she'd become. The sheet had shifted down, showing the indentation of her spine, her skin as smooth as silk. Her hair was spread across the pillow, wild and free, a representation of her personality. Sure, her breasts had me fascinated, but I feared it was so much more than that.

Unease stirred in my gut. I turned away from her and found the pile of our clothes that I'd brought in from outside at some point. I stepped into my underwear and pants, the chill of the material wiping away the warmth of last night. Sleeping with Addy didn't have to change anything. I'd treat her like I did all my friends and acquaintances. I put the undershirt on and balled the dress shirt in my hands as I approached the bed.

I needed to put her back in the box I planned to keep her in. Nothing about her confession of giving me that flower crown to keep me from being sad all those years ago could make a dent in the steel cage I had around my heart. Attachments of the heart were for other men, not me.

With that firmly decided, I flicked my wrist, swatting her squarely on the ass. She yelped and flipped to sit up, her hair a tangled mess over her face and shoulders. She swiped it back and glared at me, the familiar expression making me feel like I was on steady ground again. Her eyes were puffy with sleep.

"Rise and shine, woman."

She huffed and even that was cute. Helped that her naked

breasts bounced when she did it. "A simple pat on the shoulder would have sufficed."

I grinned, happy to be back to sparring with her. "But where's the fun in that?" I hooked my thumb over my shoulder. "I've got to get going, but I need your phone number."

Addy pulled the sheet up to cover her breasts. Damn, taking all my fun away. "Why?"

"Because you can't ride a bike to the classes anymore. Total safety violation. I'll pick you up." I glanced around the house. Her phone couldn't be too far away. Pretty sure I could stand in the center of her house and spin around, touching all four walls. "Now, where's that phone?"

Addy huffed, the rustling of sheets following. I couldn't help but look back, thinking I might get an eyeful, but sadly, Addy had ripped the sheet from the bed and wrapped it around her as she stood. "I don't know. It's around here somewhere."

We both started looking, but Addy found it a few minutes later with a triumphant, "Found it!" She was squatted down by the bed, blowing the dust off the small cell phone.

I smirked. "Seriously? A flip phone?"

Addy stood and put her hands on her hips, tucking the phone behind her. "I have no use for smartphones."

I didn't either really, but I couldn't help but keep up the teasing. "Ever heard of social media?"

"Sure, but what use is there in doom scrolling?"

I opened my mouth to argue but paused. She was kind of right. Social media had started out as this awesome invention and turned into a way to feel badly about yourself compared to everyone else's highlight reel. "Good point."

"Why, thank you, Ace. That might be the first time you've uttered those words to me."

I flicked a lock of her hair behind her shoulder when I really just wanted to wrap it around my fist and slam my lips on hers. "Might be the first time you've ever been right."

Addy's glare made my morning. "Do you want my number or what?"

We exchanged numbers and then an awkward silence hung there between us. This was why I didn't spend the night. Easier to just sneak away in the darkness and avoid the awful decision of whether to hug or high-five as I said goodbye.

I inched backward toward the front door. "Okay, well, thanks for last night. I'll see you next week at six thirty."

"Careful, Ace. That might be construed as a second date."

Nausea, the kind that hits hard and fast, swept through me. Then my brain registered the light in her eyes, and I realized she was just teasing me. "Nah. This wasn't even a first date. No dinner. No making out in my truck. We were just scratching the itch, like you said."

The light seemed to go out in Addy's face, but she flashed a smile that made me wonder if maybe I was just seeing things. "Thank the goddess. I don't need my chakras getting mixed up with yours."

I grabbed the doorknob and shot over my shoulder, "You seemed to like my chakra last night."

I ducked out the door and closed it quickly to avoid the pillow she tossed at me. I chuckled out in the open, the trees the only witness to the smile I couldn't wipe from my face. Addy was fun. And fucking gorgeous.

For just a quick second, I was going to appreciate the time we spent together. Then I'd go back to disliking her. A little time. A little space. That was all I needed to forget about last night's scratching of the itch.

As I started my truck and headed home, one thing was for certain: I was never meditating again. That shit was straight voodoo.

I GROANED. "Of all the shit timing..."

I parked in my driveway and got out, eyeing the silver convertible parked at the curb in front of my house. Mom was here.

Climbing the front porch stairs, I steeled myself for the inquisition. The door flung open and there she was, hand on hip and mouth already open like the drama queen she was.

"Where have you been, young man?"

I stepped inside and kissed her cheek before moving further into the house and dumping my shirt and keys on the tiny table where I ate meals. I seriously regretted giving her keys to my place. She had zero concept of what constituted an emergency. "Good morning to you too, Mom."

"Enough with the sweet talk. Why weren't you home last night? You were off work, right?"

I scratched my cheek and made a mental note to shave today. "My math might be off, but I believe I'm twenty-eight years old."

Mom huffed and fluttered her hands through the air, bracelets flashing in the morning sunshine streaming through the windows. "I don't care if you're eighty-eight years old, I'm still your mother. And as such, I know you don't spend the night places. Like, ever."

I moved around her to the kitchen, hearing her heels clicking behind me. Damn. Nine in the morning, and she was already in heels and questioning me. I grabbed a glass from the cupboard and filled it with water, gulping it down.

"I spend the night at the station all the time," I said when I was done.

"You were off last night!" Mom practically yelped.

I put the glass down on the counter and put my hand on her shoulder. "I love you, but I'm not answering your questions, Mom. Now what can I help you with?"

She narrowed her eyes but thankfully dropped the question I was unwilling to answer, even to myself. "I got a phone call last night."

I rolled my eyes and prepared for some Hell bullshit. The very worst of it spread like wildfire. The faster it spread, the more certain you could be that it was completely fabricated news.

Mom didn't wait for me, just barreled right into it like she did most things in life. "I heard that you and a particular woman have been hanging out, and based on what I saw last night, I would have to agree that there's something there."

Those warning bells were back, clanged loud and clearly in my head. This was not a conversation I wanted to be having. Especially when I was still trying to wrap my head around what all went on last night.

"I don't know what you're talking about," I growled, spinning around to get some eggs out of the refrigerator. Mom danced around me, but never further than a foot away.

"I think you do."

"I think I don't."

I grabbed a pan and cracked the eggs in it while she huffed behind me.

"You know exactly who I'm referring to and the fact that you won't even speak to me about it tells me everything I need to know."

My molars felt ready to crack in two. I stirred the eggs and reminded myself not to snap at my own mother. When I had my anger under control, I answered her finally.

"There's absolutely nothing going on with Addy, and that's all you need to know."

Mom's hand landed on my back, soft and soothing as she stroked circles like she used to when one of us boys was sick. "I know chemistry when I see it," she said quietly. "And I also know that kind of chemistry is rare. It would be a shame to turn your back on it right out of the gate."

I sighed and turned off the burner before my scrambled eggs burned. I knew teaching this class with Addy was a mistake. After moving the pan off the burner, I turned around.

"Thanks, Mom. I appreciate the advice, but there's nothing there except animosity. The first aid class may have forced us to accept a sort of temporary truce, but Addy and I are not suited. I promise you that."

Mom stared up at me, her soft brown eyes like truth-seeking missiles, able to detect a lie from twenty paces. All the second-guessing had to be pushed aside. What I said was the goddamn truth. I couldn't accept anything else.

She patted my arm, her face losing its vivacity, reminding me of a time long, long ago when she'd always looked like that. Like she'd had the happiness knocked out of her. "Not everybody will let you down like your father, Ace. It's okay to let your heart soften."

With that nonsense, she twirled on her heel and left my house, closing the door quietly behind her. It was just like Nikki Hellman to drop a bomb and then walk off, calm as you please.

"Fuck!" I grabbed the eggs and threw them in the trash.

Everything on my list would have to wait. I felt a sudden need to go on a long, punishing run to clear my head.

CHAPTER FOURTEEN

*A*ddy

"HOLD UP. Go back. Ace came over to *meditate*?" Meadow's inflection showed just how out of character that was for him.

I paced two steps forward, turned around, and paced back again in my house, everywhere I looked reminding me of Ace. I could still feel the way his hands had glided over my skin. Not one square inch he hadn't touched. It had nearly been a week and I was just now telling Meadow about that night, which was crazy. I told her everything. Yet with this, I'd held it close to my chest for several days, wanting to mull over every second. Dissect every word or look. But it was driving me crazy.

"I basically dared him that he couldn't."

"Oh, well, that makes sense, then. So did he? Meditate, that is?"

I glanced out the window, looking in the general direction of where we'd sat that night, knees touching. "Yeah, he did. It was kind of intense there at the end."

"Intense in a good way?" came Meadow's voice through the tinny speaker of the ancient flip phone Ace had made fun of.

My whole body went warm just thinking about how intense it got the second he pulled me into him and kissed me. "Definitely a good way."

Meadow squealed and I had to pull the phone away from my ear. "You're holding out on me. I can just hear it in your voice. Spill, woman!"

I plopped down on the beanbag and rested my head back, staring at the ceiling. "You remember that one guy a couple years ago who I met at that yoga retreat?"

"Uh, the one who rocked your world with an orgasm that went on for like an hour?" Meadow's voice was rising so high I had a feeling only animals could hear her now.

"Yeah, that's the one. He was a devotee to tantric sex." I sighed. "Ace made him seem like an amateur."

A loud crash met my ears. "Meadow?"

Her voice came back a second later. "You, Adelia Bammingford, the fervent hater of all things Ace Hellman, had *sex* with him?"

I started giggling, almost in as much disbelief as Meadow. The universe certainly had a sense of humor. "Did you drop the phone?"

"Who cares about the fucking phone, BamBam. Answer the damn question!"

"Yes. I did. And it was amazing. We barely slept all night."

Meadow had a coughing fit, rudely hacking into my ear before she got ahold of herself. "Ace spent the *night*?"

I nodded, thinking about how nice it had been to sleep in his arms. Of course, maybe he'd only done that so he didn't fall off my tiny bed. "Yeah. But before you get too excited, I haven't heard from him all week and we agreed we were just getting it out of our systems. He'll probably be back to insulting me at tonight's class."

"I...well..." Meadow sounded beside herself with shock.

"Babe, you need to come have coffee with Annie and me this afternoon. We need all the details. And I mean all. Plus, I heard the guys have been out on some big fire a couple counties over. Ace probably couldn't call you."

My heart did a little jump in my chest, pumped up by false hope. I squashed it down before it grew like a weed. "No. It was definitely a one-time thing."

Meadow made a noise that sounded like she didn't believe me. "Just meet us for coffee, okay? Two o'clock?"

I sighed. "I don't even drink coffee."

"Chai tea, then."

I wasn't really wanting an interrogation by my friends, but then again, staying at home and stewing on it by myself wasn't working either. I'd done multiple sunrise rituals and even a swim in the cold ocean at midnight to rid myself of thoughts of Ace. All I could do was go over and over the face he made when he slid inside of me. It was like looking at an Ace without all the facades he put up. He let me see a real and raw side of him that reminded me of the boy he used to be. Before his dad left. Before he destroyed my flower crown. Before we'd become enemies.

"Fine. See you soon."

I'D FINISHED my chai tea, which was surprisingly good from a place called Coffee, but Meadow and Annie were still having a field day with this new information about Ace. I'd sworn them to secrecy of course. I didn't want to start a town rumor that would make its way back to Ace. More than that though, I didn't want my name to be added to the long list of women who'd dated Ace and never saw him again, pining away for all eternity. I felt no shame for engaging in mutually pleasing sexual activity with him, but letting people think I'd fallen for him? No way in hell. I'd convinced my brain that I was fine by myself in this world, but my heart hadn't quite gotten with the program.

"So, he stayed all night? Like past sunrise?" Annie asked, her flaming red hair looking like she could be in an Irish shampoo commercial.

I kept the sigh inside where they couldn't hear it, knowing my friends were reading way too much into my night with Ace only because they loved me and wanted to see me with someone. They, of all people, knew I was lonely.

"I think he left around eight?" I couldn't actually remember, nor was I a stickler for clocks and alarms and showing up on time. All of that created undue stress.

"There you are, Annie!"

We all spun in our seats to see Janie, the woman who owned a place just outside of town that hosted goat yoga. She was a competitor of mine, but I never felt that competitive spirit with her. The woman was old, her salt-and-pepper hair more salt than pepper. And she loved yoga trends, whereas I tended to keep things traditional in my yoga practice. Right now though, Janie looked far from calm and serene. She ran over to Annie and grabbed her by the shoulders.

"I need your help! Snowflake the third is foaming at the mouth!"

Everyone around us hushed. Annie stood up and steered Janie out the door. Meadow and I grabbed our trash off the table and scurried out the door after them.

Sure enough, there was Janie's old truck at the curb, the paint job more rust than paint. Hay spilled out the back, the bleating tones of a goat with major indigestion drawing all eyes to the white and black animal. Or maybe Snowflake was just scared of the attention he was getting from everyone passing by. A crowd was quickly forming with Janie flapping her arms and hustling about.

"Janie!" Annie put her hands on Janie's shoulders and stopped her in her tracks. "Stop moving and tell me what happened."

Janie's mouth dropped open and then she slammed it shut, her spine straightening as she pulled herself together. "I ran out of raisins during class this morning, so I substituted dried cranberries. But I don't think poor Snowflake took to them. He gobbled them up and then started pawing at the dirt, snorting up a storm. I just ended yoga early and threw him in the truck. Figured you'd be around here somewhere and would know what to do with him."

Annie, being a second-year vet student and lover of all animals, climbed right into the back of the truck, not afraid of getting her hands dirty with a goat that looked ready to puke on command. I, on the other hand, got distracted by the small cage in the back corner of the truck bed. I could barely hear the hiss beyond the commotion of Snowflake, but I could see the beady eyes. Janie had brought her pet snake, Danger.

While Annie stroked her hand over Snowflake's head and talked to him in that little voice one would a human baby, I reached over the side of the truck and pulled open the cage. Danger slid forward, seeing an opportunity to get out and see the world while everyone else was distracted by the barn animal. I lifted him in my hands and let him slither across my arms. His forked tongue flicked in and out, as if tasting the air here on the outside. He was a beautiful snake, all black and white and smooth scales.

"Hello, gorgeous," I crooned, smiling as he wound his way up my shoulder.

"Addy! Put that down!"

The loud shout from down the street had heads turning, mine included. Ace Hellman was marching down the sidewalk like a man on a mission, that frown of his recharged and on full blast. People hustled out of his way and turned to look at what had him so upset. He was staring right at me, his hand outstretched and pointing. I looked down, belatedly realizing he meant the snake.

Next thing I knew, he was at my side, his commanding voice telling me to once again put down the snake.

"For God's sake, Addy, put down the wild animal. What is with you?"

I lifted my nose in the air, refusing to acknowledge how much my heart pounded out of my chest just seeing him again. "I will not. This is Danger."

Ace crossed his hands across his chest, his big body seeming to grow with each angry inhale. "I know he's dangerous. Put him down before you get hurt."

I huffed, exasperated with him. Why did he automatically think I was getting myself into danger? I'd lived twenty-eight years without his help so far and I was doing fine, thank you very much.

"No, his name is Danger, but he's harmless. He's Janie's California king snake."

Ace continued to glare at me, as if measuring my words for truth. Danger slithered to my other shoulder without a care in the world. Ace's eyes followed Danger's movements. Then he lifted him off my shoulders and put him back in the cage.

I shook my head. Why did he always have to snuff out the fun? I must have squeezed out every last drop of fun Ace had in him during our night together. He was already back to being an annoying hero I didn't need in my life.

He turned back around and that's when I noticed his face was smudged with dirt or soot. Even his hair was in disarray. A small tear in his AHFD T-shirt showed some red skin below. He looked like he'd just gotten back from a fire.

"Just..." He ran a hand through his hair, making it stand up even more. "Just stay out of trouble. Can you do that for me, Addy?"

I put my hands up. "I was just fine. No trouble at all happening here."

Ace narrowed his eyes and then marched off without another word, heading back for his truck. He'd parked it halfway into the street where it was blocking traffic. People moved swiftly out of his way, looking back at me as if to piece together why Ace was so grumpy. If I could solve that mystery, I'd be powerful enough to have command over the tides and the supernatural.

Meadow stepped up next to me, slid her eyes my way with one eyebrow lifting slowly. "Nothing going on between you, huh?"

I snorted.

There was definitely nothing going on between us. He'd made sure of that by not calling all week and then snapping at me for holding a harmless snake. We'd scratched the itch and that was it.

Itch. Scratched.

CHAPTER FIFTEEN

*A*ce

MY THUMB TAPPED out an SOS on the steering wheel as I sat at the curb staring at Addy down the street. She was in the center of the chaos, her long blonde hair fluttering in the breeze, looking as easygoing as a woman would out for an afternoon with her friends. Meanwhile, I was a ball of nerves, angry for five thousand reasons. None of which I could explain to her.

I'd spent the whole week since I left her dealing with a forest fire. It was my first one as the official captain of our station and I'd had to coordinate with other crews, feeling completely out of my depth in this new role. The fire had been intense. Shifting winds and unstable ground had made each move challenging. The feeling of responsibility for each of my crew members was almost debilitating. I could feel the muscles in my neck tightening with every hour the fire blazed on. Every waking moment had been focused on the job and the safety of my crew. And while it shouldn't have, my brain let in a few thoughts of Addy when I let my attention drift. The last thing I could afford out on a dangerous fire was to be thinking of a woman. Especially that woman.

I spent my life making things safe for people. She spent every moment without a care for her safety, incurring safety violation after safety violation. Everything was a game or something to her. It made me anxious. And I hated that I cared enough to be anxious for her. She clearly didn't care about her safety, so why did I?

Here I was using precious moments during my harrowing week to think of her and she was letting snakes wind around her neck for fun. Did she have no parents to instill some common goddamn sense in her brain? Never take someone's word for whether a snake was poisonous or not, especially if that word was from someone like Janie. The woman had been arrested multiple times for protesting in the nude. One could never be too careful.

Addy was my complete opposite, and part of me was beginning to wonder if I'd just imagined our chemistry the other night.

The breeze coming through my window brought a scent of lemon and lavender that had me blinking away my thoughts. Addy, Meadow, and Annie stood there on the sidewalk right by the front fender of my truck in a formation, staring at me from ten paces. Shit. I'd lost track of time.

"Everything okay, Ace?" Addy asked, a familiar frown on her face that made it seem like she'd already forgotten all the orgasms I'd given her.

I didn't fucking like that. If I couldn't get her out of my head, I didn't want her forgetting about me so quickly. Fair was fair. I frowned right back, clearing my throat and feeling the burn from inhaling so much smoke the last week.

"Fine," I said gruffly.

"Still plan on making the class tonight?" Addy tilted her head, studying me like I was weirder than the snake she'd had on her arm.

"Of course. I'll even be there on time," I snapped, feeling all kinds of irritated.

Meadow stepped forward, an evil smirk on her face that made my balls immediately want to climb up inside my body for safety. "You know, I saw a girl in Coffee you haven't dated yet, Ace. Why don't you go ruin her day and leave my friend alone?"

Annie's big blue eyes went round. Addy rolled her lips in and looked like she was about to laugh. At me. Red filled my vision. Exhaustion lined my bones after battling a fire all week and still these three women wanted to snap at me for being a little cranky. I opened my mouth to respond, but Annie slid her arm through Meadow's and tugged the line of them down the street. Meadow sneered at me over her shoulder for good measure while Addy avoided looking in my direction. I watched them go, my gaze on Addy. At the corner, she swiveled her neck and finally looked back. We locked eyes for a brief second and then she was gone.

I slumped back against the seat and scrubbed my hand over my gritty eyes. What the fuck was I doing just sitting here staring at Addy and her friends? I shouldn't have even stopped on my way home, but when I saw Addy holding that snake, my brain had gone offline. I needed a shower and some food and solid shuteye that didn't include emergencies waking me up every half hour.

I put the truck in gear and headed home, keeping my gaze firmly on the road and not out looking for a glimpse of Addy doing anything else that would set my nerves on edge.

"This is exactly why I don't go out with a woman for a second time," I told my dashboard. "They get stuck in my head and then my focus is shot."

Which wasn't exactly true but my dashboard didn't call me out on it. I'd never gone out with a girl a second time because I just hadn't been that interested. Not going out with Addy a second time seemed like a prudent decision for my health and safety.

I pulled up to my house and slid right out of the truck. My legs had gone rubbery while I sat there. That frequently happened after a long fire. All the adrenaline had run its course, and now that the danger was diverted, I was left with the energy of an eighty-year-old man. I grabbed my bag, shut the door, and headed inside. My phone pinged the second I threw my stuff on the floor. I fished it out of my pocket and headed for the refrigerator. The leftovers all looked a bit too old, but the bread looked fine. I made a quick cheese sandwich that would have to do until I headed back into town tonight for class. I'd get a decent meal to go at the Forty-Diner once I'd gotten a nap in.

Shoving the dry sandwich in my mouth, I finally looked down at the phone to see my brothers texting away like they always did. I swear they didn't work a full day of labor between them.

Daxon: Boys, the festival is tomorrow and I got me a hot date. Eat your hearts out.

Ethan: Who says we don't have dates too?

Daxon: I didn't hear anyone calling dibs....

Callan: I'm taking Cricket and I think she's bringing Annie too. As friends though, so don't start your bullshit.

Me: I just got off a six-day fire. I don't even know what day it is.

Daxon: So what you're all saying is I'm the only one getting lucky tomorrow?

Mom: Please, boy. I have a date too and I guarantee he'll be getting lucky before the fireworks start.

I bobbled the phone and had to beat my fist against my chest as the cheese sandwich went down the wrong pipe.

"Fuck," I swore, choking out a laugh. "Who put Mom on the text string?"

Daxon: Well, this is awkward.

Mom: Nothing wrong with a healthy sex life, darling. I hope I've taught you that over the years. Just make sure you use protection and make it good for her.

Ethan: Yeah, Dax. Don't forget the woman should orgasm before you nut.

Daxon: I'm no longer discussing this on this thread.

Callan: What? You don't want Mom giving you sex advice?

Me: Maybe next time check the thread before you start typing. Rookie move...

Daxon: GOODBYE

Mom: Was it something I said?

I chuckled, throwing the phone down and moving toward the bathroom. I swallowed the last of my sandwich and headed for the shower, turning it on and letting the steam build up before I stripped and stepped inside the stall. The warm water felt like heaven running down my aching arms and legs. The scratch on my chest burned, but I ran the bar of soap over it anyway. In the back of my mind, I knew Addy would have some sort of salve or oil to put on it, but good old-fashioned soap worked just fine for me.

Exhaustion weighed down my eyelids. When my forehead hit the tile and I was just burning through the hot water, I flipped the handle off and grabbed my towel. No use sleeping standing up. If I set my alarm, I could get a quick power nap in before I headed over and picked up Addy before class. I wasn't going to stand by while she rode her bike to and from class. Definite safety violation.

I grabbed my phone and fired off a text to her, followed by setting my alarm for five forty-five.

Me: See you around six.

I didn't wait for a response. I just tossed the phone on my bed and collapsed face-first on the mattress. I was out before I'd even quit bouncing. My brain shut off and sleep held me in a state of bliss where thoughts of Addy finally left me alone.

CHAPTER SIXTEEN

$\mathcal{A}$ddy

I WAVED to Meadow as she pulled away from my driveway. When she saw how many bottles of kombrewcha I'd bought in town, she hadn't let me walk home like I usually did. The clanking of the bottles alone would have caused a riot amongst my forest animal friends. Having Ace jump down my throat over the snake may or may not have had something to do with how much alcohol was going in my refrigerator tonight. I wasn't looking forward to teaching the class with him if he was going to revert back to grumpy Ace. I'd need something cold and strong to look forward to after, hence the kombrewcha binge.

I put the beer away in my little refrigerator and lifted my shirt to my nose, eyes watering.

"What is that smell?"

And then I remembered. Snowflake the third had finally spit up the cranberries right after Ace had walked away, showering everyone in a five-foot radius with watery goat puke. I shivered in revulsion and immediately stripped off my clothes to take a long shower outside to rid myself of the smell. I loved animals, but decided I liked them better when they were healthy. Annie could deal with the sick ones.

Of course, my brain kept circling back to Ace. It was thinking of that squinty-eyed frown on his face that had evil thoughts spinning through my brain. Ace seemed to like my boobs, so I planned to make sure they were on full display tonight, just to piss him off. Two could play this game. Seemed as if sleeping together hadn't cooled off our need to poke the bear like we thought it might.

The water sputtered out of the spigot on the side of my house, finally coming on full speed with the warm water in my tiny tank. I'd learned to shower fast over the years if I didn't want to end the shower with a splash of icy cold water.

I was just rinsing off my homemade soap when the devil appeared.

"Damn, Addy, you know how to greet a man."

My eyes popped open to find Ace standing just outside the spray of my shower, his arms crossed over his massive chest and his fist jammed to his mouth. His eyes looked like they might be having trouble not crossing as he ran them over my naked body. I felt that sweep of his gaze like an actual caress.

I cocked a hip and refused to cover myself on my own property, despite the way my heart was beating out of my chest. "I really do need to get some *No Trespassing* signs put up."

Ace's gaze flew up to mine, the heat in them making my knees wobbly. He looked good. Tired, but always more handsome than any man had any right to be. He even had a line across his cheek like he'd just woken up.

"I texted you I'd be here early to pick you up."

I tilted my head. "Not sure where my phone is."

Ace took a step forward, a flicker of a frown. "Addy."

"Is the hometown hero swooping in to drive me to and from class?"

Ace's eyes narrowed.

I reached back and flipped off the spigot before the hot water ran out. And before his dress pants got soaked. Ace grabbed the purple towel off the little half fence that created a type of shower stall. All kinds of soaps hung off the pony wall, the scent I chose depending on my mood each day when I took a shower. Ace held the towel in his hands and, instead of handing it to me, began to dab his way down my body, drying me off quite efficiently. No one had dried me off like that since I was a little child. All the sass I'd planned to throw his direction from his earlier hissy fit seemed to leak out with the little river of water draining away from my house and into the ground.

When he got so low he couldn't reach, he squatted down and blotted my legs with care. I placed my hand on his shoulder for balance and tried to quell the desire that had me wanting to propose scratching the itch again. His skin hadn't actually touched me, and yet all I could think about was getting him to run those callouses over every square inch of my body like he did last week.

Ace finally stilled, looking up at me with an expression I couldn't read. The gentle evening breeze flitted along my skin, my nipples tightening in response. He opened his mouth and I braced for a remark that would have me forgetting how sweetly he dried me off.

"You drive me crazy, Addy. I don't know whether to snap at you or toss you over my shoulder and bury myself so deep inside you I can't remember my name."

My knees let go and my hands had to scrabble along his shoulders to keep me upright. Hearing raw honesty from Ace's mouth was almost too much for a woman. "I vote for the second one."

Ace smirked, a puff of air leaving his nose. He stood up and my hands slid down his arms. He handed me the towel and I wrapped it around myself, figuring he didn't actually intend to carry me into the house to have his way with me. More's the pity.

He reached up and tugged on a curl that had come loose from the haphazard bun on top of my head. "I need food." He swatted my behind and pushed me toward my back door, suddenly in a hurry. "Get dressed so we can get something to eat before class."

Maybe it was him bossing me around. Or maybe it was the slap on the ass, but something in me couldn't just follow orders. I dug my heels in the soft dirt and turned to look over my shoulder. "Careful, Ace. Grabbing dinner might be construed as a second date."

Ace's jaw hardened and I mentally chastised myself for wiping the smile from his face. I couldn't just leave well enough alone, could I? What was it about Ace that turned all my sweetness around and left me with a snappiness that had no place amidst this newly fledged friendship?

"Like I said before, we never had a first date, Addy." He swiped a hand across his chin, the whiskers there letting out a rasp I wanted to feel against my fingers. "Against my better judgement, I'm feeling like taking you on one."

He stepped closer, his brown eyes staring into my soul with a seriousness I didn't often see on a Hellman boy's face. All the air left the vicinity, leaving me lightheaded. "What do you say? Will you let me take you to dinner at Forty-Diner?"

My heart was intent on imitating a hummingbird, fluttering around like a wild animal. "I just...I just have one question." Even my voice came out breathy, as unsure of my question as I was on letting Ace take me to dinner. Surely dinner and conversation was not what I should be doing to get Ace out of my head. And it was definitely not the right decision if I didn't want to be part of the rumor mill in Hell again.

Ace leaned in, his hand coming up to my face. His thumb traced along my jaw and then pushed hair behind my ear. "Ask your question, Addy, and I'll answer it."

I just couldn't leave well enough alone. I had to understand. Had to see who Ace was under the grumpiness he sent my way, or the bravado he sent everyone else's way. I wanted the real Ace more than I wanted my next breath.

"Why did you tear apart my flower crown? I know you didn't want it, and I know you already apologized, but why destroy it?"

Ace's head dropped, a sigh leaving his chest. When his head came up again, there was a weariness in his eyes. I opened my mouth to tell him to forget it. That I didn't need to know. That it was so long ago I was going to finally let it rest, but he cut me off.

"You're like a dog with a bone, Adelia. If you were my brothers, I'd tell you to fuck off. If you were one of my fellow firefighters, I'd assign you so many chores you'd never ask me another question again. But I promised you I'd answer, so I will."

Ace swiveled his head, looking around the clearing for something while I held my breath. I was afraid to speak lest I break the spell of Ace actually being cooperative. I knew I irritated him, but I was willing to be an irritation if it got me a real answer out of him.

"Aha!" Ace moved quickly, picking me up and twirling me around before walking away from the house. I grabbed at his shoulders and tried to keep the towel around me as we moved. I wasn't the lightest of women, but Ace didn't seem to mind as he stepped into the ring of crystals I'd left outside and had a seat, settling me on his lap.

"I have no idea what these crystals do, but if I'm going to lay my soul bare, I figure they might keep my secrets."

I grinned, knowing the crystals would do no such thing, but liking that he didn't shy away from them any longer. He may not understand them, but he was willing to sit amongst them. Progress.

Ace huffed and settled his big hands on my hips, the heat of him soaking through the towel. "Okay. Brace yourself. I might need some of your magic meditation to get this out right."

The grin intensified. "It's not magic, Ace."

He tipped his head. "It is to me."

CHAPTER SEVENTEEN

ce

THERE HAD to be a voodoo vortex that hovered in the air around Addy's place out here in the woods. Talking about the past and my feelings was equivalent to entering a burning building without protective gear, but I was willing to do it, if just to make Addy smile.

"You brought attention to me," I said quietly, wanting to get my explanation just right. I didn't intend to sit here for hours discussing things when my stomach kept letting out a hungry growl. I rubbed my thumbs over the wet towel as I held her still on my lap, wishing I could feel her silky skin instead.

"But—" Addy frowned and sat up tall. "But you love attention."

I shook my head. "No, I really don't. I deal with it, because it just seems to kind of come my way, but I don't like it." I thought back to that day of the holiday concert. That time was a dim haze in my memory. I thought about all the things I'd been feeling as a scared and confused little kid. My dad had left us, my mom was crying all the time, and I had so much rage building in my chest I didn't know what to do with it. "You brought attention to me when I just wanted to melt into the background. I felt like everyone was pointing at me up on that stage, whispering about how our dad left us behind." I made myself look her in the eyes. "I didn't want anyone's pity, so I ripped up the crown like some kind of tough guy."

Addy sucked in a long, slow breath before melting against me. She wrapped her arms around my neck and practically smothered my face in the press of boobs spilling out over the towel. As far as confessions went, I was willing to spill more of my soul if it ended in asphyxiation by boobs.

"Thank you for telling me the truth," Addy whispered in my ear. "I didn't think of things like pity and attention when I gave you the crown. Perhaps I should have."

"You were six years old," I mumbled against her soft skin. Addy had always been a social butterfly in school, flitting from friend to friend like some kind of ray of sunshine, gifting people with her presence. It was part of what irritated me about her. There I was in the depths of anger and hurt, and she was so fucking happy all the time.

Addy shrugged and pulled back. I instantly missed the boobs. "I just should have known, that's all." She pushed on my shoulders and scrambled to her feet, all without flashing me somehow in the short towel. "You need to shower before we go to dinner, mister. As much as I like hugging you, you stink."

I glared at her. "I already showered."

She reached down and tugged on my shirt collar until I stood up. "And you still smell like smoke. Come use this soap of mine. I can't sit across from you eating dinner when you smell like a forest fire."

I sighed and followed her over to her outdoor shower. "It always takes a few days to wear off. Just part of the job."

Addy grabbed a bar of dark soap off the side wall where it

hung from a rope and handed it to me. "Not on my watch, Captain."

I took the soap, eyeing it dubiously. "Soap on a rope? Seriously? It's black and has little things in it."

Addy rolled her eyes. "Just trust me. It has charcoal in it." She patted my chest and walked to her back door. "I'll bring you a towel after I get dressed."

I looked around the quiet forest, realizing I was, in fact, going to take a second shower out in the open with questionable soap just so I could take Addy to dinner at the Forty-Diner. I shook my head and stripped out of my clothes, piling them on the fence line. I caught a flash of something through the window when I turned back to the spigot. A grin spread across my face.

Addy was totally spying on me while I showered.

My dick liked that thought very much. I even forgot about the hunger pains. I turned on the water and stood under the spray. I made sure the soap traveled a sensual line down my chest before tangling in my junk. If Addy was going to make me shower, I was going to give her a show worth watching. Thunder Down Under couldn't have performed a more sensual shower than I did outside with the squirrels chattering away. By the time the water went cold, Addy had slammed out the back door and thrown a towel at me, averting her eyes. Her cheeks were pink though and that was all I needed to see.

I chuckled silently, toweling off and getting dressed again, tucking my erection away. I lifted an arm and gave a good whiff. "You might be right about that soap."

Addy spun around in a long multicolored skirt, short white crop top, and a thousand necklaces decorating her gorgeous chest. "Of course I'm right. That soap is magic. You really should think about trusting me."

I shook my head and grabbed my keys out of my pocket. "I'm starting to," I mumbled, putting my hand on her back and steering her toward my truck parked out front.

"HEY, Addy. Lovely to see you as always."

Callan popped up on the sidewalk outside of Forty-Diner like a fucking jack-in-the-box waiting there for us. I'd added my location to all my brothers' cell phones as a safety measure, but I was seriously rethinking that now. Callan flashed his white smile at Addy, setting my teeth on edge. He reached forward and pulled her in for a hug too, giving me a wink over her shoulder, the bastard.

"Why, Callan Hellman, you just get taller and more muscular every time I see you!" Addy pulled back from the hug, but squeezed Callan's bicep in a way that made me want to sucker punch my own brother.

Callan shrugged, giving her the whole aw-shucks routine that went along with his nice-guy vibe. "I've been working out recently. Thanks for noticing." Callan looked between Addy and me. "Are you on your way to class? I thought it started at seven?"

I ground my molars together. "We're grabbing dinner first."

"Oh." Then Callan's eyebrows winged up high on his forehead. "Oh!"

I shook my head and growled, "There is no 'oh.'"

Callan's mouth slid into a smirk I didn't care for. "I don't know, big brother. Kind of seems like an 'oh' moment."

Addy was watching us like she was a spectator at a tennis match. Before I could pull open the door to the diner and whisk Addy inside, Callan had to interject some more.

"You sure smell pretty, Addy. I bet it's one of those special lotions you make, huh?"

What the fuck did Callan know about Addy's lotions? And why was he still here talking when I had a hot meal that needed to be in my belly?

Addy twisted a lock of hair around her finger. "Thank you,

Callan. It's a new blend. I've been experimenting with grounding oils."

Callan bent forward as if he was going to sniff her neck. "Can I...?"

Fucking hell. "Okay. We're done here," I barked. I stepped between the two of them, unapologetically whacking Callan in the head with my shoulder. I steered Addy to the door, making sure to block Callan's access to her. "See you around, jackass."

Thankfully, Callan didn't follow us inside the restaurant, though his laughter did. Addy held up two fingers to Dot at the hostess stand. Then she twirled and shook her head at me.

"What?" I grumbled, looking around the diner out of habit. One didn't take a girl to the Forty-Diner and not scope out who was watching. There would inevitably be a rumor started and it didn't hurt to know how much time I had to squash it. If Yedda, Poppy, or Lucy were around, I might as well just accept my fate. Those ladies wasted no time spreading anything even remotely juicy.

"That's the first time I've seen you be grumpy with someone other than me."

My gaze darted back to Addy. "I'm grumpy with plenty of people."

Monroe walked us to a booth and we both followed, accepting her menus as she grumbled about getting us water glasses.

"Thank you, Monroe." I flashed the old waitress a smile that always made her smile back no matter how busy she got. She was wearing suspenders today, the straps of which were covered in a few hundred Disney buttons, some of which looked vintage. "I love the flair you're sporting today."

"Oh, you handsome devil," she simpered in that raspy voice of hers. When she walked off, I could have sworn there was renewed energy in her gait.

"No, you really aren't. I mean, look at that. You instantly flirted with Monroe."

I screwed my face up. "I did not. I was just being nice."

Addy spread her hands out on the table. "I know. That's my point! You're nice to everyone. Except me. And now poor Callan. What did he do to get on your bad side?"

I scrubbed a hand over my face and considered her words. Maybe I was only grumpy with her and my brothers. I wanted to be grumpy all the time, but I usually could rein it in and give the public what they expected from me. So what was it about Addy that got my grumpy side when everyone else got the hometown hero routine? Well, except for my brothers, but they didn't count. They knew I loved them despite the bark.

Monroe came back with our water and we gave her our orders. I was careful to be kind, but not overly flirtatious like Addy had accused me of being with everyone but her. Addy ordered a salad with chickpeas and all sorts of grass-like things only rabbits would eat. Me, on the other hand, I ordered a juicy cheeseburger and fries. I'd burned enough calories the last week to justify the plate most likely to stop your heart. Plus the junk food we ate while out on a fire left a lot to be desired. Beggars can't be choosers, and when you needed fuel, you just grabbed whatever was available, but I couldn't wait to sink my teeth into a real meal.

"Oh! My two favorite instructors!" Yedda's raspy voice interrupted Addy trying to explain to me how micro-greens was an actual thing humans should eat.

My head popped up and the sounds of the busy diner came crashing back in. There for a second, I could have sworn it was just me and Addy in our own little bubble of conversation.

"Hello, Yedda. Fancy seeing you here." I flashed her a smile, belatedly realizing Addy was smirking at my practiced response.

Yedda beamed right back, her new dentures seeming to be a better fit than the last pair. "Well, you almost didn't see me here, young man. I've been waving to you from my booth for the last few minutes. Got yourself a looker, huh?" Yedda waggled her eyebrows, her gaze darting to Addy. "Heard you gave her a pet snake but it bit you in the ass, so you killed it right there on Main Street."

Addy sputtered a laugh while I shifted uncomfortably on the vinyl seat. This right here was a fine example of how mundane things that happened in Hell got out of control once it hit the rumor mill. And here I was giving them more fodder by taking Addy to dinner. I was watching it happen right in front of me and couldn't do a damn thing to stop it. I knew taking Addy to Forty-Diner represented a huge risk, and yet I'd done it. And hell if I could find any sort of remorse in me.

"That's not...it didn't..."

"Let 'em eat, Yedda, so we can all get to class," came Poppy's holler from a booth across the aisle. Monroe came waddling over right then with a huge bowl for Addy and a loaded plate for me. God bless the woman, she'd added more fries than the meal normally came with.

"Okay, okay," Yedda grumbled, hopping out of the way for Monroe to plop down our plates. "You're looking a little white around the edges though, Ace. I'll fix you right up when we get to the community center."

Yedda winked so hard her reading glasses slid off the top of her head and hit her in the nose. I looked lower to see her holding her bright purple track suit open. Like a sidewalk hustler of fake watches, she had three pockets sewn into the inside of her jacket, each one stuffed with a shiny silver flask.

Definite safety violation waiting to happen. My blood pressure crept up at what would come out of her mouth in class once she'd nipped off those flasks, but a waft of greasy meat and fries brought me back from the brink. Yedda flipped her jacket shut and practically skipped to her seat across from Poppy.

I grabbed the ketchup bottle from the side of the table and eyed the salad Addy was already digging into. "You think we should cover binge drinking in our first aid class?"

Addy's head came up, a sparkle in her eye. "If you think

anything you can say on that topic will actually affect Yedda, sure."

I shook my head and picked up my burger. "Nah. You're probably right. I should just leave well enough alone with that woman."

Addy grinned and stole a fry off my plate. "You're not as dumb as you look."

"Hey!" I said around a mouthful of food.

If I thought scratching the itch would suddenly change things between us, I was clearly wrong. I still wanted Addy and I had a sinking suspicion that even a second or third date wouldn't get her out of my system. Her voodoo vortex was spreading and I was powerless to stop it.

CHAPTER EIGHTEEN

*a*ddy

"I'M in the break room and have exactly fifteen minutes, so spill your guts, woman."

"Well, good morning to you too, Meadow." I rolled my eyes heavenward, but couldn't help the smile that crept onto my face. I'd been doing that a lot this morning. Smiling for no apparent reason. I feared it had less to do with my packed sunrise yoga class and more to do with a certain firefighter. After the first aid class last night, Ace had dropped me off with a head nod and a clenched jaw. All that sexy flirting during his shower—yes, I was totally watching and knew he knew that I was watching—and he dropped me off as Grumpy Ace.

Like Jekyll and Hyde, Ace had two personas. The grumpy guy he reserved just for me, and then the public Ace who was gregarious and showy. Unfortunately for my heart, I was learning there might be a third persona. The one who smiled softly, spoke about his feelings, and touched me so sweetly. That Ace was rare, like a glimpse of sun coming out from behind dark clouds to stun you with his beauty.

"Fourteen minutes," Meadow barked in my ear.

I shook my head and walked inside to make a cup of tea. "Easy, killer. I'm floating on a yogasm."

Meadow snorted. "Yogasms are fine and all, but I was hoping to hear about some Ace-gasms."

I poured hot water over the tea bag and reached for the raw honey I bartered for with free yoga classes. "Unfortunately, all I have are yogasms. Ace dropped me off after class and left. I didn't even get a hug. Or a fist bump. Or a fuck you later."

Meadow sighed. "It's just so weird. I would say he's obsessed with you, always showing up uninvited and then taking you to dinner. Like, if Ace were a normal guy, that is. But a full-on naked shower show and then just dropping you off without making a move? It's weird, BamBam."

I blew on my tea and took a tentative sip. "I know. I feel like I have whiplash from all the mixed signals. Against all my better judgement, I think I'm developing feelings."

Meadow squealed so loud I had to pull the phone from my ear.

"Calm down, lady. I need you to tell me to move on. It's a lost cause. I know it is, and yet I can't seem to help myself. Ace has never dated someone long term and we certainly don't have a track record that would suggest we'd get along that way, so I just need to turn my attention elsewhere."

"Elsewhere? To like, what? Your yoga business?"

I nodded along, pacing my house with a restlessness I didn't like. "Sure. That, plus getting my tincture business up and running. I keep talking about doing an Etsy store, but so far, I haven't done it yet. Maybe now's the time to dig in."

"I think that's a great idea, but I have a better one."

"I'm all ears."

"Come to the festival with me and Judd this afternoon. Let's find you a man to distract you. Best way to get over a man is to get under another one."

I huffed out a laugh. "Did you get that from a country song?"

"Totally. It's not only poetic, but accurate. Besides. Side benefit will be that, more than likely, Ace will be at the festival and you can show him what he's missing."

I thought about trying to make Ace jealous and something about that didn't sit right with me. That, and I wasn't exactly looking forward to being a third wheel with Meadow and Judd. Seemed to be the story of my life. "I don't know, Meadow. I'm not looking to play games."

"Just a second, Bain." Meadow's voice came back loud and clear. "I gotta go, but we'll pick you up around three. Play games or don't, but don't stay home by yourself when you could be having fun with your friends. Don't let Ace take away a fun night just because he's the biggest flip-flopper in the world. Besides, everyone seeing you having a good time solo will crush the raging rumors about you and Ace after that dinner last night."

Ignoring the rumor part, she had a good point. I went to the festival every year. This year would be no different, except Meadow had a boyfriend now. I opened my mouth to agree to the plans when a noise pulled my attention out my window. A black truck pulled up my driveway. A very familiar truck.

"Um, Meadow?"

"Yeah?"

"Ace just pulled up."

Meadow whooped in my ear. "Ride that hose, baby! Text me later and let me know if you still need a ride. My money's on you getting a ride with Ace, if you know what I mean."

My cheeks went up in flames. "Yeah, I don't know about that. I'm sure he's just here to gripe at me about something."

"Push those boobs up and make him flustered, girl!"

Ace's door opened and his jean-clad legs hopped down to the ground. My brain went fuzzy and I couldn't remember who I was talking to. "Gotta go..."

I hung up the phone with Meadow hollering advice like a crazy woman. I honestly didn't know how Bain dealt with her on a daily basis. I tossed the cell phone on my bed and whipped the front door open. Leaning on the doorway, I folded my arms across my chest, nearly upsetting my cup of tea, and watched Ace approach.

He was wearing a dark-blue Henley that molded to his biceps and stretched across his broad chest. The sleeves were pushed up to show off his muscled forearms. The shirt didn't have the AHFD logo on it, which was a surprise to my eyes. I wasn't sure I'd really ever seen him without a fire department–issue shirt in years. Not that I catalogued every time I saw him or anything.

He walked over as if he knew women all over the world appreciated his masculine gait. His boots stopped just a foot away, the unique scent of him I couldn't get to leave my brain wafting over me. The damn cup of tea was rocking and I couldn't seem to get my hand to settle.

"Addy," he murmured in a low voice that did nothing to calm the butterflies that had taken flight in my stomach.

Yep. I'd caught feelings alright. Shit.

"Ace."

He stood there with his hand behind his back, looking at me without saying a word, the silence stretching out like a hard yoga pose that just wouldn't end. If he wanted me flustered and confused, he was well on his way.

"Is this going to be a daily habit now? Showing up without an invitation?"

His brown eyes lit up at the jab, the humor sparkling in them and taking him from simply handsome to downright gorgeous. His lips quirked to the side and I remembered what they'd felt like against my skin.

That was it. I'd have to dump out this tea. It was making me hot and bothered on a calm spring day.

"You never answer your phone anyway, so what's the use in giving you a heads-up?"

I scoffed. "I'll have you know I was just on the phone. Heard it loud and clear."

He made a noise in his throat that told me he didn't believe me. His hand stayed in the back pocket of his jeans and he stared right into my soul. "I need a date for the festival."

I choked on nothing and pushed off the doorway. Leaning around Ace, I tossed my tea out the door and into the wild brush outside my house. "Is that a question or a statement?"

Ace's face morphed into a smirk, the kind I'd seen him toss at women all over town. "I always bring a date to the festival, and seeing how you're no longer finding inventive ways to insult me, I'd like to take you."

I let the power of Ace's public magnetism wash over me. It set my nerve endings on fire and tightened something in my gut. Powerful, indeed. No wonder the ladies fell at his feet and begged for a second date.

But I didn't want this side of Ace.

I realized it like a lightning bolt to the brain. His mean side, the one that aimed his frown at me constantly, was not my type. Yet neither was his showboating side. I didn't find that attractive beyond a surface level. If I was going to spend time around him, I wanted the Ace who'd sat in my crystal circle and told me his pride had been at stake when his father left. The Ace who ate my pussy like he was a starving man while talking dirty and turning my cheeks red.

I shrugged. "No, thanks. I'm going with Meadow and Judd."

His face faltered, and I turned on my heel, walking back inside to put my mug down in the sink. I heard his boots come just inside my front door.

"Addy," he said, sounding just a bit stunned.

I turned to find the smirk long gone. I felt a little mean, knowing I'd been the one to wipe it off his handsome face, but I wasn't going to play games. Not now that I knew my heart was involved.

I sighed and came back over to explain. "Look, I don't want your pity invite. Or to be some girl to show off on your arm. I know how you get in public situations, and I don't want to go with that Ace."

He studied me for a long moment. "Which Ace do you want to go with?"

I tilted my head and smiled up at him. "The real one. The one who can be playful, but not boastful. The one who teases me, but follows it up by saying something so sweet I can barely breathe."

Ace's nostrils flared, which wouldn't normally be something I'd say was hot, but on him, it was. He stepped closer and brought a hand up to cup my face. His callouses scraped along my skin, bringing out a rash of goose bumps on my arms.

"How about the Ace who brings you a peace offering?"

His other hand came out from behind his back. I tilted my head down to see a ring of flowers clutched in his fist. I gasped as my knees decided to give up standing altogether.

Ace Hellman brought me a flower crown.

"Ace," I whispered, staring at the green stems intertwined with delicate yellow and white flowers. A stream of thin white ribbon fluttered at the back.

He brought the crown up to place it gently on my head. "Perfect."

Tears flooded my eyes and my heart beat out a rhythm I knew no amount of moonlight or chakra work could erase. Ace's eyes held a heat I'd come to crave and convinced myself I'd never see again.

"I didn't exactly make it myself, but the new flower shop in town had what I needed." Ace suddenly looked nervous. "Have you met the owner, Shelby? I bet you'd get along really well. She's really into flowers and plants, although I don't—"

"Ace?" I interrupted him before he used up all the words he could possibly say tonight and I was left with a silent date at the festival.

He snapped his mouth shut, his eyes guarded as he waited for me to speak.

I reached up and ran my fingers across the five o'clock shadow that always seemed to grace his face. No games, just truth. "Thank you for the flower crown. I'd love to be your date for the festival."

And then I reached up on my tiptoes and feathered a kiss across his lips like I'd been wanting to do for days. If I wanted the real Ace, then I had to give him the real Addy. And this girl wanted to kiss the handsome man who wouldn't get out of her head—or her property. Ace stood incredibly still until I lifted my mouth from his. Then he crushed me to him in a rush of movement. He took the kiss up a thousand degrees with lips and tongues and teeth and a desperation that made my heart swoop up into the sky.

This was the Ace I wanted.

CHAPTER NINETEEN

ce

ADDY LET out a soft moan that lit my veins on fire. The woman made me crazy. She held my feet to the fire in a way that previously only my brothers could. She didn't want my lines or the cheesy smile that always made women blush and stammer. She didn't want anything to do with the persona I'd cultivated over the years as a way to survive in this small town. Something about that refusal caught my attention like no one before her. I didn't just want a second date with a woman for the first time since high school, I wanted a third, fourth, and fifth.

It was the scent of the flowers on her head that had me finally pulling back. I'd come here because I just couldn't stay away any longer. Shelby from the flower shop—who hadn't even been in Auburn Hill longer than a month—had already heard the news that I'd taken Addy to dinner the night before; although, in her version, Addy had slipped her sandals off to play footsie in my lap. Which obviously didn't happen. I swear. Someone was twisting these rumors and making them ridiculous. But if even that rumor hadn't made my balls want to retreat for life, I knew seeing Addy again was exactly what I needed.

Addy was breathing hard, her lips wet from my kiss. Her neck held a blush that made me want to trace how far down that pink skin went. She was wearing a skimpy green tank top that barely contained her gorgeous breasts, cutoff jean shorts that looked softer than her skin, and a flowered kimono type thing over it all. She looked like she'd stepped off the newsfeed of a bohemian Instagram model. Which was crazy because I knew her flip phone wasn't smart enough to even have the app. This look was all Addy.

"You look beautiful. Have I told you that?"

Her eyes went soft and I made a mental note to tell her that more often. She was beautiful all right, but in a wild and untamed way. Her skin wasn't highlighted and camouflaged with makeup and false lashes and every other thing women did to their faces that baffled men. The dewy look of her skin was simply the outcome of a woman who lived off the plants of the earth. And maybe that moonlight she loved so much.

"Not since last week." An impish glow shined through her royal-blue eyes. "And you had your dick between my breasts, so I figured it might be one of your lines."

I dropped my head and tried to push away the image of Addy below me, her hands pushing her breasts together, her mouth about to welcome the tip of my cock. A few breaths later, when I had myself mostly under control, I looked back up.

"I promise you that nothing I say now, or ever, with you is some kind of line. If I say it, I mean it."

Addy studied me, apparently finding my statement sincere when she dipped her head. "Okay. I believe you. One quick question though."

I smiled. Always with her questions. "Ask away."

"Are you worried about starting a rumor if we go to the festival together?"

I let go of Addy's hips, instantly wishing I could put my

hands back on her. One night with her just wasn't going to be enough like I thought it would, but more than anything, I wanted her to trust me. To see the real me and still want to be around me. I couldn't keep touching her and not press for more, so for now letting her go was best.

"I'm sure Shelby's already spreading a rumor about your flower crown. And Yedda and Poppy already lit up the phone tree last night before we even finished dinner. So, no. I'm not worried about rumors spreading. It's Hell. Rumors will always spread."

And it was true. For maybe the first time in my life, I didn't care. Rumors were already swirling and I was still alive. Seeing Addy's eyes light up and fill with tears when I handed her the flower crown was enough of a trade-off for me. What kind of hometown hero was I if I couldn't handle a little gossip?

Addy smiled up at me so brilliantly I knew I'd made the right choice. Making her smile like that made me feel ten feet tall. Not even running into a burning building could give me a rush like seeing her happy with a flower halo on top of her head of long blonde hair. I'd seen Addy smile all my life. Granted, it was always directed at everyone but me. Seeing it now, just for me, made me want to pull out all the stops on this date to the festival. I wanted to dance with her under the stars, watch her eat something deep fried and disgusting. Maybe even try my arm at winning her a huge stuffed bear. If it was a romantic cliché, I wanted in on it.

"I'll buy you dinner if you promise to dance with me." Addy poked her finger right in my chest.

"What kind of second date would this be if I let you buy me dinner?"

Addy scoffed. "This isn't the old days where the man has to buy dinner, you know."

I put my hand on her back and steered her toward the door. "I know that, but I asked you out on this date, so I'm paying."

She shook her head, blonde hair dancing around. "Ace."

"Addy."

"OH MY GOD, THAT WAS TERRIBLE!" Addy rubbed her stomach, her tank top pulling up to show smooth, soft skin I wanted to get intimately familiar with again.

"That why you ate the whole thing?" I asked innocently, eyeing the clean stick in her hands that had held a corn dog the size of a baseball bat.

Addy gasped and backhanded my stomach, making me double over. I had my own corn dog in there, mixing with a warm beer. Perhaps the fried foods hadn't been a smart move on a date. Then again, it was kind of a tradition to eat like a jackass without a future cardiac problem whenever the music festival came around.

The current band playing wasn't my favorite. A little too rock and roll to be classified as country. Honestly, ever since the sun set and more people filed into the festival, the more anxious I got. Large crowds were never my thing and this one was getting louder by the second. I wondered if they were counting heads at the door to stay under capacity. Was it wrong to just want a quiet evening with the woman that never left my brain?

"Dude, that's no way to talk to a beautiful woman. Ignore my dumbass brother." Ethan flashed a smile at Addy that had her laughing. Fucker. He'd been trying to smooth-talk my woman all night. Just because his date left him at some point to go to the bathroom during the second band and never returned wasn't any reason to horn in on my date.

"Don't you have your own date, Ethan?" I clapped him on the shoulder a little harder than necessary. "Oh, that's right. She's MIA."

Ethan sent me a look that could have killed a lesser man.

Daxon crashed into our little circle, his arm around the waist of a woman who looked like she'd be carded all night long. Hopefully he'd made sure of her age before he invited her to the festival. He had a habit of dating women who were all wrong for him. "Are we just here to eat, or are we gonna dance, boys?"

The strawberry blonde with him giggled loudly and pulled him away to the dance floor where they blended into the crowd. Which was probably a good thing. Her short shorts hadn't covered much of her ass and the big brother in me wanted to pull them down. She just looked so young it was like watching a preschooler get ogled by grown men. Jesus. I really was getting old. Everyone was starting to look too young to be an actual adult.

"Is it me, or does she look a little young?" Ethan asked, squinting at the tops of their heads and reflecting my thoughts exactly.

"He said she was legal," Callan interjected helpfully.

Annie snorted. "Legal. When's he going to man up and date a grown woman? One who has her shit together and more to offer than a fake giggle?"

"Maybe he just needs to grow up a bit more. I find that people make better choices only when they're ready. You can't force them." Addy shrugged and stepped away to throw her stick in the trash. As soon as she stepped back into the circle, I slid my arm around her waist and tucked her in close. Of course Addy would see only the best in people.

The band shouted their thanks into the microphone and ran off stage to make way for the headlining band. The DJ threw on one of my favorite songs in the meantime, like a blessing to my ears after all that screeching of the electric guitar.

I leaned down and whispered in Addy's ear. "Time to dance off the food?"

"I thought you'd never ask," she flirted back, that little smile that drove me wild flickering across her face.

I pulled her away from the circle of my brothers and friends,

Cricket and Callan arguing over the appropriate time to use a tambourine in a country song. Those two fought like siblings, and quite frankly, I'd rather have Addy all to myself without their bickering in the background.

The makeshift wooden dance floor was packed now, but I managed to find a space for us. Long white string lights criss-crossed above our heads. Speakers set up in the four corners made the bass thump deep in your chest. Meadow, Addy's friend, was nearby with her boyfriend, Judd. She gave Addy a wink and then made some lewd hip motions that had Addy spinning me away quickly.

"What the hell was that?" I asked, pulling Addy into my arms and swaying to the music.

"That was pure Meadow. Just ignore her. That's what I do."

Honestly, I didn't care about Meadow's antics, not with Addy's breasts smashed against my chest and her hips shifting against mine. Fuck, I loved her soft curves, and my hands were having a hell of a time staying in zones that wouldn't get me in trouble. This was a family festival, after all.

Speaking of family, I saw my mother two-step right past me with some old cowboy's hands on her ass. The flirtatious smile on her face made me cringe. She should have been smacking his hands off her backside.

"Jesus," I grumbled.

Addy looked up and then over her shoulder to see what had caught my attention, spying my mom and her amorous date. "Guess those libido oils I gave her are working."

I pulled back to gape at her. "Addy, how could you?"

She took one look at me and burst out laughing. "Oh my God, you should see your face right now!"

Her laughter, at least, was distracting me from the horrific mental images of my mother and her new man friend. Addy jiggled when she laughed, like her whole body wanted in on the humor. Dammit, I wanted this woman. My hands gripped her hips harder and I let her feel exactly what she was doing to me below the belt. She gasped, her laughter cutting off as she stared up at me.

"Did you squirrel away another corn dog in your pocket?" she asked straight faced, and then burst into laughter again.

I just shook my head and kept dancing through the next two songs. Here I was sporting a boner that would have all the tongues wagging in Hell and she was laughing her ass off. She was absolutely crazy. I never knew what was going to come out of her mouth, but I wanted to be there when it did. I wanted all her words, her laughter, her beliefs in crystals and oils and salves. I wanted to hear it all.

My phone buzzed in my back pocket and I took it out with a groan. I wasn't working tonight but the guys knew to call me if anything came up that they couldn't handle. The crowd noise picked up as the headlining band took the stage.

"Need to take that?" Addy shouted over the noise.

I shook my head and read the text over her shoulder. "Nah, they'll be fine." I shot off a text in response, hoping they actually could handle it without me. A pang of guilt hit my stomach. Before a few weeks ago, before Addy had invaded my head space, I would have left the festival the second anyone at the station texted me. That kind of narrow focus was what got me the captain's job and now I was already slacking off.

I'd just slid the phone back in my pocket when another couple bumped into my back. I spun a bit to give them a friendly head nod, but stopped short when I saw it was Captain Murray.

"Hey, Captain. Good to see you," I said over the music that began to play, nodding at his wife.

He had bags under his eyes that spoke of his health troubles, but the genuine smile on his familiar face had my worries easing. "Ace! Congratulations on the new position. I'm sorry I left you a bit of a mess, but..."

I held my hand out and we shook. "I'm just happy to hear you're doing better." I turned back to Addy. "Addy, this is Captain Murray, my boss. And this is his wife, Carol."

"Hello. So lovely to meet you." Addy shook hands with them both, giving them a wide smile.

"Well, I'm not your boss any longer, son. I'm leaving all that stress to you now." Captain Murray tugged his wife a little closer, his smile fading away. When he spoke again I had to strain to hear him over the music. "Make sure you don't make the job your whole life, Ace. Have some fun. Live a little before it's too late. I wasn't able to balance it all and I want better for you."

Carol patted him on the chest with a look that still held some fear along with a lot of love. "Speaking of, tonight's about dancing, not work. You owe me a two-step, mister. The doctor said dancing was good for your recovery."

Captain gave me a wink and twirled his wife away, leaving me to pull Addy back in my arms with heavier thoughts.

"You said he had a heart attack?" At my nod, Addy kept going. "I'm going to bring over some frankincense for him this week. It's good for heart health."

I closed my eyes and pulled Addy in tight, resting my cheek on top of her head, careful to not smash her flowers. Of course, her first thought would be to help a man she'd just met. The woman had a heart of gold while I'd spent my whole life hating her over something trivial that had happened in kindergarten. Why she forgave me and wanted to go on a date with me was beyond my comprehension.

The music shifted, the beat slowing as the band began to play their first hit. A love song about finally seeing what was right in front of you. I ran my hands along her back, wishing we were alone and I could strip her out of her clothes. I wanted to see her naked skin glowing under the moonlight. I wanted to be the only person she saw. The one that was right in front of her, begging for a chance.

For the first time in my life, I didn't want to be the job. I didn't want to be the small-town hero everyone looked up to. I didn't want to be the older brother watching out for everyone else. I just wanted a chance with a girl who'd written me off twenty years ago.

"Be mine, Addy," I found myself whispering in her ear. She stiffened, but I kept her swaying with my body until she relaxed again. I should have been freaked out by what I'd just floated out there, but all I felt was desperate. Desperate for her to agree. "Be my girlfriend, little wood nymph."

She didn't answer, but her hands tightened on my neck. When the last note of the song reverberated across the dance floor, she lifted her head from my chest, eyes more serious than I'd ever seen.

"I belong to no one." My heart dipped as she rejected me outright. A part of me knew she always would. How ridiculous to think that Ace Hellman and Adelia Bammingford would be a couple.

"But for you I'll make an exception."

CHAPTER TWENTY

$\mathcal{A}$ ddy

THE WORDS WERE BARELY OUT of my mouth before Ace let go of my hips and grabbed my hand, interlacing our fingers. He walked away from the band so fast I had to jog to keep up. A blur of familiar faces flashed by as we left the dance floor and pushed through the crowd that was standing around on the grassy area of the park where the music wasn't as loud. I saw Ethan watching us leave, giving me a thumbs-up and an enthusiastic smile.

"Ace! Slow down," I gasped, realizing my yoga routine had not given me the same cardio benefit that a firefighter possessed.

Ace spun around and picked me up. I suppose I should have been glad it wasn't in a fireman's carry, but still, I didn't want to be carried from the festival like my own two feet wouldn't work. Talk about rumors.

"Is this really necessary?" I asked dryly, my hands clinging to his neck until I realized I shouldn't be worried. Ace was incredibly strong and didn't even look like his breath was coming any faster with me weighing him down. Part of me was thrilled to see him so enthusiastic. The other part of me was wondering when he'd revert back to grumpy Ace and second-guess his decision to ask me to be his girlfriend. I wasn't quite ready to trust that one-date Ace was sure about having a steady girlfriend.

"It's absolutely necessary," Ace said gruffly, his jaw clenched as he strode across the last patch of grass to the parking lot where we'd left his truck.

I rolled my eyes, but gave in to the moment. If my boyfriend —holy shiitake mushrooms, Ace was my freaking boyfriend— wanted to carry me away from the festival to have his way with me, what did I care about rumors? I rested my head on his shoulder, snuggling into his chest and inhaling as deeply as I could. The scent of grass, fried foods, the flowers on my head, and the unique scent of Ace all combined to make a sensory memory I knew I'd never forget.

Ace's truck beeped and then he was somehow managing to open the door without dropping me. He settled me on the passenger seat and pulled the seat belt around to click it in place. He hovered there, his hands on both sides of me, his shadowed face just an inch away.

"I can't remember a better North Valley Festival." His voice was barely above a whisper, the rumble of it skating along my skin and making me shiver.

"Is that why we're leaving early?" I teased him, giving in to the need to flirt with him the only way I knew how. Our entire history was filled with digs and jabs. A girl couldn't be expected to change on a dime.

His mouth hitched to the side. "We're leaving because these jeans got too fucking tight to keep dancing. And it's all your fault."

I leaned in and buried my nose in his neck, letting myself get a lungful of his scent. Every time he was around, I wanted to sniff him like some kind of curious animal. He had a pheromone that spoke to every female cell in my body. "I can help you with that," I whispered against his hot skin.

Ace cupped my jaw and pressed his lips to mine in a fierce kiss that spoke of epic levels of frustration.

"Thank fuck. Hold that thought."

And then he let me go, shutting the door and literally running around the hood of his truck to get in the driver's seat. He started up the engine and left a cloud of dust as he raced out of the parking lot. I grabbed the handle above my head and held on tight, laughing the whole way through town. The moon and the stars shined brighter through the window as we left the downtown area and headed further into the woods by my house. Ace and I always seemed to end up at my place, not that I was complaining. I liked the privacy I had out here in the middle of nowhere.

Ace pulled up to the top of my driveway and cut the engine. I couldn't seem to wipe the smile from my face. He clicked my seat belt and then hauled me onto his lap, the steering wheel digging into my back. His hands went in my hair, his fingers finding knots from dancing and driving with the windows down. His face was in the shadows, but even so I could see the hot burn in his eyes.

"You sure boss a girl around, don't you, Captain?" I teased him, secretly loving the way he seemed right at the edge of his control. I had every intention of pushing him over that cliff tonight.

"Addy?" His hands tightened into fists in my hair, slowly wrapping the strands around his hands.

"Yeah?" I replied, so breathless I sounded like I ran all the way home.

"You can bitch at me all you want later. Right now I just want you to ride my cock. Can you do that for me?"

My breath caught in my throat, and every single thought in my head went right out the window. Without even blinking, I shrugged the kimono off my shoulders and whipped the tank top over my head.

"Yeah, just like that, baby," Ace murmured, one of his hands leaving my hair and tracing a path down my collarbone and between my breasts.

I'd never been so happy to have chosen a lacy bra instead of a sports bra like I usually did if I had a yoga class that day. Ace's finger trailed along the edge of the cup before flipping the material down on one side and cupping my bare breast in his palm.

"I fucking love your breasts."

I fucking loved Ace's dirty talk. I never would have guessed the frowning, always-in-control firefighter would say such filthy things when the clothes came off. Meadow would have said you always had to watch those brooding quiet ones.

Ace's hand left my breast to reach around back and flick my bra open. I lifted an eyebrow at how quickly he got it undone, but his gaze remained firmly on my breasts. The fist in my hair tugged, arching my neck to his mouth. He thoroughly kissed his way along my throat and then finally made it to my lips. His kiss was hungry, the little grunt he made in his throat desperate.

I pulled at his shirt, getting my hands underneath and on his skin, feeling every bump and dip of muscle along his torso. I pulled away and tugged harder on his shirt. He took the hint, reaching behind his head to tug the offending material off his body. My hands eagerly traced a path from shoulder to shoulder, then down lower until Ace growled deep in his throat.

His hand smoothed across my belly and I refrained from sucking in. All the yoga in the world wasn't going to give me a flat stomach, and based on the way his gaze was eating me up, Ace didn't care. Those fingers inched below the waistband of my jean shorts. My heart began to hammer inside my chest. How had I ever thought sleeping with Ace once was going to get him out of my system?

"Addy," Ace huffed, his gaze snapping to mine. His fingers stilled inside my shorts.

I bit my lip and shrugged, knowing exactly what had gotten his attention.

Ace dropped his head to my forehead, his eyes squeezed shut. "If I'd known you weren't wearing underwear..."

I wiggled my hips, begging him to get over it and move those damn fingers. He slammed his mouth on mine, teetering on that edge and falling over it as his fingers split me open. His thumb found my clit and flicked it. I gasped into his mouth and he easily slid two fingers inside me. His tongue kept the same rhythm as his fingers, moving in and out with less finesse with each thrust and more desperation. I'd been ready for this moment since we arrived at the damn festival.

My hands found their way into his hair, pulling at the strands until he grunted. I felt myself tightening, reaching for that first orgasm that was right around the corner. Ace pulled his hand out of my jean shorts and set me away from him.

I blinked my eyes open, moaning out loud. "Dammit, Ace."

"Lose the shorts," he bit out.

I was desperate enough for him I didn't even give him shit for ordering me around. Besides, as I scrambled to get my shorts pulled down, he pulled down his jeans and his erection sprang out to greet me. I can pretty much say I was fully distracted.

I lifted my hands to take the flower crown off, but Ace interrupted. "Leave it on, wood nymph."

There comes a moment in every good sexual encounter when a woman feels like a fucking goddess. This was that moment for me. The moon was shining through the windshield, highlighting the incredible body of the man who'd just asked to be my boyfriend. Ace was looking at me with heavy eyes, as if I was an actual wood fairy sent to destroy him with my sexual prowess. I felt like a goddess.

I lifted a leg and climbed onto his lap straddling him, my hair surrounding us like some kind of private tent. My hands pushed on his shoulders and I lifted my hips up high, letting his cock run along my pussy as I slowly shifted down. Ace let his head drop back to the headrest. His hands skimmed along my sides, never settling for long on my hips, waist, or breasts before traveling to a new area, like he couldn't decide where to land.

Taking him in my hand, I gave him one hard stroke that had his abs flexing. Then I notched him at my entrance and ever so slowly inched my way down his length.

"Fuck, Addy. You feel so fucking good on my cock." His head came forward and his hands cupped my breasts, lifting them up to his mouth. His tongue darted out to flick my nipple.

Then he dropped them and grabbed my hips, helping to lift me up and down as we both got caught up in the frenzy. My thighs began to burn and still I rode him hard. The feel of him filling me over and over again was doing something magical to my head. I felt like I was floating away, riding a tide of pleasure so exquisite I was having an out-of-body experience. I could hear our flesh slapping together with each slide down his cock. I could even feel the warm heat that fogged up the windshield. But it wasn't until Ace flicked his thumb over my clit again that I came back to the moment in startling clarity.

A white-hot poker of painful pleasure seared up my spine and exploded behind my eyes. I cried out something unintelligible, my body shuttering as the first waves of the orgasm hit hard. I leaned back and the steering wheel bit into my skin. I blinked my eyes open and saw Ace staring down at my body like he was catching a glimpse of heaven. A single bead of sweat dripped down his temple and he clenched his jaw.

His hands gripped me hard enough I'd probably find bruises in the morning. He slammed his hips up and it pushed me into the steering wheel, setting off his horn as my ass connected. Like a man possessed, he slammed into me over and over again, the horn blasting out a honk with each thrust.

Ace let out a loud growl and stilled, hot liquid emptying into me before he collapsed across my torso. The horn was now going off on a constant wail, but I didn't want to shift and disturb Ace at this exact moment. I'd never been so thankful not to have nearby neighbors. I was spread out on the steering wheel, staring up at the night sky with the horn going off and Ace buried deep inside. I hoped to goddess no one would come over to investigate all the noise. A giggle bubbled up my throat and I let it go. Some girls cry after sex. I laughed apparently.

Ace finally lifted his head and pulled me upright, the horn instantly going silent. He shook his head at my continued laughter, the edges of his lips tilting up despite himself.

"What's so funny, wood nymph?" he mumbled, pushing my hair back from my face.

I ran my hands over his chest, tracing the outline of the red mark just below his left collarbone. Every time I saw him, he had a new injury of some sort. Maybe one day I could get him using my oils to help them heal faster.

If he'd been so far gone in the moment he hadn't heard the horn as my ass repeatedly hit it, I wasn't going to mention it. "I'm not even sure. Just happy, I guess," I answered him.

Ace pulled me into a tight hug, his arms banded around me. "I wish I could stay, but I have an early shift tomorrow. Working the next few days in fact."

My heart sank. I was hoping to sleep wrapped in his arms again tonight. But I understood he had to get to work.

Ace pulled back enough to place a quick kiss on my mouth. "I was thinking...could I come to your yoga class on my next day off?" He paused, looking a little sheepish. "If my ineptitude won't be a distraction, of course."

I pushed on his shoulders, my disappointed little heart bubbling over again. That little organ was catching a lot of feelings these days.

"Ace Hellman. You want to come to my yoga class?"

"Well, Jesus, Addy, don't make a big deal out of it." The adorable grump wouldn't even look at me. "And definitely don't tell my brothers."

I snort-laughed and began to pepper kisses all over his face. "I'm totally telling your brothers."

He poked me in the side and I yelped. Thus began the tickle session which led to my second orgasm of the night. When Ace's truck finally pulled away from my house, the worries about him regretting his decision to date me faded away. I thought he just might make for a very good boyfriend. Maybe the best.

CHAPTER TWENTY-ONE

$\mathcal{A}$ ddy

"IF YOU'RE GOING to make us hold a plank for three minutes again, I ain't coming back, missy. My back can't take that bull-shit," groused Lenny as he shuffled up to me after class. He had his yoga mat rolled and tucked under his spindly arm. He'd started coming to my sunrise class after I gave him that ankle bracelet that matched mine. He still hadn't caught on to the informal dress code that existed for yoga. He had sweat bands on his head and both wrists, as if I just might toss a tennis ball at them when they were in down dog.

I winced, knowing my brain had been a bit preoccupied the last few mornings. Calling out the change in poses had slipped my mind as I went over every second with Ace at the festival on repeat. And everything that happened later in his truck, of course. It wasn't until later that night when I cleaned myself up that I realized we hadn't used a condom. It was late in my cycle, so I didn't anticipate a problem, but apparently Ace hadn't noticed either because he hadn't said anything. I really needed to get my head out of the clouds and be more responsible.

"Nobody actually holdth the pothes she calls out, dumb ath," Yedda cackled, the lack of dentures making for a deep lisp that had me biting my lips to keep from laughing.

"Well, no need for name-calling, Yedda." Lenny turned to her, forgetting about me entirely. "Some of us like to actually follow the class instead of sneaking peeks down everyone's shorts."

Yedda's mouth gaped open before she snapped it shut again and lifted her little nose in the air. "I do no thuch thing."

Lenny batted his hand through the air. "Why do you think no one sets up their mat in front of you anymore, you sick little—"

"Okay, well, thank you both for coming today," I interrupted, not wanting a fight to break out. Meadow assured me that Ace and I were the topic of the town gossip right now and I didn't need a geriatric cat fight to add to the rumors. "We'll have a much livelier class tomorrow, Lenny."

"Well, thank the goddess for that," he mumbled, shuffling off to his vintage golf cart to head home. I grinned, charmed by the grumpy Lenny using one of my phrases. He really was quite good at yoga, especially for someone of indiscernible age. No one really knew how old he was, but based on the wrinkles that stacked up above that sweatband, he had to be pushing eighty at least.

"Like I'd want to see whatever that guy is packing." Yedda did a full-body shiver and then, as she passed me on the way to her ancient light-blue Lincoln that was way too much of a car for her to drive, she gave me a wink.

Now it was my turn to shiver. I'd have to keep a better eye on her in class. I couldn't have a Peeping Tom making people uncomfortable, even if she was five feet of harmless old lady. That's how people dropped out of classes and I'd just gotten my class to a good size. One that was manageable but also made me enough money to keep me in tea and tofu without financial help from my parents.

I heard my phone ring from inside the house. My heart leaped into my throat and I made a run for it. I'd started actually listening for the dang thing since Ace began to text me at fairly regular intervals after the festival. Just simple good mornings and what he was up to. Each one was a treasure I looked forward to. Was that pathetic so early on in a relationship? Maybe, but I felt powerless to stop my heart from racing each time I heard that little beep of a notification. He'd told me they were super busy, so I wasn't expecting him to reach out.

Unfortunately, my parents hadn't bothered to text or call in well over a month. I had no idea where they even were in the world right now. Talk about feeling like a forgotten third wheel.

"Hello?" I gasped into the phone, hoping I answered it before whoever it was hung up. Dang, I really needed to add some cardio to my routine.

"Addy?" I heard a female voice ask through the phone.

"Yes, this is Addy." My heart began to slow now that I knew it wasn't Ace.

"Oh good. This is Lucy Sutter. I need your help if you're available today. I realize this is quite short notice, but these things can't be helped."

I didn't know Lucy all that well, but everyone in Hell knew who she was. You don't get to be an owner of a sperm bank in a small town and not make a bit of a name for yourself. She was also married to Bain, the warden at the prison in town. Also known as Meadow's boss. They had two kids in elementary school and Judd was teaching the youngest one this year. Lucy was also known for being a little bit off her rocker, if you know what I mean. Friendly, but a bit of a wild card.

"Actually I do have time. I just finished my yoga class and have the rest of the day." I had planned to go to the library and use one of their computers to work on my Etsy site, but that could wait.

"Fantastic! Meet me at Coffee in an hour and I'll explain everything?"

"Sure. See you shortly. Wait! What should I wear?" I wasn't sure if she needed help at her clinic or if we were volunteering our time painting the picnic benches at the park.

"Oh, just something casual. No manual labor, I promise." And then she hung up before I could ask another question. I shook my head, a little bit nervous about what I'd just signed myself up for. Knowing Lucy, it could be anything.

"MY TREAT!" Lucy trilled, shoving me toward the barista with a smile that was too wide for innocence. My stomach clenched. Shit. She was now bribing me with coffee for whatever she had in mind for today. Not a good sign.

"Just a chai tea, please," I told the barista weakly.

"And I'll take a double-shot espresso with whole milk, frothed not cold, six pumps honey blend, cinnamon powder, and a little zip of that caramel drizzle if you would."

Lucy's smile didn't falter, even as the barista's eyes widened a bit at her order. I nearly choked at the dollar amount that drink cost. I could buy like fifty tincture bottles with that same money. Lucy passed over her credit card and then we moved down the line.

"So, what's in store for us today?" I asked as we waited for our drinks.

Lucy's smile somehow intensified. She smoothed a hand down the blouse she wore over tight dark blue jeans. Her boots had a heel that put her towering over me. I felt a little too youthful in my cutoff jean shorts, tank top, and faux leather vest with a fringe that made me want to twirl in a circle just to see it fan out.

She put her hands up like a movie director. "Picture it. Twelve hunky firefighters with no shirts on, snuggling animals." She put her hands down and elbowed me in the side a little harder than I would have guessed from a middle-aged mom who smelled like peanut butter. "Are your ovaries squeezing?"

There was definitely something going on in my torso region, but I didn't think my ovaries were to blame. "Firefighters did you say?"

Lucy cackled. "I knew that would get your attention."

The barista called out Lucy's name and we stepped over to grab our drinks. Lucy glanced at her watch. "Oh, we better get going if we're going to have enough time to oil them all down."

I almost walked right into the glass door of the coffee shop. "Oil them down?"

Lucy pushed the door open for me since I clearly lacked the motor coordination and exited, pointing to her minivan. "Why do you think I need your help? I'll be behind the camera, but I need someone to prep the boys. That's where you come in."

I closed my eyes briefly, wondering how I'd gotten myself into this. I wasn't sure I wanted to be oiling down a bunch of men. What if Ace was one of them? Did I act like we weren't a couple? We hadn't discussed this dating thing. We'd been too caught up in *hide the corndog* in the front seat of his truck to discuss how to act around each other in public.

"Get away from my vehicle, Penelope Fines!" Lucy shouted, my eyes flying open to see her shooing the meter maid away from her minivan. "It's parked legally, so shove that ticket book up your ass."

Damn. I'd never had an issue with Penelope, but then again, I didn't own a vehicle. I hurried over and gave Penelope my best smile to help diffuse the situation. I shouldn't have bothered though because she was glaring at Lucy and didn't know I existed.

"One day you'll slip up and I'll be waiting, Lucille."

Lucy scratched the bridge of her nose with her middle finger and opened the driver's door. "Get in, Addy. We have some men to ogle."

I slid inside the passenger side, careful to avoid the sweatshirt on the floor of the car and the candy bar wrapper on the seat. Lucy kind of scared me.

"Oh, sorry. My kids treat this car like a dumpster." Lucy swept everything into the back seat and drove us to the fire station, keeping up a steady conversation about the fundraiser she was supporting by printing and selling a town firefighter calendar. When I asked about the timing of putting out a calendar several months after the new year, she shushed me and said people weren't actually buying it for the calendar function. They just wanted to look at the hot firefighters. She probably was not wrong.

But something about that didn't sit right with me, most likely because I was now wondering if my own boyfriend would be one of the men being ogled by the whole town. By the time we bounced into the fire station parking lot, I'd talked myself down. What Ace did with his six-pack was his business, not mine. If he wanted to use his ridiculously nice-looking body to help raise money, then I would support him. Even if I had to start wearing a blade to cut any woman who made eyes at him after this damn calendar came out.

"Yoohoo! Let's get this photoshoot started!" Lucy hollered as soon as she hopped from the car. I thought Meadow was a handful, but Lucy was giving her a run for her money.

Several firefighters exited the open bay and waved. They all had shirts on, so maybe Lucy got that part of the calendar wrong. Ace stepped outside, looking all kinds of hot in his AHFD T-shirt and navy pants. He did a double take when he saw me. I pasted on a smile and gave a single-finger wave, unsure how he wanted to handle the situation and not wanting to press the issue on his turf.

"Gentlemen, my assistants for the day, Keva and Addy. Now get naked so we can start!" Lucy pointed to me and another woman I vaguely recalled seeing around town. Pretty sure she was the receptionist at Lucy's sperm bank.

My cheeks went hot at the attention.

"You heard the lady," Ace said loudly to his firefighters, though he didn't take his gaze from mine as he walked over. He reached behind his head and took his shirt off, looping it over his head and throwing it to the side with a sexy flourish that had his fellow firefighters whooping and hollering. His muscles rippled under the warm midday sun. If I wasn't envisioning things, I thought he might be flexing a bit too, making those pecs jump as he approached.

He stepped right up, his boots kissing the toe of my sandals. I couldn't seem to look away from the most beautiful sight I'd seen in days. I kind of felt like I had a front-row seat to a Magic Mike show. Was this real life?

"You are exactly who I wanted to see," Ace said just for my ears. Then his hands cupped my face and he was kissing me, pushing me back against the minivan as he devoured me. His tongue demanded entrance and I was powerless to stop him. His warm skin pressed into me and I forgot where I was. I slid my hands up his chest and around his neck, needing him closer.

A wolf whistle split the air and Ace pulled back with a cocky grin. The exclamations from the other firefighters finally registered and my face went up in flames. I guessed we were letting everyone know about us dating after all.

"Well, shit. I thought I was helping set you two up," Lucy grumbled from somewhere over Ace's shoulder. "Way to steal my fun."

Ace's lips cocked up in a lopsided grin that definitely had my ovaries squeezing. "At least one person in this town isn't up on the latest gossip," he muttered.

Lucy gasped. "That was just mean, Ace Hellman."

Ace ignored Lucy's antics and let go of my face to put his arm around my waist. "Let me introduce you to the guys." He pulled me over to the open bay, that smug smile not leaving my face even as his buddies ribbed him about laying one on me like that.

"Guys. This is Addy, my girlfriend. Addy, this is Joe and John and Ian."

"Don't forget me, bossman!" Another guy came out of the bay and clapped Ace on the shoulder.

Ace's smile seemed a little forced. "And this is Ronnie, the new guy."

"Ah, come on. I've been here a month. I can't still be called the new guy," Ronnie whined.

"Dude, do you see any other new hires around here?" Joe asked, effectively shutting Ronnie up.

Or maybe it was John who said that. Their names had flown right out of my brain. Honestly, I quit listening after Ace called me his girlfriend. It sounded so strange to my ears, it was currently echoing around my brain on repeat. The guys all shook my hand, easy smiles and acceptance on their faces.

"Here's the oil, Addy. Get that man of yours greased so we can get started. I'll have Keva check on the animals." Lucy thrust a bottle at me and walked off, directing everyone like only an experienced mom could.

John took his shirt off and threw a smile at me that screamed of flirtation. "I'm ready for you, Addy."

Ace's hand smacked him in the chest and shoved him back a foot. Ace stepped in front of me, blocking my view. "How about you start with me?"

I looked down at the bottle, then up at Ace's mile-wide chest, my heart tripping over itself in excitement. "Thank the goddess."

CHAPTER TWENTY-TWO

$\mathcal{A}$ce

I'D ALREADY TOLD Joe about Addy yesterday when he caught me texting again with a stupid smile on my face. He'd been happy for me, which had prompted me to let everyone else know Addy was my girlfriend at the first appropriate time. I probably could have done it in a little less in-your-face way, but when she showed up at the station looking all adorable in a Woodstock hippie vest, cutoffs, and sandals that had straps winding up her gorgeous calves, I went on instinct. And everything in me said to kiss the hell out of that woman and make her mine publicly.

Dibs, assholes.

"Okay, Ace, I think you'd do best to go first with the snow leopard. Her blue eyes and white coat would look great against your dark hair and eyes."

Lucy nodded to the zookeeper who had a van backed into our parking lot with five animals on board Lucy wanted to use for the photoshoot. Apparently, we were raising money to get a small satellite zoo built right here in Auburn Hill. Our county didn't have a zoo and many of the parents were petitioning and fundraising to get one so their kids didn't have to take a two-hour bus ride into the city to see some exotic animals.

"I think I need more oil, Lucy," I replied, not taking my eyes off the blush that had spread from Addy's cheeks to her neck.

She massaged my chest as she ran her hands over me again. If I had any more oil on me, I might just shoot out of the bay like a slip and slide, but I wanted Addy to keep touching me. Then again, I didn't want to sport an erection in the city calendar and I was well on my way there.

Lucy snorted. "Get your fine ass over here and show your firefighters how it's done."

I leaned down and stole a kiss from Addy before stepping away and trying to adjust my pants without anyone seeing. Without realizing it, John helped me out by putting his hand up and winking at Addy.

"I'm next."

I gave him a death stare that had his smile fading faster than my erection.

"Maybe I'll do the oil myself," he said, taking the bottle from Addy and moving away from her.

Happy with that situation, I stepped over to the backdrop Lucy and Keva had set up. The fire truck was right behind me, and even though the sun was right in my eyes, I knew the lighting would be perfect for the photos. The zookeeper had a white and gray fluff ball in her hands.

"Let's have you lie down on your side," she said quietly. "I'll place Zelda in front of you. She is trained to lie quietly, but please don't touch her. With their sharp claws, even domesticated snow leopards can cause harm when they play."

I swallowed hard, the erection I'd been sporting completely gone. When I'd been told about this photoshoot, I hadn't been informed I'd be posing with deadly animals. I was thinking more like puppies and turtles, not leopards that could maim me with one swipe. Seemed a bit beyond the safety standards if you asked me.

The zookeeper gave me a confident smile and I didn't want to upset Lucy so early on in the shoot, so I moved into place and lay down on my side like I was directed. I put my head in my hand and followed Lucy's guidance from behind the camera on how to pose. When Lucy was satisfied, the zookeeper placed the snow leopard cub right in front of my hips. Jesus. Talk about feeling vulnerable.

"Okay, Lucy," I said quietly, not taking my eyes off the cub. "Take those pics fast, huh?"

I turned on my public persona and hammed it up for the camera. Lots of smirks, smolders, and of course, flexing of the muscles. The cub was actually quite cute, just lying there while Lucy took hundreds of shots. At the very end, the cub turned her head around to look at me. We locked eyes and I held my breath. I'd never stared down a wild animal at such close range. She was beautiful in a dangerous kind of way. I couldn't help but smile at her and that's when Lucy told the zookeeper she got the money shot. The cub was picked up and our staredown was broken.

I got up off the ground and realized we were drawing a crowd. Seemed like half the town was gathered on the sidewalk, their cell phones out snapping pics. I ducked my head and quickly searched the ground for the T-shirt I'd taken off earlier. Addy had it in her hands, handing it to me with a knowing smile.

"Got a few admirers here, Captain."

I growled low in my throat and got that shirt back on as quickly as I could. "I'm going to see if Lucy can move this shoot inside the station."

Addy drilled her finger into my chest. "Oh, come on. Let the people have their fun. Besides, you're all done." Her finger stroked across my chest and then down to my stomach where my muscles tightened at her touch. "I don't know. This shy side of Ace might be one of my favorites."

I leveled a look at her that reminded me of how we'd sparred up until a few weeks ago. "I'm not fucking shy. I just don't feel the need to be center of attention."

"There's the grumpy Ace I remember," she teased me. I snatched her hand off my stomach where she'd been toying with me. I brought her hand up to my mouth and kissed the back of it just to get my lips on any part of her soft skin I could.

"Okay, we have the porcupine next!" Lucy called out. "Who do you want paired with Porky, Ace?"

I kept hold of Addy's hand, but spun around to survey my guys. I saw Joe inch his way back into the bay. John looked like he wanted to be anywhere but here.

"I think that honor should be Ronnie's, don't you think?" I announced with a smirk.

"Ah, come on, guys," Ronnie moaned.

A few of the others smacked him on the back and pushed him toward the backdrop with snorts of laughter. He tossed me a glare, but took off his shirt, resigned to his fate. Someone from the sidewalk let out a wolf whistle. Ronnie's head popped up and his walk turned into a swagger. Can't keep a cocky young guy down for long.

The photoshoot continued for hours with the rest of the zoo animals, then a few of Janie's goats, a couple snakes—that I made sure Addy stayed far away from for obvious safety issues— that slithered across the broad shoulders of Joe who looked like he might shit his pants, a few rescue dogs, and then a whole crapton of cats from Yedda's National Cat Protection Society. She was quick to correct us that it was called a crowder of cats, but Lucy kept shushing her and telling her to get out of the picture frame.

Thankfully no urgent calls came in and we were able to get all the shots Lucy wanted in one day. By the time the sun was setting and Lucy packed things up, my shift was over. Addy stuck around, though she never did oil up any of the other guys. The bottle of oil was conveniently lost after she oiled me up. Strange how that thing got lost.

"Give me just a second to grab my stuff and then I'll take you home?" I asked Addy, giving her a quick kiss on the nose. She nodded and turned to chat with my buddies. After I'd told my inner caveman to shut the hell up and stop being jealous, she'd hung out with everybody today and it was remarkable how well they got along. I'd spent so many years hating her I hadn't fully appreciated how personable she was. People genuinely gravitated toward her sunny disposition. When I'd grabbed my things and walked back out, she was giving each of them a hug goodbye.

"Make sure you come visit again," Joe told her. "Ace is a hell of a lot less grumpy when you're around." I rolled my eyes, but Joe only had eyes for my woman.

"I'll come by next week with that salve for your back," she promised him.

I frowned. What the hell was wrong with Joe's back? I'd have to ask him about that later. I slid my arm around her waist and tugged her into my side. "Ready to head out?"

She smiled up at me and all the other guys faded into the background. I could get used to this. Ending my shift and having Addy to look forward to. I suddenly understood why my brothers were so eager to find a woman they could wrangle into more than just one date. I'd been missing out all these years. Then again, I hadn't found Addy until recently. Thank fuck I saw her naked breasts and decided to mend things between us.

I helped her up into my truck and rounded the back. I heard John whisper loudly from the bay, intentionally letting me hear him.

"Never thought I'd see the day Ace tied himself down."

I didn't bother defending myself. I just lifted my hand in the air and gave him a wave goodbye with a single finger. The middle one.

John and Joe both busted up laughing. I climbed in the truck and Addy grabbed my hand to lace our fingers together before I even got out of the parking lot.

"I really like your buddies. You know, I never really understood the camaraderie that you must have at the station. You're like another family. It must be nice to have a place you belong."

Her voice almost sound wistful as she said it, but she was right. They were my family and that's why I made my job a priority. A mistake could put my family at risk.

I pulled out of the lot and headed to Addy's place. I didn't like the sad tone of her voice or the way she now looked out the window like she was deep in thought. Despite her professed love of meditation and yoga, perhaps Addy was lonely from all that time spent by herself. She hadn't mentioned her parents much and I suddenly wondered if she missed them. Those seemed like things I should know about my own girlfriend. Shit. I needed to talk to Ethan. He'd know all the right things to ask to get a woman talking.

Until then, I needed to find a way to pull Addy back into her normal state of sunshine and daisies. I was finally off work and we had an evening together. I didn't want to waste it being sad when we had each other now.

I brought her hand up to my lips and kissed it again. She shifted her attention to me, blinking like she'd forgotten I was here with her in the truck.

"It is nice to feel like you belong somewhere. That's how I feel about you and me. We belong together."

Her eyes softened and that smile was back. "Are you sure you haven't done this boyfriend thing a lot? I feel like you're pretty good at it."

I kissed her hand again and settled our hands on my thigh. "I'm just highly motivated when I see your beautiful face."

She laughed softly. "Wow. Laying it on thick. Are you hoping for a repeat horn-honking session in this truck, or will we make it all the way to my bed tonight?"

My pants got infinitely tighter, the erection I'd been pushing down all day finally getting to blossom now that we were alone. "Horn honking? I've never heard it called that before."

Addy's mouth dropped open. "You seriously didn't hear us honking the horn?"

I wracked my brain, but came up empty. "No idea what you're talking about."

She shook her head and laughed. "Wow. Okay, well I vote for the bed this time."

"I'm good with anything you want, baby," I answered smoothly, shifting in the seat to ease the ache in my groin until I got us back to her place.

She untangled her fingers from mine and reached over to stroke my cock through my pants. I released a groan on top of a full-body shiver. "Damn, that feels so good."

She kept stroking and I pushed on the accelerator harder. We almost didn't make the turn into her driveway. Pretty sure I displaced some gravel I'd need to fix in the morning. I could barely see straight, and if I didn't get her naked soon, I'd explode in my pants, which was not how I saw the evening going.

"Oh shiitake mushrooms," Addy whispered, her gaze focused out the windshield and her fingers freezing.

"Huh?" I hit the brakes and assessed her house, which was lit up like a Christmas tree. "Did you leave all the lights on?"

Addy's shoulders slumped and she snatched her hand from my lap. "Nope. But I recognize that RV."

I looked over to where she was focused, just now realizing there was a thirty-two-foot RV parked next to her house. Damn, I should probably ban hand jobs in the truck. For safety reasons. A plane could have landed right in front of me and I wouldn't have noticed.

Addy slid out of the truck and I scrambled after her, trying to run with a fucking lead pipe in my pants. She marched right up to her house and flung open the door, letting it hit the wall with a bang. Jesus. This woman had no sense of danger, just barging in without taking proper precautions.

"Mom? Dad?" she called out.

I cringed and shifted quickly so I was behind her, thereby hiding my erection. I didn't know much about being a boyfriend, but I knew that was not the way to meet the parents for the first time.

A mostly bald head popped up from behind her bed where the sheets had been mostly pulled to the floor. Her dad didn't have a shirt on, but he looked just like I remembered him. Gray hair ringed the dome of his head, the long, straggly hair in back pulled into a ponytail, the epitome of an aging hippie.

"Hey, Daisychain!" he called out. He stood, sporting a pillow over his groin, naked as the day he was born. His spindly legs had a healthy sprinkling of dark hair.

"Oh shit," I muttered, turning around to give him some privacy.

"Is that you, Addy, honey?" I heard her mom call out.

"Seriously?" Addy yelled from behind me. "You're having sex in my house when your RV is right there?"

I bit my lip and tried to hold the laughter inside. Addy did not sound like she'd appreciate me laughing right now. Though the sight of a naked Mr. Bammingford had instantly rid me of the erection problem.

"Ah, Daisychain, sex is as natural as peeing," her dad said, the slow cadence of his voice telling me he was probably already high.

"Maybe so, but I don't want to have a front-row seat to peeing or sexing." Addy's voice was climbing higher with each word out of her mouth. "And ew. You need to wash my pillow and sheets now before I'll sleep there."

Pretty sure sexing wasn't a word, but I wasn't going to correct her. I wanted to focus on the "washing sheets" idea. No way in hell was I getting back in Addy's bed until those things had been washed. In boiling hot water. Bleach wasn't a bad idea either.

"She's got a man with her," I heard her dad whisper in a voice louder than Ronnie when he whined.

"Sorry, honey. We'll let you two have the bed as soon as I find my thong."

I looked up at the dark sky and prayed for patience.

Tonight was definitely not going as planned.

CHAPTER TWENTY-THREE

ce

ADDY SHUT the door and looked up at me, her eyes reminding me of the puppies from the photoshoot. Vulnerability shined through, like she needed me to solve the world's problems, or at least all of hers. And fuck if I didn't want to try.

"I'm so sorry you had to see that," Addy began, her gaze dropping to my chin.

I cut her off by tucking some of her hair behind her ear, waiting until she looked into my eyes again. "It's okay. I take it you didn't know they were coming?"

Addy cringed. "I never know what they're up to. That would require them to actually call me and inform me of their plans."

Ah shit. There was some family drama there. I could see it in the way Addy's eyelid began to twitch. I knew the look of a kid dealing with issues involving their parents. Before I could convince her I'd make things better, the door flew open and Mr. Bammingford stepped out.

His hair was still a bit of a mess, but at least he was fully clothed. He put an arm around Addy's shoulders and held his hand out to me. We shook as he eyed me up and down. I could smell the weed wafting off of him. Reminded me of that one time my brothers and I smoked a joint in the woods when I was a senior in high school. I hadn't liked the way it made me feel loopy, but Daxon and Ethan had loved the stuff just a little too much. I made them swear not to buy any more of that shit. If they had, they certainly hid it from me well enough.

"I'm Cornelius, but you can call me Neil. You're one of the Hellman boys, right? Let me guess." He tapped his chin and studied me some more before breaking out into a grin. "Must be Ash, the oldest one, right?"

I nodded. "Close, sir. It's actually Ace. What gave me away?"

Neil started chuckling and I could see why everyone in town liked the guy. Beyond the fact that he always shared his stash of weed with anyone who asked. "I could say the hair or the upper body, but it was the fireman shirt." He pulled his arm from Addy and grabbed ahold of my biceps, giving them a squeeze. "My goodness, youngster. You take those steroids to get this big?"

Addy stiffened, looking like she wanted to be anywhere but here.

"No, sir."

Neil let me go. The door opened again and Addy's mom joined the group. Neil instantly put his arm around her as she snuggled into his side.

"That's good. You know steroids shrink your nuts, right?"

"Dad!"

"What? They do. If you're going to be dating Aaron here, you want to know he has a nice pair on him, right?"

Addy buried her face in her hands, groaning.

"Oh goodie! My favorite topic," her mom giggled, looking a lot like Addy. Just twenty years older and maybe a little more nutty. Speaking of nuts. "I'm Jaqueline, but you can call me Jackie. Hello, handsome."

Jackie didn't try to shake my hand. She slipped out from

under Neil's arm and went up on tiptoe to plant a kiss on my cheek. Awkwardly, I patted her shoulder, not sure what to do in a situation where my girlfriend's mom was flirting with me and her dad was standing there, high as a kite.

"Got something for you, Alex." Neil slid a hand into the pocket of his shorts and pulled out a baggie of green stuff.

"It's Ace, Dad."

"Sure it is." He handed the baggie to me and I pushed it back.

"No, thank you." When he looked like I'd kicked his favorite puppy, I tried to clarify. "I can't have that in my system with my job."

His face cleared and he shrugged. "A-okay. Just means more for me. Right, Daisychain?"

Addy forced a smile. "How long are you guys in town?"

"Oh, honey, you know we don't make plans. We'll just see where the spirit takes us." Her mom poked me in the chest with her index finger. "Huh." Then she poked me in the other pec. Then ran her finger down my abs.

I jumped back and Addy looked ready to yell something she might regret later. I grabbed her around the waist and pulled her into my chest as she tried to lunge forward. She fought me for a few seconds, but I successfully held her back.

"Have you two eaten dinner yet? How about we go get some food together?" I gave them the Ace Hellman smile. The one that had everyone agreeing to whatever I suggested.

Neil covered one eye with his hand and just stared at me in a stupor. Jackie bobbed up and down on her toes, clapping. "Oh! A double date!"

That wasn't quite how I'd put it. "Sure. Like a double date."

"I know just the place. It's Addy's favorite restaurant."

Addy tilted her head. "The Forty-Diner?"

Jackie laughed. "No, silly. Tofurky Yourself. In Blueball."

"I'm sorry, what?" I interjected, thinking maybe that was some sort of family inside joke I wasn't a part of.

"Oh. Yeah. That sounds good too." Addy tilted her head to look back at me. I wasn't letting go of her waist until her parents were out of sight. "Do you mind eating vegan?"

"No, I don't mind at all." Fuck. Yes, I did mind. That vegan shit was nasty. But for Addy and keeping the peace with her parents, I'd choke it down somehow.

"Can we take your truck, Axel? I probably shouldn't be driving and Jackie hates driving at night, don't you, snookums?"

"Sure thing." I spun Addy around and walked to the truck.

"I'm so sorry," she whispered, looking like she could use a long meditation session.

"It's fine, okay? Seriously. I'm happy to get to know your parents, so stop apologizing," I grumbled back. I mean, I was happy to get to know her parents, if only to understand Addy better, but I wished it didn't have to be over a plate of grass and seeds and shit.

We all climbed in the truck and I headed off to Blueball, the next town over from Auburn Hill. The Bammingfords kept up a steady conversation of where they'd been the last six months or so. The only time Addy was able to get a word interjected was when she snapped at her dad to put the joint away, which I appreciated. Didn't need to show up at work with my truck smelling like a high school pothead's vehicle. I found it curious that neither of her parents had stopped their verbal diarrhea to ask Addy what she'd been up to. If they hadn't seen each other in awhile, you would think they'd have at least asked how she was doing. Shit, I couldn't keep my mom out of my business no matter how hard I tried to keep my personal life private.

I parked the truck right outside the hole-in-the-wall restaurant in Blueball and shut off the engine. "We're here!" I tried to inject some enthusiasm into my announcement, but the only person to cheer was Jackie. Neil looked like he could use a nap and Addy looked ready to commit a misdemeanor.

We all climbed out and got a seat at a table in the corner of the little restaurant. My chair was a goddamn exercise ball. If it weren't for Addy looking up at me with those doe eyes, I would have kicked it into the kitchen and demanded a fucking real chair.

"Oh, lucky ducky, Andy. You got the bouncy seat," Neil said with a seriousness that scrambled my brain.

"Here, I can switch with you," Addy offered, already scraping her wood chair back.

"No, thanks. You stay on the chair. I got this."

Addy slowly sat back down, still not meeting my gaze, which bothered the shit out of me. "Are you sure?"

I leaned over as much as I could while still staying seated on a round fucking ball, put my arm around her and whispered in her ear. "I already told you to quit apologizing. Now would you please stop looking down and be the Addy who knows every healing plant on the planet and tells grown firefighter captains to go fuck themselves?"

Addy's lips twitched. Her gaze came up and locked with mine, a real smile finally growing on her face. "Okay, bossy."

I brushed a kiss across her lips and promptly felt the ball tipping too far to the side. Without thinking, I slammed my hand on the table to keep my perch atop the ball, but sent all our water glasses sloshing.

"Whoo!" Jackie shouted, every patron of the restaurant looking our way. "Slap that table, Ace!"

"Dear goddess, this is a nightmare," Addy grumbled under her breath.

And we hadn't even been served our grass and seeds yet.

"WELL, thank you for dinner, Abel. You didn't have to pay for it." Neil clapped me on the shoulder, looking a bit more alert than when we'd left. And I did have to pay for it since neither of Addy's parents brought a wallet.

"It's Ace, Dad," Addy sighed.

Jackie kissed Addy on the cheek. "We're going to stay in the trailer tonight, honey. Call it an early night. You and Ace take the cabin."

"Why, thank you, Mom, for giving me my own house."

"You are welcome, honey." She patted Addy's cheek, either oblivious to Addy's sarcasm or she just didn't care. I didn't know which.

Neil walked off with his wife, already lighting up his joint. "Let's braid each other's hair tonight."

"Oh! And facials!" Jackie said loud enough for all the squirrels in a ten-mile radius to hear.

The trailer door slammed behind them, but I could still hear Jackie talking loudly. A window opened on the side of the trailer and smoke puffed out like a chimney.

Addy kicked a rock, looking like she wanted to be anywhere but here. I stepped closer and put my hand on her face, tilting her head up. "Hey. Are you okay?"

She sucked in a deep breath, her eyes filling with tears. Ah, fuck. She was going to cry. Tears were every man's kryptonite. I'd have to channel my inner Ethan to know the right thing to say.

"You saw them." She tried to shake her head, but my hand was still holding her. "They're ridiculous. Over the top. They embarrass me and I sound like a horrible daughter for even saying that."

I frowned. "No, you don't. Your parents are definitely...unique."

A single tear slipped down her cheek and my heart rate sped up. "That's an incredibly kind way to put it. My dad can't even remember your name."

"I have a feeling that's intentional, baby."

Addy got a little frown line between her eyebrows. I leaned

down and kissed it, wishing I could do a lot more than that, but not with her parents right next door.

"I'm sorry they ruined our night."

"I swear to God, Addy, if you apologize one more time, I will punish you in ways you don't like."

Her eyes flared with something other than sadness. Shit. Maybe I did know how to handle a crying woman.

"What ways would that be, Captain?"

And the erection was back. "Force-feed you red meat."

"Hey!" Addy laughed softly and I gave myself a high five in my head.

"Kidding, baby. I'd probably start with a spanking and see what progressed from there."

"I feel the sudden need to apologize again," Addy whispered, pressing those tits into my chest in a clear invitation.

"Ouch! That's too tight!"

We both looked over at the trailer and winced.

"How about we save that thought for another day?"

Addy's shoulders sagged, her gaze dropping to my chin again. "Fine."

"Hey." I tilted her head back and made her look at me. "I'm leaving to be respectful to your parents, not because I don't want to sink into your heat and see what color your ass turns when my palm slaps it. Do you understand me?"

Addy swallowed, then gave a quick nod. "A kiss goodbye wouldn't be disrespectful, would it?"

"Fuck no," I murmured. And then my lips were on hers, showing her exactly how much I wanted her and how none of that had changed since having dinner with her parents.

When we were both breathing hard, I pulled back. "Go inside, Addy."

"But—"

"Inside," I barked, needing her to be out of sight or I wouldn't physically be able to drive away from her.

"Okay, grumpy," she snapped back, walking to her front door

and giving me more hip action than normal. Fuck. This woman was trying to kill me.

"Goodnight, Ace."

"Night, Addy."

It took the entire drive home plus a cold shower to tame the erection. I debated with myself, believing that the Bammingfords wouldn't have cared if I spent the night with Addy. They didn't seem to be the type of parents who put a moral judgement on sex. Then again, I'd just started dating Addy and didn't want to fuck it up just because I couldn't seem to control a part of my anatomy. Probably best that I left.

Besides, having some time alone gave me the head space to analyze her relationship with her parents. Neil and Jackie were a hoot, but I could see how they tended to overlook Addy. I could practically feel the hurt feelings building in Addy as we sat at dinner. They'd finally asked about her yoga class, but it was because they wanted to know what time it started so they could join the next day, not because they cared about how her business was going.

The time spent with the Bammingfords tonight made me realize that while my own parent shit had been pretty obvious when my father left us, there were other families dealing with their own shit that maybe wasn't as obvious.

My phone dinged and I picked it up, thinking it might be from Addy with another fucking apology.

Blaze: Hey, bro. Had an accident at work last week. Can you call me tomorrow?

I sat down on the couch, stunned. Blaze had actually reached out and he wanted to talk?

Me: Sure. I work tomorrow, but I'll call you on my lunch break. Are you okay?

Blaze: I will be. I hope. Just call me and I'll explain. Oh, and don't say anything to Mom or the boys.

Me: Will do, man. Miss you.

He didn't respond after that, which I was expecting. Blaze

didn't do feelings like a normal person. If Addy thought I was grumpy, she clearly hadn't spent much time around Blaze. Although it wasn't so much a grumpy nature as just being quiet. Closed off. An island. Probably why he and Ben were best friends. They both were the strong, silent type.

I had to work a short shift tomorrow and I'd probably have to drink a whole thermos of coffee to jump-start my brain. I stayed up later than I should, thoughts swirling about Addy, her parents, and what might have happened with Blaze. I knew none of that mess was my responsibility, but I still felt compelled to jump in the middle and fix what needed fixing. It didn't even occur to me that maybe none of it was within my power to fix.

CHAPTER TWENTY-FOUR

*a*ddy

THE COMPUTER SCREEN FROZE. I shoved the mouse and banged on the enter key with enough force to cause the San Andreas Fault to rumble, but nothing moved. Thank the goddesses I'd practically bathed in hemp lotion this morning to calm my nerves.

Dad had woken up in the middle of the night and decided it was a good time to start a bonfire and try out his new ukulele. I got him to put out the fire lest a certain firefighter found out I was burning on a no-burn day again, but he'd sung three songs before I got him to give up the impromptu concert. Of course, by then I was so angry I couldn't get back to sleep.

When would I simply accept that my parents lived in their own little world and would never open their eyes to how their actions affected me? When they were gone, I missed them, but I was starting to realize that I only missed the *idea* of parents. The kind who listened, asked questions, and demonstrated they loved me. That sounded harsh. I knew my parents loved me in their own way, it was just that they never made me feel special or like a priority in their lives.

"I'd hate to find out what the computer did to you."

I looked up from the screen, eyes feeling like they were burning after several hours of grappling with my new Etsy site. Ethan, Ace's youngest brother, stood across the table from me, a warm smile on his bearded face.

"Hey, Ethan. Sorry you had to see that. My zen up and walked away the second I sat down behind this computer."

He shrugged. "Happens to a lot of people when they're on those things. Anything I can help with?"

I let out a deep breath. "Only if you know how to connect this bank merchant with my Etsy site."

Ethan winced. "No can do, lovely lady. If you need a leaky faucet fixed or drywall repair, I'm your guy." He looked around the library and then had a seat, leaning halfway over the table. His voice dropped to a whisper. "Although I've been meaning to talk to you."

Oh no. My boyfriend's brother wanted to talk to me? Sounded like I was in trouble, or maybe his family didn't like me and he drew the short stick to be the one to tell me.

"Sure," I said faintly.

"I've got a side project I'm working on and I need to ask you a few questions about natural scents. Like from plants and things. I figure with your tinctures and lotions and stuff, you'd know which natural substances make for the best scents in other products."

I blinked a few times. That was not what I was expecting to come out of his mouth.

"Well, what products are you trying to give scent to?"

Ethan scratched his beard and grimaced. "I can't say."

I couldn't help but smile. The guy was weird but in a really friendly way that made me like him. I was weird too.

"Okay..." I tapped the table and then shoved the keyboard out of my way. I could work on my site later. "Let's start with essential oils. That might be the easiest way to get the scents you're looking for. Do you know anything about them?"

Ethan smiled, looking relieved. "Can't say that I do, but I saw my mom has some on her counter. She slapped my hand when I picked one up, saying they were for her gentlemen friends."

I cleared my throat and moved on quickly, not wanting to explain that comment. "Well, they work in all kinds of ways. You can put them on your skin, in lotion or oil. Many of them you can ingest or diffuse into the air. Maybe you could come by my place sometime and I'll show you all my oils and you can see if they might work for your supersecret project?"

Ethan slapped the table with his palms. "Perfect. I knew you'd be able to help me." He shoved the chair back and stood. "I was surprised to see you dating Ace, but I'm really happy my brother pulled his head out of his ass finally."

"Thank you?"

Ethan spun around and left the library, laughing as he went, not caring at all about the old librarian shushing him from her desk at the front. When the front door closed behind him, she swiveled to turn her birdlike gaze on me. I could feel the waves of judgement coming off of her. Damn. I remember seeing that face when I was a kid coming to the library to escape into the pages of a good book. Why did librarians have to be so scary? I gave her a weak smile and turned back to my computer, which was still frozen.

I needed a chai tea before I could tackle this project again. Instead of being productive, I picked up my phone and flipped it open to pound out a text to Ace. It took me forever to get it written, having to hit each button up to three times to get the right letter. Maybe I should upgrade to a smartphone, just for the texting function. Gah! No. I would not sell out and shackle myself to a device that was designed to addict me to technology.

Me: Just chatted with Ethan. Made me miss you. He's up to something but won't tell me what.

I shut down the computer and hoped what I'd worked on

had saved before the dang thing froze. Gathering my things, I decided to stop at Coffee before heading home. Actually, maybe I'd do a little shopping. Anything to delay actually going home and having to deal with my parents' latest shenanigans.

I gave a smile and a wave to the librarian—who did not reciprocate—as I walked out the door and into the early afternoon sunshine. The library wasn't far from Coffee, so I put my tote bag in the front basket of my bike and walked it down the sidewalk through downtown. After I'd ordered and sat down at a table outside, I pulled out my phone to see if Ace had texted back. Sometimes he was quick to text back and other times it took hours. Just depended on how busy he was at work.

Ace: I'll call him tonight if I get off before midnight. Sorry I can't see you. Something came up at work and I'm stuck here for the time being.

My heart sank. I had been hoping to see him tonight. Just us. I had visions of sneaking away from my parents and spending the night at his place. I knew where he lived—this was a small town after all—but he'd never invited me over. We'd always spent our time together at my place. A flutter of vague unease hit my stomach, but maybe that was just hunger. I'd skipped lunch as I tried to set up my storefront online.

Me: No worries. See you at first aid class tomorrow?

Ace: I'll be there for sure. ;)

I flipped the phone closed and smiled my thanks at the barista who brought over my chai tea. I took a sip and tried to pinpoint what emotion was making me feel uneasy. Disappointment that I wouldn't see Ace tonight. Dread regarding what my parents were getting up to on my property since I'd been gone. Boredom with my life in general? And maybe, tucked in the corner, doused in shadows, was an inkling of fear. Fear that Ace didn't have time for me. Fear that once he got to know me—and not the bright happy shiny Addy that I showed the world, but the Addy who had crazy parents and a nontraditional job he didn't understand—Ace might not want anything to do with me again.

Poppy plopped down in the seat across from me, startling me out of my thoughts. Yedda stood behind her, smiling from ear to ear at me like we were old pals.

Poppy folded her arms across her chest and stared me down. "Heard you turned Tofurkey Yourself into an orgy with your parents the other night, Addy."

I nearly spit out my tea. "Ew. No. Ace and I went out to dinner with my parents, but clothes stayed on." I was getting really sick and tired of this rumor mill in Hell. They got everything so wrong I was starting to think they exaggerated on purpose.

"Hey, no judgies here, missy. I'm just happy your father is back in town. I got restocked this morning." Yedda gave me a wink, her black eyeliner wobbling away from her eye and making more of a droopy cat tail than winged eyeliner. My money was on Yedda being too baked this morning after paying a visit to a certain trailer to apply it properly. Thanks to dear old Dad and his plentiful stash of weed.

It would be funny except when your second-grade teacher was one of his customers. And don't forget my harp teacher (because of course Mom couldn't pick a normal instrument for me like piano). Or my first yoga teacher when I was fifteen who'd been introduced to Dad when he dropped me off. She partook in his lit joint and spent the entire class in savasana pose instead of teaching me.

My parents never stopped to wonder what having the town weed dealer for a father did to me as an impressionable child. Dad just did what he wanted to do and didn't give a damn about me. And for some reason, today was the day I was sick of it. I'd had it up to my eyeballs with their interference in my life.

For the first time ever, I just wanted to be a normal girl with a normal boyfriend, living a normal life in a small town. I didn't want to be known as the weird one. I didn't want to be the center of all the town gossip.

I stood so fast my metal chair scraped on the concrete,

letting out a sharp squeal that had heads turning. "Excuse me, ladies. I have somewhere to be."

A better exit would have included getting in my car, slamming the door, and revving the engine as I left them in my dust. But because I was Adelia Bammingford and didn't believe in expanding my carbon footprint, I had to unlock my bike with one hand and try to ride it down the sidewalk while holding a hot tea. I only clipped one person and dribbled the tea down my leg, so maybe my exit wasn't too humiliating.

By the time I biked home, I'd lost my head of steam. It wasn't my responsibility to clean up my father's act. I was a grown adult who could only control my own life. About the only thing I could do was ask them to move their trailer off my property, which is what I intended to do as soon as I got home. There was a camping site just a few miles down the road that would be perfect for them. And would give me just enough privacy to live my life like I wanted.

I left the bike on its side at the end of the driveway, too preoccupied with the spots of color by my front door to bother putting it away properly. I gasped, seeing that I now had an even row of perennials planted outside my house. Even the pine needles were brushed away. Did Mom take the time to add some beauty to my property? She knew I loved flowers. I suddenly felt guilty for all the things I'd been thinking about my parents today.

I was just about to head around the house to find them when a square of white on my doorstep caught my eye. Picking it up, I didn't recognize the handwriting on the front. I pulled a card out of the envelope and flipped it open.

Thought a few flowers would brighten your day. Also...call me and explain why I'm the last to know about you and my oldest son dating. Love, the Plant Fairy, aka Nikki.

My mouth popped open. I didn't know whether to laugh or cry. My parents hadn't planted the flowers. Ace's mom had. She went out of her way to do something nice for me. That felt really good. The warm fuzzies left quickly though. She might be mad at me for not telling her about me and Ace.

That anger I'd felt toward my parents was back, but this time it was dipped in hurt. How come they didn't do nice things like that for me? How did a woman I barely spent any time with know I loved flowers?

I tucked the card in the back pocket of my shorts. A feminine yelp came from the woods behind my house. Steeling myself for something that would probably make me angrier than I already was, I walked around the house to go find my parents.

It didn't take long to find them. When I came around the rock outcropping that led to the river, my mother was naked as the day she was born, running full speed for the river bank. I opened my mouth to say something—what, I didn't know—but the next second she leaped, grabbing her knees to her chest, and splashing into the river as my dad cheered from the embankment. A haze of smoke covered him in a bubble and his back was to me, thank the goddess. Because he was naked too.

I slapped my hands over my eyes and felt the anger festering into a cauldron of rage. My throat chakra felt like it was about to implode, the damage either going to overflow out my mouth, or lodge in my throat, forever cutting off my ability to communicate. I chose to spew.

"What the actual fuck are you doing?" I yelled.

I heard Dad scramble to his feet, hopefully to find some fucking clothing. Mom splashed in the water and I couldn't tell if she was getting out, or enjoying a cold bath.

"You're home, Daisychain," Dad sang to a song the rest of us didn't hear.

Great. He was high. Because of course he was.

"Yes. I'm home. This is *my* home, by the way. My property." I kept my hands over my eyes, feeling like I was yelling at no one since I couldn't see them. "You're squatting on my land. The least you could do is keep things decent. No child needs to see their parents naked." I thought about the day they arrived. Naked then too. "Repeatedly."

"Oh, honey. It's just skin," came Mom's voice from right in front of me.

I jumped back. Wow, she moved quick. "Yes, I know, but I don't need to see it, okay? Can you please just keep clothing on? For me?"

Mom sighed, but put her arm around me, getting me wet in the process. "Okay, fine. We'll do our best."

"Thank you." I wasn't sure how much I could trust "their best," but that was better than nothing. Maybe tonight over dinner I could discuss with them how long they intended to stay. If it was more than a week, I'd gently steer them toward the campground. For everyone's sake.

When Mom let me go—and thank the goddess she did because I was pretty sure she was hugging me naked—I turned around and headed for my house, finally removing my hands from my eyes.

I needed a meditation session. ASAP.

CHAPTER TWENTY-FIVE

*a*ce

"I'M SO SORRY, Ace. Depending on how quickly the doctor sees us, maybe I can still come in halfway through my shift."

I squeezed my eyes shut and forced a level of kindness in my voice I didn't really feel. "Don't worry, man. Just be there for your kid. I got your shift covered."

"I really appreciate it. I'll shoot you a text when I know what's going on."

Dave was a good guy. Not his fault his five-year-old son fell out of a tree and possibly broke his arm. It just came at a really bad time. With fifteen minutes before his shift started, there wasn't time to find a replacement. Which meant I'd be staying on another twelve hours.

"We're almost out of here. You coming?" Joe poked his head into my office. The place still felt like Captain Murray's office, but once I got my head wrapped around all my new responsibilities, I would make it my own.

I tried out a smile, but it was brittle as hell. Even Joe looked at me a little weird, his easygoing smile fading.

"Nah. Dave's kid might have broken his arm. I'm covering his first twelve."

"Are you sure? One of us could probably stay on."

I shrugged, trying to look like I had things handled. I mean, I did, but only at my own expense. "Nah. I got it. Go enjoy some well-deserved time off."

Joe rapped his knuckles on the doorframe. "Okay. If you're sure."

I lifted an eyebrow. I appreciated his concern, but I wanted my guys to know I'd always have their backs. "Get out of here, would you? Go find a girl or something to occupy your time."

He laughed. "I'm waiting on that calendar to come out. They'll flock to me then."

That brought a real smile to my face. "That's why I agreed to Lucy's plan. Knew you jackasses needed a little help in the romance department."

"Dude, shut the fuck up. You get a girlfriend for the first time and suddenly you're an expert."

I nodded and gave him a wink. "You know it."

He rolled his eyes and backed out of the doorway. "You might be right. Addy's hot."

I jumped out of my chair but he let out a whoop and ran off. Fucker. I loved the guys I worked with, but we clearly knew how to push each other's buttons. I plopped back in the chair and sighed, staring at the blank walls. When I'd signed on as captain, I'd mostly been thinking about the title and the honor to be picked for the position. I hadn't realized all the other work behind the scenes that had to be done. Reports, work schedules, ordering of new equipment, scheduling trainings, filing on-the-job accident reports. It was a steep learning curve, taking me away from my fellow firefighters and sticking me in this tiny office more than I wanted.

"Come on, Ace. Suck it up and do it." I scrubbed a hand

across my face and decided more caffeine was a must to get through the next twelve hours.

My phone buzzed on the desk and I picked it up immediately, seeing Blaze's name on the screen.

"Hey, brother."

"Ace. How are you?" His voice sounded deeper than I remembered. It was familiar, but not, which made me sad. I should instantly recognize the voice of my own damn brother, shouldn't I?

"Just living the dream."

Blaze huffed out what sounded like a laugh. "Yeah, it's all unicorns and puppy dogs until it's not, huh?"

I nodded, knowing exactly what he meant. "Yup. Want to tell me about it?"

He sighed, but started talking. "You heard of Cal Steele?"

"Of course." Every female on the planet was drooling over him and his ridiculous physique he was all too happy to show off in his movies. You couldn't convince me it was all natural, even with Hollywood trainers and a private chef. Now that he'd separated from his wife, the women online were going crazy, thinking somehow they'd be plucked from obscurity to date Cal.

"Well, I was tagged to be his body double for this movie set in the woods. I was supposed to be jumping from up in a pine tree to a crane. Unfortunately, the metal of the crane iced over while we were setting up the shot and on the first run-through with the cameras rolling, I slipped and ended up falling about twenty feet."

"Shit, man. Did you break anything?" I stood up, pacing my office. When the fuck did this happen and why was I just now hearing about it?

"Yeah. Fractured my femur and dislocated my shoulder when I tried to grab on to the side of the damn crane to keep from falling. It probably slowed my fall enough to keep me alive, but fuck."

"When did this happen? Are you in the hospital?" My brain

was swirling, thinking we needed to send someone to Los Angeles to help him.

"It was exactly a week ago. I'm out of the hospital now."

I rubbed at my chest. "Dude. It happened a week ago and you're just now telling me?"

"Ace..."

I knew that tone. That was his warning that he was about to shut me out if I kept up that line of questioning. I squeezed my eyes shut and tried to focus on the fact that he did finally call. That had to count for something. "Listen, never mind about that. What can I do to help?"

Blaze was silent for so long I thought the call might have dropped. When he finally answered, he sounded more lost than I'd ever heard my little brother. The guy had always been so confident growing up. Where I'd been faking it, he'd been for real. He'd gone into law enforcement straight out of high school and then left that for stunt work when he realized he wanted to do that.

"I just...I guess I just wanted someone to know. I'm rehabbing fine on my own, but it might be pretty slow going before I'm back to work. The doctors won't even give me a definitive yes that I'll be back to work at all."

"Fuck." I rubbed the back of my neck, trying to release the tension there. "Do you think you should just come back to Hell for a few months to rehab? Maybe sublease your place so you're not losing money?"

"No, I don't want to stress out Mom. Just...keep this between us for right now, okay?"

He wanted me not to tell our family about his very serious injuries? "Dude. I think they should know."

"No way, Ace. I told you this in confidence."

I sighed and flopped back in the chair. "Fine. But I think you should tell them yourself. And I think you should move back. Just for a few months. 'Til you're back on your feet. Think on it."

"I will and my answer will still be no. But thanks for listening. I'll let you know how things are going."

"Okay. Love you, man."

"Love you too."

He hung up and I set the phone on the desk slowly. Fuck. If he couldn't go back to stunt work, that probably meant he couldn't go back to the police force either. The stubborn mule wouldn't let me help him, so I guess he'd have to cross that bridge when he came to it.

My phone immediately buzzed again, but this time it was a text from Callan. Not on the brothers' string of texts either. Just to me.

Callan: Hey. I know you're just getting off work. I wanted to get this out there, but not in person because you'd probably just coldcock me and that's not how I wanted this to play out. Once you've cooled off, let's get together and chat about it. Without fists.

I frowned at the screen. That was a long lead-up to nothing.

Me: What the fuck are you talking about?

Callan: I want to reach out to our father.

I dropped the phone on the desk and stood, putting both my hands on the back of my head. What the fuck else could go wrong today? I felt like the weight of the world was on my shoulders. I could hear the next shift filing into the station. I had a shift to run but all I wanted to do was put on gloves and hit the shit out of the punching bag in the back of the station. It was probably too much to hope for, but if we didn't get a bunch of calls tonight, that's exactly what I was going to do.

Callan: Ace?

When I felt like I could respond without typing something that might actually damage our relationship, I picked the phone back up.

Me: Obviously, I think that's a very poor idea. Let's discuss later. Please don't do anything until we talk face-to-face. I'm working the next shift, so maybe tomorrow sometime?

Callan: Sounds good. Call me when you have time to meet.

I left the office to make sure the next crew was ready to go. Once all that was as it should be, I stepped outside to call Addy. She was probably expecting me to come over, thinking I was now off work. She answered on the first ring.

"Hey, handsome."

"Wood nymph." Just hearing her voice helped settle some of the rage and exhaustion that was threatening to pull me under.

"Are you off?"

I leaned my head against the stucco wall behind me and looked up at the darkening night sky. It was almost a full moon again, reminding me of the night I'd walked in on Addy topless in her backyard. Almost felt like I'd been a different guy back then. A little more carefree, a lot less responsibility. And yet, I'd felt stressed then too. Maybe I was just built to be the one who carried the weight of the world. Someone had to do it, right?

"Unfortunately no. Someone called in last minute, so I'm filling in for them. I'll be done tomorrow morning, but I'll need to crash for a bit."

"What are you doing?" she shouted. I pulled the phone away from my ear. "Hold on a second, Ace."

I realized she wasn't yelling at me. I waited, listening to her rant to her father.

"Dad, you can't just set up your pot plants in my house! This is a very small space. I don't have room for these and all the lights. Look at all the extension cords!"

"Daisychain, they don't fit in our RV either."

"Then you need to get rid of them! Not clutter up my house too!"

"You want me to destroy them?" That almost got a chuckle out of me. Neil sounded like Addy had suggested he kill a real live human.

"I don't care what you do with them, just get them out of my house."

Addy was breathing hard into the phone. A door slammed and then she was back.

"I cannot believe the nerve of that man. Do you know I caught them skinny-dipping in my creek yesterday? And now my house has been turned into a cannabis greenhouse! I can't take it, Ace. I need them to go back on the road. Or get their own place. Something! At this point, I'll never have peace in my life ever again. Mom came to sunrise yoga today and started singing during savasana. Yedda accidentally whacked her with her rolled-up yoga mat. I thought I might have to pull the two of them apart."

Addy finally paused to take a breath. Honestly, I felt bad for her, but I couldn't take on anything more. I was mentally and emotionally spent. Between my professional life and my own family, I had enough shit to deal with. Jackie and Neil were a level of crazy I'd only take on if I had an unlimited supply of time and patience. Both were running severely short in my life.

"Ace? Are you there?"

I pushed off the wall and walked back to the door of the station. "Yeah, I'm here. I'm sorry about your parents."

Addy paused and then, when she spoke again, her voice came out quieter. More calm. "Is something wrong?"

Hell, what *wasn't* wrong might be the better question. But Addy had enough on her hands with her parents. I didn't need to burden her with more.

"No, nothing's wrong. Just busy with work. And I'm sorry I can't make the first aid class tonight like I wanted to. Can you have your parents drive you to class?"

"Oh, you can't do the class?" Addy sounded disappointed in me and that cut deep.

"No, not tonight."

"It's okay. I get it. Call me tomorrow?"

"Sure. Goodnight, Addy."

When she hung up without saying goodbye, it only added to my worries. A woman didn't just hang up on her boyfriend unless she was upset. Even I knew that. We'd only been together for a week and already I felt like I was failing at this boyfriend thing.

"Fuck!" I said into the night air.

"Watch your mouth, asshole!"

I looked over to see old Lenny shuffling down the sidewalk with a basset hound who looked equally as old on a leash. Lenny flipped me the bird and I lifted a hand in apology to the back of his head.

Going back into the station where I wouldn't offend the senior citizens of Hell, I hightailed it to my office, not wanting to have to put on a fake smile for the rest of the guys milling about doing their jobs. I had a change of clothes in my bag. If I didn't get a workout in, I might just explode.

My computer dinged as I dug around for the sweats that were in my duffle bag somewhere. I moved the mouse to bring the screen to life, seeing I had a new email.

From the chief.

Shit. I dropped the bag and had a seat to give it a read. I kind of wished I had a punching bag handy though when I read it. Apparently, I'd forgotten to submit a report that was due this morning. The line that threw me over the edge was the one that stated I needed to be more on top of things. That gutted me. I'd never had a superior tell me I wasn't pulling my weight. Not ever. Usually their comments were about me going above and beyond the job description.

I felt like an absolute failure at life.

I dropped my forehead to the desk and took some deep breaths. I could really use one of Addy's meditation sessions right now, but I was afraid if I asked for a favor now, I'd find itch powder in my uniforms.

When we were kids, Mom had bought us a vintage muscle man figurine that you could stretch. Said to take our frustrations out on that thing instead of each other. Supposedly, it was inde-structible. We'd pulled on his arms and legs like we had an ax to grind, which we did considering we all grew up knowing our father had left us behind. And one day it finally broke. I felt a lot like that doll. Pulled in every direction. Stretched to the max.

And while I operated under the assumption that I'd never break, I probably had my limits too.

Long minutes later, when I had myself mostly in control, I lifted my head and lectured myself on getting my shit together. This was not me. Ace Hellman handled his responsibilities and everyone else's. Quit wasting time thinking of Addy's gorgeous tits and focus on the job.

Report first.

Grovel to the chief.

Then it was punching bag time.

ddy

I LOOKED outside at the line strung from the antenna of my parents' RV to the huge pine tree in my backyard. Clothes hung haphazardly from it, which wouldn't normally be a problem, but my father's underwear was flying in the breeze, holes and all.

"Maybe let's just meet in town," I told Ace, who'd called me after he got some sleep.

He sounded like he could use some more though. His sigh was audible, as was the scrape of his hand across his beard. "I don't want you riding your bike, Addy."

"It's still light. I'll just ride it there and you can bring me home?"

I'd read my parents the riot act before I left and demand they have the clothesline taken down by tonight. I couldn't have Ace seeing just how ridiculous my parents were. It had taken me until fifth grade before I even invited Meadow over to see our dilapidated house in the woods that my parents managed to rent from an old man who didn't care what they did with the place as long as they stayed current on their rent check. She'd taken one look at the place, and from then on, she never suggested play dates at my house again. No judgement from Meadow. She just knew I was embarrassed and she didn't want that for her best friend. My own place was small, but it was clean and well taken care of.

"Okay, fine. That works." Ace didn't sound happy about it. More resigned than I'd ever heard him, actually. "I'll meet you at Forty-Diner and then we can check the movie listings in Blue-ball. See if there's anything we want to see."

"Sounds good." I paused, wondering why I felt a huge gap between us. It wasn't that he'd missed last night's first aid class. Or even that he had to cancel a few dates recently. Ace was usually tired after a long shift, but today felt different. "I can't wait to spend time with you."

There was a pause, but when he came back, his voice had dropped to that sexy growl that made me wonder if I'd made up an issue between us where there was none. "I can't wait either."

I was late getting to the diner as I'd had to explain multiple times to my parents that I didn't want their dirty laundry strewn across my yard. They, of course, protested that it wasn't dirty. It was quite clean. It had gone back and forth like that for awhile before I'd lost my cool and yelled at them to just take it down. I didn't condone yelling at people, but I sure was doing it a lot lately. It didn't make me feel good about myself. Maybe I needed to increase my daily meditation to an hour.

Forty-Diner was lit up from inside, warm yellow light spilling out onto the sidewalk. The charm of Main Street, with its old-fashioned lampposts and unique storefronts, eased some of the tension from my shoulders as I pulled up to the restaurant and got off my bike.

A couple with two kiddos with them stopped on their way into the restaurant. The woman glanced over with a warm smile. She looked familiar, but I couldn't quite come up with a name.

"That bike could use some greasing up. I heard the squeak a mile away."

I laughed. "Yeah. It's a bit on the rusty side, but she still rides."

The woman pulled a bottle out of her huge purse. "May I?"

I stepped aside, surprised by her kind gesture for a stranger. "Sure, by all means. You carry bike lube with you all the time?"

The husband let out a guffaw. "I'll just grab us a table." He ushered the two kids inside while the woman squatted down to squirt something on my bike chain.

"Well, it's not bike lube, but it is lube," the woman drawled.

I frowned. And then the lightbulb went off. "Oh, you must be Lenora from the Hardware Store!" I was still in school when that business opened—and no, they didn't sell hammers and nails—but I'd heard about it plenty. It was all anyone talked about for awhile. Lenora's dad was the preacher in town at the time and she and Jayden, the owner of the sex toy business, started dating. Then he gave her the business as some kind of romantic gesture. It was a crazy story, actually.

She looked up and gave me a smile that only someone truly happy in life could give. It was something in the eyes. "That's right. And you must be Addy? I've been hearing rumors about you and Ace Hellman. Not sure if any of it's true, but you two would make an adorable couple."

I felt my face heat. "Well, thank you. We just started dating, so we'll see, I guess." It felt weird that Lenora had already heard about me through the rumor mill. In actuality, I felt pretty confident about Ace and me dating despite what I said. In fact, during my meditation this morning it occurred to me that I could very easily fall in love with the guy. If I hadn't started sliding in that direction already.

Lenora stood and popped the sparkly bottle back in the bag. "Should be good as new. All organic too."

"Really?" It was rare that I met someone else who cared

about things being organic. "I might have to stop by and check out your products."

She linked her arm through mine and held the door to the diner open. "You do that, but make sure you mention you get the friends and family discount."

"And if you ever take up yoga, make sure you come to my class. I have a friends discount too."

Lenora shot me another one of those smiles and waved good-bye, walking to the right where her family was seated in a booth. I looked left and saw Ace in a booth in the corner, his head leaning on his hand, looking bored. Or half-asleep. I hustled over and slid into the booth on his side, my whole body sighing with relief as I pressed against him.

He jumped, his head coming up. "Hey, gorgeous."

He leaned in to kiss me and I noticed dark circles under his eyes. The kiss was quick, almost distracted. Not at all like the ones he'd given me when he pressed me up against a tree. I chalked it up to working too much.

"Oh man, maybe we should skip the movie and just get you fed. You look like you could use some more sleep." I ran my hand over the hair on the back of his head, trying to massage the muscles there that frequently knotted up due to tension. Ace sighed and dropped his head, giving me access to his neck too.

"That feels so good," he moaned.

I kept up with the massage as we caught up. He was just getting to the part about missing some report when the little bell over the door rang again and the voices I didn't want to hear tonight called out.

"Daisychain! Arlo!"

I groaned an entirely different kind of groan and dropped my head on Ace's shoulder. "Please tell me my parents aren't here at the diner."

Ace kissed the top of my head. "I don't want to lie to you, baby."

I grumbled some more but lifted my head and swiveled to my

parents who now stood by our table. "Hi. Imagine running into you here. After I just told you I was meeting Ace here. Huh."

"We started getting hungry and you didn't have much in your refrigerator, honey. We figured we'd grab some food to go, but it looks like you have room for more, huh?" Mom pointed to the empty bench seat across from us.

My eyes popped open at the idea of enduring another dinner together. "Actually! That's, um, not a good idea. You two have quite the project at home to get to. Right?"

Ace put his hand on my thigh and squeezed. I wasn't quite sure what message he was trying to get across, but I couldn't do it. I couldn't sit across from them and pretend everything was fine between us. Couldn't a girl just have one night to herself with her boyfriend? Parents shouldn't be cockblockers once their kids were adults.

Dad ran a hand down the buttons of his Hawaiian shirt that I was pretty sure he'd had since I was a little girl. The thing was faded, the palm trees just barely visible after thousands of washings. He believed clothes should be worn until they fell apart. I liked the motive behind his philosophy, but also believed looking nice in clothes that didn't look like they came from the bottom of the bin at a secondhand store had value too.

"Oh, so you actually wanted us to do that *tonight*?" He looked confused. As if me saying "take down the clothesline before I get back from dinner" wasn't clear enough.

I nodded, determined to keep my cool in front of Ace and everyone in this town who just so happened to be at Forty-Diner tonight and watching us. "Yes, please."

Dad just shrugged. "Okay, we'll get the meal to go. More naked time for you and me, my little love puppet." He slung his arm around Mom's shoulders and the two of them walked off to the counter to place their orders.

"Ew," I said under my breath, watching them go.

I felt something shaking and looked over to see Ace laughing silently, his shoulders jumping up and down. "How would you like it if your parents did that crap in front of you?"

He put his hands up, trying to control his laughter. "Hey, I get it. You gave my mom libido oils, remember?"

My hand covered my mouth. "I did, didn't I?" I put my hand down and squeezed his muscled thigh. "I'm so sorry."

He put his hand on top of mine and everything seemed right with the world. "It's okay. But maybe next time let's go to a different town for dinner. Or maybe take it to go and head back to my place. I want to take you out for an actual date with privacy, but it seems kind of impossible in a small town."

I opened my mouth to say going to his place sounded great, even for tonight, when he cut me off with a snarl.

"For fuck's sake."

I jumped, not expecting that kind of tone, but he wasn't looking at me. Following his angry gaze, I looked over my shoulder. Nikki, Poppy, Yedda, Penelope, and Lucy were crowded in the doorway of the diner, their eyes scanning the restaurant and then snagging on us. Nikki's face lit up and I knew she'd be on her way over.

"How about we get our dinner to go too?" I whispered.

"Most definitely." Ace started pushing me out of the booth. I stood, right when Nikki made it to us.

"Where are you kids going?" she asked, pulling me in for a hug and a kiss on the cheek.

Ace stood up behind me, placing his hand on my lower back. Despite it not being appropriate with his mother standing there, I shivered at the touch. It hit me that I'd missed him. We'd only been dating a short while and I'd already come to rely on him. Already come to crave him.

"Placing a to-go order, Mom," Ace offered, giving her a quick one-arm hug.

"Well, that's lovely. Running from your mother. Dodging my calls." She gave Ace the stink eye, looking beautiful even with the scowl.

"Thank you so much for the flowers, Nikki," I rushed to say, trying to diffuse her anger at Ace. He seemed stressed enough. "They make the front of my house look amazing."

She turned back to me, her face morphing into a smile that reminded everyone she'd once been a beauty queen. "You're welcome, dear. But let's be real. I came over to get the scoop on you and Ace, but you foiled my plan by not being there. I couldn't just let the flowers die."

She sounded so put out by the whole thing it made me want to laugh. Ace put his arm around my waist and tried to steer me to the counter that my parents had just vacated, eager to place our order and get out of here.

"Can I get a picture of you two?" Lucy tapped Ace on the shoulder, startling us both. "I'm making an Instagram account with all the couples I've helped set up."

Ace's jaw went tight and I jumped in again. Seemed like the grumpy act he used to use only with me was starting to spread to interactions with other people.

"But you didn't set us up, Lucy," I said gently.

She pouted, looking remarkably like her youngest daughter. "But I did set you up at the photoshoot. Not my fault you took matters into your own hands and got together before then."

"I've got your order, Ace." Dot's voice interrupted, sounding like rusty metal scraping together. She held up a white to-go bag, her Mickey ears askew. Ace's face transformed beside me.

"Have I told you you're my favorite Hell citizen, Dot?"

The old woman's ruddy cheeks went even redder. "Ah, you're one of the good ones, Ace."

Ace took the bag from her, leaned down to kiss her cheek, and pulled me with him as he rushed to the door of the diner. I looked behind me to see Nikki frowning at the back of Ace's head, Lucy looking like we made fun of her minivan, and Dot waving a laminated menu at her face as if she was about to faint.

The cool night air was a balm to my overheated self. I didn't like making scenes like that, or disappointing people. Ace's long legs ate up the sidewalk and I nearly had to jog to keep up with him. He threw the bag of food in the back seat and opened the passenger door for me, stepping close.

He pushed some of my hair behind my ear and traced a finger across my bottom lip. My stomach went aflutter and I forgot all about our audience at the diner.

"Let's go have a picnic."

I nodded, entranced by the way he was looking at me, those brown eyes practically sparkling in the light from the streetlamps.

"Oh! My bike!"

He smirked. "Get in. I'll get it."

By the time we made it to the lookout over the ocean, we were both starving. Ace bit into his burger like it was the last meal he'd ever eat. My salad was just like the last time I'd been there. I had to admit, Dot may be old, but she had a memory like a bank vault. The whole time we ate, I was hoping for a repeat of the last time I was in Ace's truck. Even if my ass hit the horn, I was up for it. When I was done, I put the remains of the salad back in the bag behind our seats and waited for Ace to finish his mound of fries.

He dipped one in ketchup and popped it in his mouth, chewing quickly. "This was just what I needed. Good food and some quiet time."

My smile faded a bit. I was hoping he'd say spending time with me was what he needed, but maybe that was implied in the quiet time comment.

"You want to talk to me about what's bothering you?" He'd been so distant the last few times we'd talked. We hadn't dated long enough for me to know if that was just how he was some-times, or if something was actually wrong.

Ace flipped the to-go box closed and shoved it in the bag. When he spun back around, he leaned his head against the head-rest and looked out at the ocean spread out in front of us.

"I guess I'm just realizing how much work this new job is. And then my family has laid some stuff on me that—"

His phone dinged from somewhere in the console on the floor between us. He sighed and sat up to retrieve the phone.

"Sorry. I have to make sure it's not work." The cell phone screen came to life, illuminating the cab of the truck. And highlighted those under-eye circles of his. The pit of my stomach was not happy and it had nothing to do with the salad I just ate.

"Fuck," he muttered.

The ache in my gut gathered steam. I had a feeling about what he'd say next.

"Sorry, Addy." He clicked the screen off and winced looking at me. "It's Blaze. I have to go home and take care of this. Mind if I just drop you off now?"

I swallowed down the disappointment. "I was hoping you could spend the night?"

Ace looked back out at the ocean. "I can't. I have to go in tomorrow and submit another report. I can't be late again."

I found myself nodding and telling him it was okay when I felt like this situation was anything but okay. This felt a lot like my parents when they showed me over and over again that they just didn't want to make time for me. How many times did I need to get shoved aside before I realized I wasn't someone's priority?

The drive home was silent, both of us lost in our thoughts. When Ace pulled up to my house, he put the truck in park, but didn't get out. He leaned over and kissed my cheek. My freaking cheek.

"I'll call you tomorrow," he said, already shifting back to his seat, expecting me to get out, his mind already elsewhere.

"Okay." There was that stupid word again.

I slid out of the seat and closed the door quietly. I got my bike out of the back, struggling with it and wondering why he didn't get out to help me like usual. His truck took off down the driveway, not even a tap on the brakes to make sure I got safely inside. That wasn't like Ace at all. Nothing about the last few days felt like the guy who'd given me that flower crown and called me his wood nymph. Even his angry barbs from before we buried the hatchet were better than this half-assed distracted sham of a relationship.

I turned and walked into my dark house, plopping on the beanbag and dialing Meadow's number. I needed a fellow female's help to figure this thing out.

"Hey, BamBam," she answered right away, her familiar voice already easing some of my worries.

"Hey," I said softly, my voice already warbling. "Do you have a—?"

She giggled and then said something muffled that I couldn't hear. I heard a deeper rumble and realized she was with Judd.

"Sorry about that. What did you say?" Meadow asked into the phone, then broke into a peal of laughter.

I leaned my head back and stared at the wood beams above me. Hello, third wheel, been a hot minute since we hung out.

"It's nothing. Have a good night with Judd," I said, infusing as much sunshine in my voice as I could.

"I'll call you tomorrow."

She hung up right as I said "okay" to the empty room.

CHAPTER TWENTY-SEVEN

 ce

I SLAMMED the door when I got home, taking out my frustration on a slab of wood that didn't do anything but keep people from robbing my house. Exhaustion like I'd never felt before had sent me into a state of paralysis. I was out on a date with Addy and thinking about work. I was at work and I was thinking about Addy and my brothers.

The couch beckoned. I sank into the pillows and settled into a good wallowing session. The cheeseburger had been a mistake. It sat like a brick in my stomach. My phone was buzzing and I couldn't even bring myself to check it. Probably Addy. Or at least it should be, ripping me a new one for being an absolute jackass on our date. I wouldn't blame her if she was done with me. I squeezed my eyes shut, wondering if somewhere down deep, I'd been hoping she'd break up with me just so one of my stressors would be eliminated. Fucking hell, I was an idiot.

I opened my eyes and stared at my wall, trying to regroup.

Trying to forget the disappointment in Addy's tone when she said it was okay to just drop her off early. She deserved better and it pissed me off that she was putting up with that kind of behavior. Even if I was the one doing it.

My phone buzzed yet again and I pulled it out to check the notifications.

Blaze: Hey, man. If you're free, call me.

Blaze: I changed my mind.

Blaze: Seriously. I need you to call me, Ace.

"Fuck." I scrolled to his contact and called, now on hyper alert. Did something happen to stall his recovery? It was not like Blaze to reach out at all, let alone admit he needed someone.

"Hey, thanks for calling me back." His voice sounded as tired as I felt.

"Man, you're freaking me out. What's going on?" I stood up and began to pace my living room. It felt like my sternum was going to crack under all this weight life was piling on me lately. Is this what an early heart condition felt like?

"I thought I could do this on my own, but I'm waving the white flag. I need help. Lots of it."

I nodded. "Done. I can pick you up and bring you back here. But I need to talk to Mom and the boys first so they have a heads-up." I mentally went through my work schedule the next week. "I can get you in two days, or once I tell the family, one of the boys can probably get you sooner."

Blaze didn't hesitate. "The sooner the better."

"Okay. Let me talk to them tomorrow morning and we'll make the arrangements. Were you thinking you'd stay at Mom's house?"

I could practically feel the pain in the silence that followed. Blaze was more independent than us all. It would kill him to have to move back in with Mom, even if he did need to be nursed back to health.

"Nah. I'm going to ask Ben and see if he'll let me stay at his place."

It had to be asked. "Will that be enough help? Are you sure you don't need someone around all the time to help out?"

"Ben will be my nursemaid." Blaze chuckled and I realized I hadn't heard him laugh in a very long time. "He works from home, so it shouldn't be a problem."

"Alright, then. We'll call you tomorrow and make firm plans to bring you back to Hell."

Blaze's voice held a resignation I didn't like to hear. "I knew Hell would always pull me back."

We hung up and I texted Mom to make sure I could swing by tomorrow to tell her the news in person. One didn't tell Nikki Hellman news about her boys over a text and live to tell about it. Probably why she'd been pissed that I hadn't told her about Addy and me. So I'd tell Mom what was up and then text the boys to see if anyone could make the trek south to pick up Blaze.

That decided, I headed to bed early. The extended nap I'd taken this morning when I got off shift hadn't worked. It had only made me more tired. Maybe with some adequate sleep under my belt I could deal with Mom, Blaze, write that report, and also find a way to make things right with Addy.

"My baby?" Mom's red-painted nails fluttered so fast as she grabbed at her chest, they blurred.

"He's twenty-six, Mom." I folded my arms across my chest and refused to give in to drama hour with Nikki. This is why certain things had to be communicated in person. She needed to vent or she'd take her frustrations out by swooping over to someone's house to pull her plant fairy routine. Sometimes I wondered if she was solely responsible for keeping the nursery in town in business.

"I don't care how old he is, he's still my baby!" Mom cried, turning an angry glare on me. That's what I got for being the one to deliver bad news.

"He's done with the surgeries. He just needs to recover. He's going to be fine." I dared to put my arm around her shoulders, inhaling the jasmine scent of her perfume. The one she'd worn her entire life. The one that evoked memories of home, and love and acceptance, and burned chocolate chip cookies every Friday night.

"I still think he should move in here," she grumbled.

I squeezed her tighter. "I know, but let's just be happy he's coming home."

She let out a dramatic sigh. "You're right. Okay." She clapped her hands. "So go get him, sweetie."

I shook my head. "I can't. I have a report to write and a shift to cover tonight. I was going to text the boys and see if one of them can."

Mom pulled away from me, her jaw dropped comically. "What is this? My oldest boy actually delegating?"

"Enough, Mom. Let me text them."

I got out my phone, ignoring Mom's antics while I texted the group chat.

"You should do that more often, you know. Delegating. I worry about you sometimes."

I hit send and looked up to see her eyeing me in all serious-ness now.

"I do."

She snorted and it wasn't delicate. "Sure you do."

"I do," I insisted. "I just punted this to the boys to take care of, and I delegate at work all the time."

"Speaking of work, how's the new position going?" The coffeemaker let out a beep and she spun to fix us up two cups.

I leaned against the counter. "I won't lie. It's a lot more work than I thought. I messed up and didn't get a report in on time. And now Addy's probably mad at me because I was a bit preoc-cupied on our date last night."

Mom handed me my cup, her eyebrow lifting. "But did you shit your pants?"

A smile tugged on my face and I went with it. If felt good to invite some levity back in my day. Mom had been asking us that question as long as I could remember. Whenever one of us boys would complain about something, she'd throw the question out there like shitting your pants was literally the worst thing that could happen to a person. Thankfully, none of us over the years ever answered her with an affirmative. Unfortunately, I also knew that it wasn't the worst thing that could happen. I'd already lived through the worst thing when I was six years old and my father forgot about me.

"I did not shit my pants." I took a sip of the coffee, loving that she made it strong. Kind of like her personality. "But I really need to manage my time better. I'm spread thin and not doing any of it well. Hell, I couldn't even make the last first aid class."

"I noticed that, but don't worry. Addy ran it so smoothly we hardly missed you. Well, the female half of the audience missed you, but..."

I groaned.

"Oh, don't take things so seriously, Ace. Be flexible. Learn when to give it your all and when to half-ass it."

"I don't half-ass anything," I said indignantly. And it was true. Anything doing was worth doing right.

"You give it your full ass every time, which is why you're gonna lose your ass if you're not careful." Mom smirked at me. "And the females in Hell would be really sad if that happened."

I placed my mug in the sink, feeling highly irritated. "Okay, I think that's my cue to leave. Thanks for your infinite wisdom."

I kissed Mom on the cheek—because even if I was irritated with her, she was still my mother—and headed for the door.

"See? Too serious all the time!" Mom yelled after me. I flipped her the bird and she just laughed harder.

I hopped in my truck and headed home to work on that report on my laptop. If I went into the station, I'd get pulled into something that would turn into me being there all day. Addy's bike was lying on its side by my front stoop. The woman herself was sitting on my welcome mat, knees pulled up to her chin, head resting on her knees.

Adrenaline pulsed through me, thinking she was hurt. Then again, she had ridden a bike all the way over here, so the injury couldn't be that bad. I barely got the truck in park before I was hopping out.

"Addy?"

Her head popped up and the redness of her eyes didn't help my heart rate one bit. I ran over and pulled her to her feet, scanning her bare legs and arms for blood or broken bones.

"What happened? Are you hurt?"

"No, no. I'm fine." She pulled out of my grasp and twisted her fingers together, staring at my chest.

"You...don't look fine. Want to come in?"

She tried out a smile but it wobbled. "That would be great. Yes."

I unlocked the door and led her to my couch, having a seat and waiting for her to sit too. Those fingers, the ones that gripped my hair so tight or kneaded my sore muscles, wouldn't stop twisting in her lap. I put my hand over hers and squeezed.

"Just spit it out."

She let out a huge breath and looked me dead in the eye. "It could be nothing, but I did the math this morning and my period is late. Like, almost a week late. And I know that one night in the truck we didn't use a condom but the timing was all off, so I didn't worry about it. You know? But now that my period's late—which is not usual, by the way—I'm a little freaked out. I know you have a ton of stuff going on, but I felt like this was important enough to tell you about right away. Just in case. You know. It's something."

Her words finally dribbled to a stop, but my brain was still stuck on the first sentence out of her mouth. Little black dots danced in the periphery of my vision. In the back of my head, I was thinking how funny it was that I could face a five-car pileup with certain fatalities and not break a sweat. But Addy possibly being pregnant was knocking my knees out from under me.

"Ace? Say something." Addy leaned forward and cupped the side of my face, turning me so I was looking at her.

I jumped up from the couch and began to pace the same trail I'd made in the carpet last night.

"I know this isn't ideal timing, but..."

"Stop!" I barked, not recognizing my own voice. I sounded like a wounded animal that smoked a pack a day.

Addy jumped but stayed silent. I felt bad for yelling at her. I felt a lot of fucking things right then. But mostly I was angry at my own egregious lapse in responsibility. I couldn't believe I'd forgotten a fucking condom. Getting a girl pregnant in the front seat of my truck? That shit was high school-level bullshit I'd never even stooped to when I was in high school. The whole town looked up to me to save them in horrifying circumstances and yet I'd just walked myself into one?

"Ace. Say something, please."

I looked down and saw that Addy had begun to cry again. I was even fucking this up.

I hurried to sit back down, careful that no part of me touched hers. That's how I got into this mess. One touch of her soft skin and I didn't think of anything but getting inside her like some hypnotized idiot.

"It's, um, definitely not a good time, but I'll do the right thing here, Addy. Whatever we find out."

Addy bit her lip, tears still slipping down her cheeks. Fuck, I wanted to hug her to me and tell her I'd marry her tonight if it would ease her mind, but something held me back. Something dark and desperate that told me I was in over my head.

"Do the right thing?" Her voice was carefully controlled.

I knew my answer right now was very important. It felt like

it could make or break this situation. "If you take a test and it's positive, I'll step up and be a dad. Hell, I'll marry you if that's what you want."

Addy huffed and jumped to her feet. That was not a good sign.

"Wow. What a romantic proposal. Just like I dreamed of." That heavy sarcasm was also not good.

"Addy..."

"No. Don't you Addy me. I'm not some girl who needs your pity. Or your last name. I refuse to be an afterthought. A girl you have to settle for."

I stood too, feeling like I was in quicksand and sinking fast. "You wouldn't be."

She stepped right up to me, her breasts brushing across my torso. Her eyes pinned me like a laser. "Then tell me right now you're ready to make me your number one priority."

Fuck. I just offered to marry her for Christ's sake. What more did she want from me? How can she expect me to push everything else in my life aside? I'd juggle a baby and a wife just like I was juggling things now. Maybe not well, but it was the best I could do.

"You know I can't do that. I just got promoted. My brother's injured and needs to move back home. You—and a baby if there is one—will be some of my top priorities. You know that. But I can't drop everything in my life because you need some reassurance."

Addy stepped back and began to shake her head. "No. Not good enough. I don't want you to marry me out of obligation, and for the first time in my life, I refuse to settle. I want to be someone's first priority and I don't think that's too much to ask."

She put even more space between us and the dark and desperate drumbeat in my gut got even louder.

"What are you saying?" I said quietly.

She licked her lips, and even with red eyes and tear-streaked cheeks, she was the most gorgeous woman I'd ever laid eyes on. "I'm saying that until you can honestly say I'm your first priority and you're happy about it, we're done here."

She spun, her long blonde hair fanning out, and walked to my door while I stood there in a stupor. What the fuck was going on here? She comes by to tell me she might be pregnant, and when I offer to marry her, she breaks up with me? Every single worry and stressor in my life converged at once, making me angrier than I'd ever felt before.

"What the fuck, Addy?"

She didn't even stop, just wrenched the door open and stepped out. "Back to grumpy Ace, I see." And then she left the door open. I could see her grab her bike and pedal off down the road.

I walked over on numb legs and shut the door. Leaning my head back against it, I went over what the hell just happened. Every which way I looked at it, I didn't understand why she was upset. I said I'd do the right thing and that just wasn't enough. She walked away from me.

Some twisted, negative side of me whispered in my ear that we always knew she would. True love didn't exist. At least not for a Hellman. People always walked away from us. I'd learned that lesson in kindergarten and somehow Addy had made me forget it.

Well, I sure as fuck learned that lesson again tonight.

My phone dinged in my back pocket and I took it out, brain still caught on the image of Addy crying, her nose held high in the air as she told me I wasn't good enough.

Callan: So I emailed our father last night and he emailed me back today. We're setting up a day to meet. Can I assume you don't want to be there?

Rage, the kind that makes you feel superhuman right-eousness while also switching off all logical thought, lit up in my body like a blowtorch.

Motherfucker.

I threw the phone, watching as the screen shattered against the fireplace and tumbled to the floor.

CHAPTER TWENTY-EIGHT

*A*ddy

CANDLES CAST THEIR WARM, flickering light against the four walls of my home. Sage burned in the shell-shaped dish in front of me. Essential oils were being diffused into the air from all four corners. Even the pillow underneath me as I sat on the floor was packed with fresh dried lavender inside, letting out calming puffs of scent every time I shifted. I was supposed to be meditating but the mental calmness required for such an activity escaped me, irritating me further, and thus continued the downward spiral.

After leaving Ace's house, the tears had dried up as I confronted the wounds at the forefront of the problem. Realizing I wasn't even in the top five priorities for Ace had made me come to some other realizations too. I'd put up with poor behavior from those around me as a way of keeping the peace. I'd grown up thinking that was the right thing. Conflict was ugly, wasn't it? But trying to keep everyone happy all the time had led to a watered-down version of myself with the people I loved the most. I hadn't been truly showing up as me, a woman with boundaries that couldn't be trampled over.

My eyes popped open and I rubbed my sternum, feeling the heartbreak like a physical injury. Perhaps all the years being seen as the odd one in this town had made me yearn for something that wasn't right for me. Or perhaps, some*one*. Ace Hellman was a hell of a catch. The local hero, the handsome oldest brother who never dated a woman twice, let alone took on a serious girl-friend. When he gave me attention, I'd eaten it up, just like every other woman in Hell would have done. Ace had opened up his true self to me and the man I saw underneath the frown or the public persona was exquisite. But he was also still human, dealing with his own childhood hurts that clearly still affected him.

My hands drifted lower, naturally coming to rest on my stom-ach. I squeezed my eyes shut and tried to connect with the little life form that could be burrowed in there, but I felt just as empty and lonely as always. I didn't feel pregnant, but then again, it was pretty early on if I was. Maybe I shouldn't have said anything to Ace. Maybe I should have waited until I knew for sure, but there I was, reaching out and trying to connect with someone. I didn't want to be alone, and in my excitement, I hadn't considered that this news might not only be unwanted by Ace, but also that he'd already been pulling back from this relationship in his head.

I heard Ace's words echoing in my brain.

I'll step up and be a dad.

At first, they provided relief from the panic of realizing my period was late. But then I'd examined them further. He didn't say he'd step up and be the best husband in the world. No. I was nowhere in that equation except as the carrier of said baby. I wanted more for myself and I wouldn't apologize for it, dammit.

I thought of all those years being the third wheel in my parents' relationship and the heartache that caused me. If I wasn't careful, I could find myself the third wheel again, this time with Ace and a potential baby.

I didn't even know I was crying until the tears splashed onto my bare thighs. The back door of my house crashed open and my parents came in without a single knock, their conversation loud and boisterous.

"I'm telling you. Susan said they don't even wear clothes in this community," Mom was saying with glee in her tone.

"Sounds perfect," Dad purred.

Then I heard the unmistakable sound of wet kisses and whispered sweet nothings. I swiped the tears from my face and spun around.

"Do you mind?"

They broke apart, only Mom having the good graces to look guilty.

"Sorry, Daisychain. We just dropped by to make those almond butter bites your mother loves so much. You have more counter space than we do."

My heart felt like it was literally trying to claw its way out of my chest on the worst day of my life and these two wanted to bake in my kitchen? Did they bother to knock? No. Did they ask if now was a good time for me to host a baking session? No. Did they even see my red, puffy eyes? Nope again.

They never truly saw me.

The straw, the one that broke the camel's back, snapped. Or landed. Or did whatever the straw did to piss off the camel. I was fucking enraged. And so, so done.

I scrambled to my feet and pointed at the door. "You two. Get out. Get out of my house right now!"

Dad stared at me like he was tracking a friendly ghost from the safety of his cannabis cloud of chill. Mom's mouth dropped open and a tiny part of me was glad to see her dismayed. Maybe, just maybe, she would feel a tiny fraction of the hurt they'd caused me all these years.

"You have literally no idea how much you trample all over me. My property. My house. My time. You just prance your way in here, naked as the day you were born, and expect me to turn myself inside out for you. Meanwhile, you never ask me anything. Hey, how's your day, Addy? How's the business going? How's your freaking life?" I grabbed my head with two hands, feeling like it was going to explode. "Nothing! You're all about you two and nothing about me. Are you sure you're my parents because you don't act like you give two shits about me."

The silence was deafening, but the ball of fiery anger in my gut didn't seem to care. It was alive and well, having festered for twenty-some-odd years.

"Addy," Mom whispered, finally snapping her mouth shut. Her eyes held something closer to shock than remorse. She literally had no idea that they ignored me ninety-nine percent of the time, which only made me angrier. How can two parents be so oblivious?

I folded my arms across my chest and stood firm on a boundary for the first time ever. "I need you to leave my property. Take your RV elsewhere. You're no longer welcome here."

"But...but my clothesline," Dad whined, clearly missing the critical aspects of this confrontation.

The rage bubbled inside, whispering in my ear that I was in the right with my anger. "Get. Out. Now."

"Okay, honey," Mom said quietly, tugging on Dad's arm. "Maybe it would be best to talk tomorrow after we've all settled down."

I shook my head. "No. I'll let you know when I'm ready to speak to you again."

Mom blinked repeatedly. I got the feeling she was looking at me like she would a rabid animal, unsure how to proceed without getting bitten. "Okay, honey."

She pulled Dad's arm again and they went out the door. Mom looked over her shoulder at me, for once really looking at me. When it was too late, of course. I shut the door and turned away. Then I spun back around and opened the door enough to yell at their retreating backs.

"And just so you know, no one likes to see a naked person

over fifty! And you should stay out of the sun! It's colluding with your lack of collagen production to do bad things to your skin."

Mom gasped so forcefully a little shriek whistled out of her throat. Dad shoved her into the RV, gave me a dirty look, and slammed the door when he got behind the wheel.

I slammed my door too.

Good riddance.

Okay, maybe that part about their skin was a little too far, but someone had to say it. Devil's advocate came out to play, a niggle of guilt surfacing for yelling at my parents that way. Nothing else had seemed to work though. The only way to penetrate their little bubble of happiness for two was to pop it in spectacular fashion. And pop it, I did.

I paced my house until I got sick of my own home and the sun had set. Thinking I needed some advice more than another fizzled meditation session, I found my phone and called Meadow.

This time when she answered, the giggles were gone and so was the masculine voice in the background.

"Addy, hey. I've been meaning to call you back."

"Is now a good time?"

"Yeah. Judd's out picking up Chinese takeout from Blueball."

"Oh, well, maybe we should talk later, then." I sniffled and hoped the tears weren't coming back. I was kind of digging the rage. The last thing I needed was to be deep into my story with Meadow and have Judd come home and cut me off. I couldn't take any more rejection, even if it was just a break for hot takeout.

"Are you—are you *crying*?" Meadow practically shrieked the last word, making me regret calling in the first place.

"No, at least I don't think so. Though I was before. Then I yelled. I may be back to crying soon though. It seems to come in waves."

"What the hell is going on, BamBam?"

I sighed. Where to start? "Well, I think Ace and I broke up? And my period is late?"

"Oh fuuuck..." I heard a bunch of noise on Meadow's end and then she was back. "Okay, hang tight. I'm on my way with reinforcements."

"With what?"

But she'd already hung up.

I tossed the phone on my beanbag and spun in a circle. I wasn't quite sure what to do with myself now that I was fairly certain my parents and Ace weren't going to be showing up unexpectedly any longer. I was truly on my own. Which was kind of the opposite of what I wanted when I thought about it.

My chakras were all fucked up.

By the time I moved the candles to the table and doused the sage, Meadow came screeching into my driveway. I opened the front door and watched her pull a grocery bag out of the back seat of her car before rushing toward me.

"I've come with everything you need!"

My mouth hitched to the side in some semblance of a smile. I highly doubted she had anything that would help this ache in my chest, or the guilt cloud that hung over me about the way I'd gone about enlightening my parents.

Meadow gave me a fierce hug, swept inside, and nearly set the brown grocery bag on fire when she plopped it on my crowded table. I quickly pulled my hair back and blew out the candles. Last thing I needed was a blaze to catch that required a firefighter to put out. Been there, done that, had the heartache to prove it.

"First, we have pregnancy tests." Meadow gave me a dry look. "And by now half the town is talking about me being pregnant, thank you very much."

I cringed, knowing exactly how quickly juicy gossip could spread in Hell. "Thank you for your sacrifice."

"What are besties for, right?" Her arm disappeared back in the bag. "Up next is kombrewcha." She plopped a six-pack of it on the table with a clink. I opened my mouth, but she cut me off. "That's for if it's negative. If it's positive..." She pulled ice cream out of the bag. "Mint chocolate chip. Your favorite. And this is for how our conversation about Ace goes."

She held up two objects, one in each hand. A tissue box and a tiny bottle of red dye. The smile on her face was decidedly devilish.

"What's the red dye for?"

"We sneak out to his house and put it in his main water line. Worst-case scenario, he washes some clothes before he knows about his water situation and they come out pink. Best-case scenario, he takes a shower and looks like a Skittle for a few days."

I shook my head, honestly a bit worried about someone I'd been calling my best friend my whole life. "Where do you come up with this stuff?"

"It all started when I read a book by Pippa Grant about a woman and her brother doing these pranks on each other. He glitter bombed her with booby traps all over her house. Can you imagine? She'll be ninety and still pulling glitter out of crevices. Anyway, it kind of got me thinking about diabolical revenge scenarios. I have a list if you want to see it."

I grabbed one pregnancy test. "No, I'm good. Though I'll be sure never to cross you." I think working with inmates all day long was not good for her mental health. She was developing a dark side the older she got.

Meadow snorted. "You could never, my dear. You and me are going to be in the nursing home whistling at the hot male nurses." She wrapped her arm around my shoulders and steered me toward the toilet closet in the corner that was barely big enough to sit down and do your business.

"Whatever this thing says, I'm going to be right by your side through it all. You know that, right?" Meadow said softly, laying her head on my shoulder.

Tears blurred my vision.

That was the answer I'd been hoping for from Ace.

Meadow ended up having to help me. My hands were shaking so badly I couldn't get the box open or read the directions. She drew the line at helping me pee, saying friendship only went so far, which I agreed with. She kept up a steady stream of conversation that was so entertaining I managed to get the job done and not bawl my eyes out at the same time. It's not that I didn't want a baby. Eventually. I just didn't think it would be happening now. Without a partner in life.

We waited the prescribed three minutes which felt like at least ten yoga classes back-to-back with the amount of shaking my muscles were doing as I stared at Meadow's watch. When it was time, I handed the stick to Meadow and made her look.

"Negative," she said evenly.

My eyes popped open and I snatched it out of her hands to study it closer. Hmm. Only one line.

"Now the insert says you're on the cusp of taking this thing too early just depending on how long your cycle was this month, so I'd do another one in a few days just to make sure."

My brain was spinning and I wasn't sure what to feel. Relieved? Sad? Let down? Confused?

"Well, shit. Now I'm not sure if I should hand you a kombrewcha or ice cream." Meadow pursed her lips and eyed the goodies on the table.

I put the test in the trash and took a cleansing breath. "I'll stick to ice cream just in case."

"And I'll take kombrewcha. Maybe getting tipsy will stop me from going over to his house and engaging in the type of revenge that will have me arrested. I've seen those holding cells at the prison. Mama doesn't need a bacterial infection."

I snorted, pulling a bowl out of the single cabinet I had in my mini kitchen. "I think getting tipsy might give you the courage to go over there and actually use that red dye."

Meadow smiled like the devil and I wondered if Judd knew what he was getting into dating her. We headed outside with our treats, lighting the wood in my fire pit in defiance of Ace and his "burn days" precaution, and having a girls' night. Meadow tried to bash Ace to make me feel better about the breakup, but we both knew the truth. There wasn't much there to bash.

If I really thought about it honestly, Ace was a great guy with a paralyzing amount of daddy issues. And while I understood it since I had my own issues because of my parents, I wasn't going to stick around when my needs were not being met.

I was proud of myself, but I still cried myself to sleep that night.

CHAPTER TWENTY-NINE

$\mathcal{A}$ce

THE FOLLOWING week passed in a blur of shifts, paperwork, and sleepless nights wondering if I was going to be a father. Probably a really horrible one, if the saying *the apple doesn't fall far from the tree* was accurate. After three days of silence, I'd finally texted Addy, looking for some answers on that front. She hadn't texted me back.

Which was how I found myself up early on my day off and calling her incessantly. In my sleep-deprived mind, leaving me hanging was the worst form of cruelty. A woman shouldn't drop a pregnancy bomb and then walk away without a word. I was dying here.

Midway through listening to Addy's voicemail again—which was just a mechanical voice reciting her phone number because the woman probably didn't ever set up a proper voicemail recording—my front door flew open with a bang.

I hit end call and turned to find my mother standing in the doorway with sunlight lighting her up like an Avenger coming to save the day. She swept in, dumping a canvas grocery bag on the kitchen counter, and walked right up to me. She looked up into my eyes, making me think I was about to receive one of her bonebreaking hugs. Instead, all I got was a whack on the back of my head.

"You're an idiot."

I rubbed the back of my head and stepped back. "Wow. Thanks for that, Mom. What would I do without your loving embrace?"

"That comes after. After I'm done setting you straight." She looked around my house, her nose wrinkling comically. "And after I clean this place. Jesus, Joseph, and Mary. You live like this?"

I glanced around too, as if seeing my place for the first time in a week. "Uh, yeah. I was just getting around to cleaning today."

Mom snorted and spun on her high-top Air Jordans with a swoosh that matched her bright red outfit. She grumbled under her breath about her not raising me to be a pig. I rolled my eyes and maybe dislodged something in my head. An idea hit me, one that should have hit me days ago, but I'd been in a fog thinking about Addy and my absent father and my own abilities if I found out I'd be a father soon too.

"Hey, Mom?" I called out, watching her take paper towels and bottles of cleaner out of her bag on the kitchen counter. She'd come prepared to clean an entire third world country.

"I'm not doing toilets, mister. You can't aim properly, that's on you. I cleaned up after you boys for two decades. It's time for you to clean up your own piss."

It was my turn to grimace. "No, that's not what I was going to ask."

She shrugged and snapped on rubber gloves. "Just making myself clear."

I came up next to her, hoping she'd take my question seriously. "How did you survive after our father left?"

She stilled, taking in a deep breath and letting it out before she spoke. "How about we start with the dishes? You can dry."

I followed her into the kitchen and grabbed a clean hand towel, waiting as she started the hot water and squeezed a ridiculous amount of soap over the dishes filling up the sink. I really should get to renovating this place so I could put in a dishwasher.

"How about you tell me what happened with Addy first? I've heard about the breakup, of course, but I'd like my own son to tell me what happened."

So I did. I told her everything, probably more than one should tell their mother, but Nikki wasn't like most parents. She could handle storms better than any grizzled seafaring ship out there.

"And I haven't heard from her since. I think I might actually be losing my mind." I dried the last dish and set it in the drying rack.

Mom snapped off her gloves, laid them on the counter, and pulled me into the best kind of hug. The one you can only get from your mom, the kind that offered comfort and unconditional love.

"I'm sorry for snapping at you last week," I said quietly. Her arms tightened around me.

"I'm sorry I joked around and didn't realize the pressure you're under," she whispered.

She finally pulled back, her hands on my biceps. "Do you see yourself falling in love with Addy? If you didn't have these other pressures?"

I told her the truth. My ribs practically ached with it. "I already know I love her, I just can't see a way to do it all. She'd be better off without me. She told me that. She needs to be someone's first priority."

"And how did that make you feel?"

I pulled back from her, needing to move. I couldn't talk about all this feelings crap without pacing the room. Without burning off the uncomfortable feelings that felt like they were strangling me.

"I felt terrible. I'm not good enough for her and she walked away."

There was silence then. Mom knew me well enough to know I needed time to think about that statement. Time to come around to the same conclusion she'd already come to.

I sighed, turning to face her. "This is about childhood shit, isn't it? Abandonment?"

Mom grabbed me by the arm and pulled me into the living room. She had to move a dirty towel to sit down—giving me the stink eye of course—and patted the seat next to her. I sat, preparing myself for a conversation I didn't want to have, but knew I needed.

"It's my fault. I've beaten myself up about it for years. Your father leaving created some beliefs in your head that just aren't true. I was so caught up in my own shit those first few years, I wasn't there to help you. But I'm here now." Mom sniffed, looking close to tears. Come to think of it, I hadn't seen her cry since elementary school. It was almost like she'd used up all her tears when our father left and didn't have any left for the rest of her life.

"Your father didn't leave because he didn't care about you kids, or you made too much noise, or you were too much to handle. He left because he didn't love me. That has nothing to do with you." Mom grabbed my hand in a tight grip. "When I found out he had a whole other life a state over, I flipped out. Told him to stay gone. In my mind at the time, a man who could do that had no business being a father. I didn't want him rubbing off on you boys, and come to find out, he already had, no matter what I tried to do to protect you from him. Look at you, Ace. You think you have to solve the world's problems, be a leader to every citizen in Hell, and never ask for help. That's a fool's mission right there."

My mind was spinning, trying to see the event from kindergarten through the lens of an adult. I was trying to separate the old hurts and see things from a logical perspective.

"I can see why you told him to stay away, but shouldn't a father fight for his kids?"

Mom squeezed my hand tighter. "I only know what I would do and I'll tell you right now, kiddo. There's nothing you could do that would make me walk away from you. I'd fight every damn day until things were right between us."

I knew that to be true. The second Addy told me she might be pregnant, I knew without a shadow of a doubt that I'd be there for that child.

"Some people are just born wrong. They have twisted ideas in their heads. A level of selfishness one can't understand. A man who can keep an entire life—a whole family—a secret...well, he isn't exactly right in the head, now is he?"

I brought my gaze back to Mom, the worry in her eyes making me feel like I needed to say the right things to alleviate it. But isn't that kind of over-responsibility what got me to this place? Where I was so overwhelmed I walked away from the best thing that ever happened to me?

"I think I need to work on that delegation thing you talked about," I said quietly.

Mom nodded. "I bet your brothers would love to step up. You just have to give them the chance."

I hadn't thought of it that way, that I was taking away their chance to be a leader by always stepping in, but it made a lot of sense. They were grown adults. I needed to trust them to handle things.

"I will. I promise."

Mom patted my hand and let go. "I've got a coffee date to get to, but one last thing for you to think about. In my opinion— and I'm your mom, so you know my opinion matters more than most—Addy is exactly what you need in your life and you need to make things right. For the first time since your father left, I saw your real smile again this last month." Her eyes filled with tears. "Any woman who can do that is worth fighting for, son."

She popped off the couch and headed into the kitchen, immediately clearing her throat and muttering about dirty laundry and boys and their toilets.

"Make sure you use those cleaning supplies!" The front door slammed shut and she was gone.

I stayed on the couch, sifting through all the truth bombs she'd dropped, trying to figure out just how I felt now. I thought about Addy calling and saying she wasn't pregnant. Instead of feeling elation at being off the hook, I felt disappointment. When I'd offered to marry her, I hadn't meant it as a solution to the baby problem, I'd mostly just seen it as an acceleration of the path I already saw us on. I thought about my shitty father and how he'd just left us behind without fighting for us. The baby wasn't even confirmed and I knew I'd fight to my last breath to stay in his or her life. Maybe if I was different than my father in that way, I'd be different than him in other ways. Maybe I could be a good husband and father.

A knock came from the door, interrupting my epiphany. I thought it might be Mom, having forgotten something, but then again, she'd just bust through the door without knocking. I looked down at my sweatpants and dirty T-shirt, thinking I probably should have brushed my hair before getting the door, but it was too late for that. I grabbed the doorknob and swung it open.

And for the second time that morning, got hit in the head. This time it was a fist to my nose, the impact not even snapping my head back, but painful just the same.

"Shit!" I grabbed my nose and closed the eye that smarted the most.

Addy's father stood on my doorstep, shaking out his hand. He had on pink swimming shorts and a red plaid long-sleeve shirt. At least his hair was brushed back into a tidy ponytail.

"I would have hit you harder, but I don't believe in violence, Andy."

"Pretty sure punching me in the nose is violence, even if you pulled it," I grumbled, stepping away from the door to find a bag of peas in the freezer. Neil followed me inside, shutting the door. When I got the peas on my face, I turned around carefully, ready to duck if he came swinging at me again.

"That was for Addy," Neil said, pointing at my face before tucking his hands in his shorts pockets. "Mess with my girl, mess with me."

I sighed, realizing I deserved it. If we had a little girl together, I'd do the exact same thing if some asshole didn't put her first. Fuck. I'd straight up told Addy she wasn't my priority. I'd messed things up with Addy so much I wasn't sure if I could fix it. And I just realized now how badly I wanted to fix it.

I pulled the peas from my face. "Go ahead. Punch me again. I deserve it."

Neil stared at me and I wasn't sure if he was tempted, or simply wondering where he'd put his latest joint. "My hand likes peace, not war. How about we have a chat instead?"

I gestured toward the living room and found myself on the couch again, this time with Addy's parent trying to talk some sense into me.

"Listen, before you get started, I have to tell you. I love your daughter. I think I've always been drawn to her, but I also have a pretty thick skull. Took breaking up for me to see how much I love her. And yes, I was an ass. I didn't handle things well at all, and I'm not sure what all she's told you, but I'd like to make things right."

Neil rubbed his hands down his shorts and over his knobby knees. "She hasn't told me anything. She kicked us out."

I tossed the bag of peas on the end table. "What?" I'd avoided the gossip floating around Hell this last week, not wanting to hear the verdict from my fellow citizens about our breakup. I had no doubt they'd side with Addy.

"Yeah, she yelled at us about not seeing her and then kicked us out. We've been staying at the campground north of the lookout." Neil leaned back on the couch, looking older than I remembered. "Here's the thing, Alec. I learned a long time ago that you can't control life. Did I ever tell you Addy was an oops baby?"

My head popped up. "No, I didn't know that."

Neil nodded, the shiny top of his head reflecting the sunlight streaming through the window. "Yep. Total surprise. I learned real quick that you can't control the shitstick of life. It's gonna do what life's gonna do, whether you want to be on the ride or not."

His metaphors had me a bit lost, but I got the gist of it. "I know that feeling."

"Here's the kicker though. Adelia was the best thing that's ever happened to me." Neil beamed, the kind of smile that made you want to smile along too. "If I'd tried to control where life took me, I would have missed out on everything that makes life worth living. So now I just smoke weed and go with the flow, man."

"Go with the flow," I repeated absently, trying to envision myself doing that. It was almost laughable. I wasn't a go-with-the-flow kind of guy.

Neil nudged my arm, a joint held in offering between us. "I'm just saying...it helps."

I opened my mouth to decline, an automatic response drilled into me from years of being the responsible one. *Go with the flow.* I didn't have to work the next day.

"You know what, Neil? Light it up."

He whooped and produced a lighter, letting me take the first drag. I choked right away and I think I coughed before anything really got in there, but it made me feel like maybe, just maybe, things would be okay in the end. I handed it to Neil and we sat there sharing it until my house stunk and we were both giggling like little boys, telling stories that couldn't possibly be true.

By the time he got up to leave, it was mid-afternoon and I was starving. "Are you sure you should drive?" There wasn't enough weed on the planet to stop my responsible brain completely.

Neil laughed and made his way to the door at the pace of a sloth. I followed him, just to make sure he was steady on his feet. "Nah. I walked."

He walked right out and shut the door behind him without another word. I leaned against the door, laughing until tears were streaming down my cheeks. He wasn't going to get back to the RV until midnight at that pace. I pulled my phone out of my back pocket and pulled up the chat with my brothers. I had a seat on the floor. Too hard to stand and type at the same time.

Delegate, Mom had said.

Me: Can one of you pick up Neil and take him home? He's walking from my place to the campground.

Ethan: I'm just leaving a job two streets over, so I can swing by. But why don't you take him?

Me: One, he punched me in the face. Two, I'm too baked to do it.

Daxon: Holy shit, I'm on my way over. I have to see this.

Me: fuck off. Actually, if you're coming over, bring snacks. I'm so fucking hungry.

Callan: Seriously?

Me: Oh, it's serious. My stomach is growling so hard it's talking to me.

Daxon: bahahaha This is amazing.

Callan: For fuck's sake. I'm coming over too just for photo proof of this momentous occasion.

Ethan: I see him. He just tried to pet Mr. Jenkins's rottweiler. Oh shit, the dog's off his chain and Neil's running now. I'll come over after I get him dropped off.

I slid the phone back in my pocket but I heard it hit the floor. I'd have to get that later. When my limbs had bones in them. Fuck. No wonder Neil did this all the time. All my problems felt like they disappeared into the ether.

My phone dinged and I almost didn't fish around behind me to pick it up. Probably just my stupid brothers. Then a little voice in the back of my head reminded me that my problems were still there, despite the marijuana telling me different. And maybe that was Addy finally texting me back. My heart decided to gallop away from me at the thought of Addy, thundering as it pressed against my chest.

I had to squeeze my eyes shut twice to make sure I wasn't imagining her name on my phone. I put in my code and tried to slow down my breathing. If I was going to have a heart attack, it couldn't be when I had drugs in my system. Mom would bring me back to life just to kill me again.

Addy: False alarm. Not pregnant.

My skull banged against the back of the door. I waited for the relief to hit me, but it never did. Just more heartbreak over opportunities lost.

It was a long time before I got myself up off the floor.

CHAPTER THIRTY

*A*ddy

EMOTIONS WERE SUCH FUNNY THINGS. My brain could demand that today was the day I got my shit together and focused on all the many positives in my life, but emotions would suddenly burst forth like a geyser, soaking all my best-laid plans. The second and the third pregnancy test came up negative, and just that morning my period came. I vowed I would have a baby someday, but today was not that day. And Ace was not the man I'd do it with. That much was clear.

"Gently fold forward and let your head, neck, and arms hang there as they will. Deep breath in through the nose. And exhale."

My sunrise yoga class was packed today. I was even having to raise my voice so the yogis in the way back could hear me. Most were familiar faces, but there were a few I'd never seen before. I hoped they weren't here to see firsthand how I was handling the breakup. It wouldn't surprise me if the Hell gossip grapevine had forked over money to get a front-row seat to the disaster.

Meadow had told me one of the checkers at the grocery store had given her a nasty judgmental look yesterday when she bought a bottle of wine with her dinner ingredients. Hell wasn't a town for the faint of heart.

It took all the energy I possessed to keep focused on calling out the positions when my brain kept jumping ship to reminisce about Ace and the brief glimpse of a future I found out I very much wanted.

"Whoo! Blood rush!" Yedda cackled from upside down, undeterred by the rest of the class being dead silent.

"Hands on your thighs and let's roll the upper body back to a standing position." I kept an eye on Yedda to make sure she didn't fall over like a goat playing dead. She'd dropped twice before I learned her warning signals and swooped in before it happened again.

"When you're ready, let's have a seat on the ground, legs crossed, hands on knees. Close your eyes and focus on your box breathing. For any new members, that means inhaling for four counts. Hold at the top for four counts. Exhale for four counts." I demonstrated, breathing louder than I normally would, and then let the class take over on their own.

This was normally the time in each class I enjoyed the most. The quiet, focused breathing, when I could enter a state almost like a trance, with zero problems plaguing me. It was nature's high. This time, all it gave me was a body swirling down the toilet bowl of emotions. Focusing back on my breathing, I tucked everything to do with Ace and the breakup into a big black box and focused on the emotion left over.

Guilt.

I felt horrible over the way I'd treated my parents. I'd spent years bottling up everything I felt, instead of sharing it with them. It was hardly their fault I'd exploded like a shaken can of soda pop. Yes, their behavior had hurt me, but that didn't give me the right to yell at them like I had. A healthy adult daughter would have calmly shared how she felt and asked them to abide by her boundaries.

"Anybody else feel like they're flying on a magic carpet?" Yedda whispered at the level of a bomb detonating.

My eyes flew open and I cleared my throat. "How about we gently roll down to our mats and get into savasana on our magic carpets?"

The group tittered, half highly amused by Yedda and the other half irritated. I vacillated back and forth on a minute-by-minute basis.

By the time everyone left and the forest was back to being my quiet little sanctuary, I had a firm plan in mind. I was heading to the campground to make things right with my parents.

IT WAS a beautiful spring day in Hell. The birds were singing, the sun was lighting everything up with an optimism I was desperately trying to feel, and even my bicycle was pedaling without a single squeak. Which reminded me of sweet Lenora and the magic lube she'd put on my chain. I'd have to stop by the Hardware Store for more of it. And maybe a few toys since I was now officially single. It appeared I'd have to scratch my own itch from now on.

As I hit the roundabout outside of the downtown area, I started to see white fliers on every single telephone pole. There was even one affixed to the forehead of the iron bust of the old mayor in the middle of the roundabout. I screeched to a halt, needing to focus on the traffic. It had been years now with this roundabout here and people still didn't know how to drive around it properly. It was estimated that nine out of every ten accidents in Hell happened in the roundabout. As a cyclist, I always took extra precautions and only crossed when no vehicles were present.

After a VW van with more stickers than paint passed me, I zipped across and went straight for the first lamppost on Main Street to see what was going on. I wondered if maybe Bain messed up again and Lucy was exacting her revenge. I was still in high school when she blackmailed Bain with a picture of his sperm deposit. It was a long—and weird—story, but suffice it to say, couples get together in the strangest of ways.

My bike almost took me down when my hands left the handles and gripped the edges of the piece of paper taped to the pole. I righted the bike and held the paper with one hand. It was a picture of me, in a complicated yoga pose I'd mastered two years ago. Mom had taken the photo, saying I looked like a gloriously buttered pretzel. It was an advertisement to come to my sunrise yoga classes. What the hell?

I didn't make these flyers.

As I went through town on my way to the campground, I saw them posted absolutely everywhere. Even cars parked along the curb had them under their windshield wipers. My brain was spinning as I left town and got closer to the ocean.

I ended up having to ride through the campground loop a couple times before I found my parents' RV. They were trying to get into a hammock that was tied between two pine trees. Dad got on first, but before Mom could even lift a leg to join him, he flipped and landed in the dirt. My face stretched into a grin. God, I missed those weirdos.

"You okay, Dad?" I called out as I came to a stop by their RV.

They both looked up, pine needles sticking out of Dad's ponytail like the plumage of a peacock. Mom reacted first, running to me full speed. I scrambled to get off the bike before she hit in a full-body hug that would leave bruises.

"Oh, thank the goddess you're here." She pulled back and

pressed her hands to my cheeks making my lips pucker in what I could only assume was a highly unflattering manner.

"Daisychain!" Dad called out, getting to his feet and brushing himself off like the last week of tense silence between us never existed.

My eyes watered and Mom put her arm around me, pushing us toward the three camping chairs set up around the fire pit. "Come. Sit. Let's talk it all out."

"We just—"

"I'm—"

Mom and I talked over each other and she put her hand on my arm. "You have to know how sorry your father and I are. We've been talking this whole week and we realize that we have been leaving you out while also invading your physical space. We'd like to be there less physically and more emotionally for you from now on. If that's okay with you."

I nodded, relieved they took what I said seriously. "I'd love that actually. But I'm also sorry for how I yelled at you. I should have said something before now so it didn't come to that."

"You know, Daisychain, I don't know if we would have listened if you didn't yell. I have a pretty thick skull. Takes a bit of a whack by a two-by-four before I'll listen." Dad smiled sheepishly.

"Hey, Bammingfords!" a voice called out.

We all swiveled our necks to see a guy who looked suspiciously like one of the yogis in the back of my class this morning.

"Thank you for the recommendation! Best yoga class I've taken in years. You have a way with you, Addy."

"Oh, I'm delighted to hear that. Have a good day, Brian." Mom looked positively giddy.

The man waved before walking over to his RV that was two spaces over from my parents. I brought my hand up too late in a wave, shock making my reaction time slow.

"Wait. Are you telling people to take my classes?" I asked, turning back to them.

Dad slapped his knee. "Darn right we are. How else can you get a high without my special stash? That breathing thing you have people do is right up there with my good stuff."

I turned to Mom. "The flyers?"

She smiled and shrugged. "I learned how to use a computer and printer. I think the old bat of a librarian wanted to kill me by the end of the day, but I got the flyer done. Did you like the picture I used?"

Mom didn't even have a cell phone she hated technology so much. "You did that for me?"

"Of course I did, honey." Mom leaned forward and put her hands on my arms again. "I probably don't say this enough. Or ever, really. You were a gift from the universe, Addy. We never set out to be parents, knowing we'd be bad at it. The goddess knows we're flighty as a butterfly, but we did our best. And we screwed up a lot too. I'm sorry for ever making you feel like you weren't worth our time and attention."

"You are quite literally the best thing that's ever happened to your mother and me, Daisychain." Dad looked me right in the eye, looking like he wasn't even high yet today.

Tears spilled over and I didn't bother wiping them away. I'd shed too many this week to chafe my skin with more wiping.

"I grew up with unconventional parents for sure, but I'm just now seeing that wasn't a bad thing. You taught me to live off the earth. To look to nature to heal. To question the normal way of doing things. I'm the lucky one."

Mom let out a soft sob. Dad stood up, and instead of going to his wife to give her comfort like I expected, he held his arms out wide for both of us. Mom gave me a wobbly smile and pulled on my hands. I stood up and joined her, making a circle of three. The hug from them both was not only loving, but healing. We swayed there for a bit, just enjoying having the peace reestablished between us.

"I should probably apologize now for punching Ace. I know

you broke up and I probably should have kept my nose out of it, but a father's gotta do what a father's gotta do."

I pulled back sharply, studying his face to see if he was serious. "You punched him?" I'd never even seen my father swat at a mosquito.

He grinned, looking ten years younger. "Yeah. It hurt like a son of a bitch, but he got me some ice while we shared a joint."

I screwed my eyes shut and opened them again. "Ace smoked weed?"

Dad lost the smile in a split second. "Well, I wasn't going to share originally, but when he said that he loved you and he'd screwed up, I figured he needed some male bonding time and there's no better bonding than a shared joint, am I right?"

I honestly didn't hear the rest of what he said. Not after the part about Ace confessing he loved me. He never even said those words to me. I suspected I'd been in love with him all along, but after we break up is when he confides his feelings to my *dad?*

Goddess, that man made me so angry. It took meditation sessions to get him to even open up to me about his feelings about his father. I couldn't even get him to share about his workday or what problems he was dealing with with his family. Getting him talking about his feelings was like squeezing blood from a turnip, a phrase I'd never understood until now.

And Ace just dropped the l-word on my pot-smoking dad?

Forget seeing red. The world was painted in a technicolor neon color that wasn't even discovered yet.

I gave my parents another squeeze. "I love you and I'm so glad we worked this out, but I have to go. My Etsy store is waiting on me to build it."

They had their arms around each other, big smiles on their faces as they waved until I was out of sight. The bike ride was a welcome form of exercise. I needed to exhaust the anger that was sitting in my gut like molten lava. By the time I got to the library in town and got my first frown from the nasty librarian, I realized it wasn't even anger so much as hurt. I'd tried so hard to get Ace to open up to me and be his authentic self and I hadn't succeeded.

Maybe I had to accept the fact that I was not the girl Ace needed in his life. He needed someone who could open Fort Knox. Not even my essential oils could help me with that.

CHAPTER THIRTY-ONE

*A*ddy

THE DAY I was dreading had arrived. Thankfully, I was able to keep my brain occupied well enough when almost double the number of people showed up for my sunrise yoga class. Goddess bless my parents. What they lacked in parenting skills they made up for with their marketing skills. I should have asked them to help me years ago when I started teaching.

Several people stayed after class and sounded enthusiastic about adding in a second class a little later in the morning. I liked that idea too as part of a joyful yoga experience required a more intimate setting. The bigger the sunrise class got, the less magical it felt.

That decided, I spent most of my day putting the newly printed labels I'd had designed onto my glass tincture bottles. Once I had a decent inventory ready to go, I'd make my Etsy debut. Meadow warned me that I would probably need to get a smartphone, or goddess forbid, a laptop if I wanted to market my wares successfully, but so far I'd held out. The exercise of biking to the library for the free computers—along with a lack of appetite due to heartache—seemed to be helping that cardiovascular endurance I'd been lamenting.

I stood up from the floor and stretched my neck. In just a few hours, I'd need to be down at the community center teaching the last first aid class. I wasn't sure if Ace would be showing up since he'd been completely silent since the big breakup. The thought of seeing him again was doing bad things to my stomach. I wasn't sure if I needed to eat, throw up, or ask my dad for one of his joints.

A knock on the door had my head lifting. I stepped over the beanbag and opened it, seeing a brunette woman around my age with the most brilliant blue eyes I'd ever seen.

"Addy Bammingford?" she asked with a friendly smile.

"That's me," I said cautiously.

She thrust a pink box toward me and I wondered why she was delivering donuts from Coffee. "I was a little rusty the first time around, but I think I really nailed it on this one. I hope you love it!"

I took the box. It was too light to contain much more than a single donut. "I—I'm sure I will?" I opened the lid and then slammed it shut again. My mouth dropped open and my stomach decided no on the vomiting, eating, or smoking. It wanted to act like it contained a kaleidoscope of butterflies, all taking flight at the same time.

"I didn't have a box for a flower crown, so I had to borrow one from Coffee next door. He wrote the card while I got it packed up and I swear I didn't peek, but I've heard the rumors about the breakup." The woman cringed. "He looked pretty rough to be honest. Seemed like he was pretty desperate. I hope you two can work things out."

"Shelby, right?" I remembered Ace telling me about the new florist in town.

She nodded and smiled shyly. "Shelby Thorn, nice to meet you. I know it's none of my business, so I'll shut up now. Come by the shop sometime. I'd love to talk plants." Shelby gave a little wave and walked back down to the little van with her Petals & Thorns logo plastered to the side. The logo below made me smile: Hell Bent on Love.

"Thank you!" I called after her, brain scrambling to make sense of what was happening.

She waved and shut the door before backing down my long driveway. I went inside the house and put the box on my kitchen counter. I stared at it, as if a snake might pop out and bite me if I opened it. The brief glimpse had told me everything I needed to know.

Ace wasn't silent anymore.

Finally I couldn't handle it any longer and threw back the lid. I blew out the breath I'd been holding. No snake jumped out, just the most beautiful flower crown I'd ever seen with white tulips, purple hyacinths, dotted with lilacs, all nestled in a bed of greenery that had my nature-loving heart skipping a beat. Ace was right. I should get to know Shelby. She'd artfully woven in all the flowers that had one meaning in particular: forgiveness. Nestled in the middle of the floral masterpiece was a single white envelope with my name on it.

My hands shook as I picked it up. Stupidly, I brought it to my nose, as if I could get a whiff of Ace's scent from something he'd touched. I still had his torched AHFD T-shirt, but the embers had burned away his scent. Believe me, I'd already tried to sniff it more than once the last two weeks.

I lifted the flap of the envelope and pulled out the card stock with his handwriting in black ink.

Addy, I know I don't deserve your time, but if you'd be willing to give just a bit more of it, I'd like to apologize in person. Meet me at the park under the old oak tree at six?

I squeezed my eyes shut against the pain in my chest. The damn organ was pulsing with the need to go to him. As much as he'd hurt me, I still had feelings for him. I was still drawn to him as if nature herself had designed us to be a synergistic pair. A hummingbird to a flower's nectar. Sharks and the pilot fish that swim with them. A seagull cleaning up a picnic left behind on the sand.

My phone rang and I nearly jumped out of my skin. I picked it up, heart in my throat.

"Hello?"

"Hey, BamBam. I know you just got a delivery." Meadow rushed to say everything before I could interrupt. "You need to go change into your favorite skirt. You know that long purple one with the slit up the side that you love? Pair it with the white tank and all your necklaces. Okay? And then get your butt over to the park."

I glanced around my house as if that would give me the answers as to why Meadow knew exactly when I got the flower crown.

"Um..."

"What do you tell me when I can't settle into a meditation session?"

I sighed, knowing she had me there. "Clear your mind and go with your heart."

"Exactly right, my friend. Stop your brain asking all the questions that don't matter and lead with your heart. Get dressed so you feel like a million fucking bucks and meet that man like the absolute queen that you are. You got me?"

A grin tugged at my face and I went with it, finally remembering who I was with just a simple pep talk from my best friend. I knew what I wanted in a relationship and if Ace couldn't give that to me, I'd wish him well and send him off with love. I'd reacted horribly to my parents, saying things I wished I could take back. And yet they'd welcomed conversation with me, accepting my apology and making accommodations to meet my needs. I needed to stop ignoring Ace and face the problem head-on.

"The only question is whether I should wear a bra or not."

Meadow whooped in my ear. "That's my girl. Haul ass,

BamBam!" And then she hung up, leaving me to rush around the house and get ready in time to bike down to the park. I didn't want to have to rush and show up sweaty.

I probably got there late, seeing as how I didn't wear a watch or bring my phone, I had to rely on the descending sun. I saw the back of Ace's head, sitting on the bench under the oak tree where he'd pushed me in second grade when I accidentally stumbled into him on one of our class field trips. I'd fallen onto the bench and his face turned red. Then he ran off with his friends and I'd added another reason to hate him to my list.

I tied up my bike to a light pole and ran a hand over my face to make sure I wasn't sweating. Goddesses standing on their own two feet in front of the man who broke their heart don't sweat like a pig. Okay, fine, maybe this one did. I strolled over quietly, seeing that his head was dropped in his hands as he sat there. Crap. I really was late.

Reaching up, I took the flower crown off my head and held it out as I came in front of him. "Looks like you need the cheering up more than I do."

His head popped up and those brown eyes of his drank me in. "Addy," he breathed, not even sounding like he meant to say my name.

His uniform shirt looked crisp and clean across his broad chest. Even his navy pants looked like they didn't have a single wrinkle in them. But his five o'clock shadow was more like a midnight shadow. Even his hair looked like he'd run his hands through it more times than a teenage girl. He looked like a man holding it together on the surface, but a mess underneath. I could relate.

Ace finally looked down at the crown and took it gently from my hands. To my surprise, he put it on his head, looking just a bit ridiculous, if I was honest. He stood from the bench, the white ribbons in the back fluttering behind him in the breeze. In sudden clarity, I realized why he hadn't wanted that on his head in kindergarten. He would have looked just as ridiculous as he did now. But this time around, he didn't seem to care. He shot me a smile that didn't quite cover the dark circles under his eyes.

His mouth opened and all the words came tumbling out. "I'd be proud to wear it. That's what I should have said all those years ago, but I was just a scared kid. And I've stayed a scared kid for far too long. I thought trying to control everything was the way to stay safe in an unpredictable world. Turns out I can't control a damn thing, and being a town hero feels pretty damn empty when I destroyed the one person's confidence I actually need. I was so busy trying to be somebody to everyone else that I missed out on being somebody to you. You were right to want to be my priority, as I want to be yours. I didn't know that making someone a priority doesn't mean dropping everything else. It just means you have a home base together. A place for both of us to drop the stress of everything else and recharge. A place without performance reviews and expectations. A place where we can just be us."

He reached out and took my hand in his, his thumb sweeping back and forth across my knuckles. His touch lit my skin on fire and made my legs feel like the ride over had been at least a hundred miles. His eyes begged me to listen. Begged me to not write him off like I did in kindergarten.

"Can you forgive me, Addy?"

My heart was still thundering just being in his presence and hearing him pour his heart out, but the woman who'd just learned to stick up for her boundaries came to the forefront. My eyes misted over, knowing that even this amazing confession from Ace wasn't enough. They were just words, designed to win me back, whether they were true or not.

"Yes, I can forgive you."

The lines of tension on his face didn't dissipate. As if he knew I still guarded my heart. "Can you give me another chance?"

"I want to, Ace, but I don't know if I should. We're just so different. I truly don't know that we're right for each other in the long run."

He dropped his head and I fought myself to keep from reaching out and sliding my fingers into his thick, dark hair. The nurturer in me wanted to comfort him, but that wasn't my place. Not anymore.

When his head came back up, his eyes had changed. There was a fire in them that reminded me of the Ace who charged into danger and gave the town a reason to call him a hero.

"I can see why you'd think that, as I've been an ass. But I happen to know we're right for each other and I'll believe it enough for the both of us." He tugged on my hand. "Come with me to class."

I frowned at the sudden change in conversation. I'd been late, but not that late. The sun hadn't even set fully yet. "But it doesn't start for another half hour or so."

"I know I keep asking things from you, Addy, but this one is important. Maybe the most important of all." Ace looked at me like he was trying to read my soul. "Do you trust me?"

It was an easy one to answer, despite everything. "I do."

His lopsided grin turned my butterflies into molten lava. "Then come with me." He tugged again, and this time I went with him, the two of us walking side by side, holding hands.

He kept up a steady stream of conversation the whole way to the community center about what he'd been up to since we last saw each other, making me wonder if maybe I'd created a monster. He was talking more than I'd ever heard come out of his mouth before. He stopped at the door to the normal classroom, his words finally drying up and the sheepish smile returning.

I opened my mouth to ask him what was wrong, but movement caught my eye. I looked through the little window in the door to the classroom and saw two whole rows of men and two women. Half of them had AHFD T-shirts on.

"What is this?" I hissed. That wasn't our normal first aid

class audience. That was all of Ace's firefighters. His peers. His employees. Everyone who looked up to him.

He ran a hand through his hair and cringed. "I put out the word about an essential oils class and all the guys were interested. Figured you should teach it though since you know way more than I do. Although, I used the lavender you gave my mom on a mosquito bite the other day and the itch went away in seconds, which was pretty amazing. Maybe you could teach us some more tricks like that?"

My jaw did drop then. Ace Hellman, the one who'd shot down all my suggestions on the first day of the first aid class was not only now using the essential oils himself, but he invited all his peers to a class that he was just now telling me he wanted me to teach?

This guy had some balls on him.

And I fucking loved his balls.

"You're damn lucky I could teach this class in my sleep," I whispered back, snatching the flower crown off his head and putting it back on mine. I couldn't have him going in there looking like that, even if he was willing.

"I am damn lucky, my wood nymph." His gaze said he meant more with those words than face value. He leaned in and placed a kiss on my forehead. "And they'll be lucky too to have a peek at all that knowledge in here."

My eyes fluttered, wanting those lips to keep kissing their way down to my mouth. I missed the way he made me feel safe with just a simple touch. I ached to feel his arms around me again.

But Ace pulled back and swung the door open. His hand gave my lower back a little shove and I found myself walking into a classroom with twenty pairs of eyes on me. I stood at the front while Ace had a seat in the back, a proud smile on his face.

I faced the crowd and saw friendly faces. My voice may have shook there at the beginning, but before long I got into the subject and time flew by. Quite a few of the firefighters stayed for the first aid class after, saying they were fascinated and wanted to learn more. Ace joined me at the front for that class, swooping down to place a kiss on my cheek that made my face flame and the gossip mill go crazy.

At the very end of class, Ace surprised me by taking the lead and talking a few minutes about common driving mistakes, mostly due to driver distraction. That wasn't part of the curriculum I'd given him at the start of this series.

"I know driving may not seem like a first aid topic, but I've been to so many car accident scenes that I felt I should mention it." Ace stood up straight at the front of the class, all eyes on him. Not a single noise came from the audience, not even sarcastic commentary from Yedda. He was so handsome standing there, my heart fluttered, forgetting I was going to give him some time to prove that I was now his priority in life. I wanted to just forgive him now and jump his bones after class.

"Actually, losing someone I love in a car accident is one of my worst fears," he continued, voice dropping. "As many of you know, my father abandoned us kids a long time ago and that left a mark on me. Losing someone you love in the blink of an eye is a tough loss. Please don't text and drive. Put the phone away so I don't have to be the one to tell your loved ones the bad news. Be safe out there, folks."

My heart nearly cracked in two at his raw honesty. Shocked wasn't even a strong enough word to describe how I felt watching him talk about his past in front of half the town. None of his usual grandstanding and flirty comments made from behind a facade he felt he had to maintain. I stepped up next to him and put my hand on his back in support. I turned a bright smile to the crowd, noticing a few ladies dabbing at their eyes.

"Thank you so much for joining us for this series. If you liked it, make sure you tell Mayor Rip, so when I come to him with my next crazy idea for a community series, he'll say yes!"

The crowd tittered as I knew they would, putting a positive end note on the class. Everyone began to grab their things and

Ace stood off to the side, letting me receive all the thank-yous and well-wishes from people as they left.

When most had left the room, Nikki swished up to Ace and I watched the two of them out of the corner of my eye. She put a hand on his crossed arms and leaned up to place a kiss on his cheek. "Proud of you, son."

My eyes flooded with tears and I didn't hear a damn thing anyone said to me after that. I simply smiled and nodded and hoped I hadn't agreed to anything I didn't intent to do.

When the room had cleared, and Ace and I got everything cleaned up, he held his hand out. I took it, giving him a squeeze. I needed some time to think about everything that had happened here today, though I had a feeling my heart was sold on Ace already.

"May I take you and Rusty home?" he asked with a sly grin.

I knew exactly who he was talking about. A part of me that had been droopier than a week-old flower rejoiced at having the teasing back between us. I lifted my nose in the air, unable to wipe the smile from my face. "I'll have you know she got a lube job the other day and rides like a dream."

Ace snorted. "I'll believe it when I see it. And I still don't like you riding home in the dark."

He held his free hand up. "I know I can't control everything, but that doesn't mean I'm going to let the people I love be reckless when I can help."

My breath caught in my throat. For all his beautiful words tonight, he hadn't said he loved me. Certainly implied it just now though. Ace shot me a wink and tugged me out of the building without another word.

CHAPTER THIRTY-TWO

ce

I WAS A BUNDLE OF NERVES, crashing in the early morning hours after tossing and turning for far too long. Dropping Addy off last night with a simple kiss on the cheek had taken every hard-earned ounce of discipline I possessed. I'd wanted to drop to my knees and beg her to take me back, fuck my pride. I'd wanted to pull her in for the kind of kiss that would show her just how suited we were for each other. I wanted to touch her silky skin and make her gasp as she came apart with my mouth between her thighs. I wanted to pull her out of that brain of hers and remind her that we were pure fire together.

But I hadn't done any of those things. I'd dropped her off and waited until she went inside and locked her door. Then I went home and hoped like hell everything I was doing was enough to get me that second chance. The kicker was that opening myself up tonight in front of everyone had had an unexpected consequence. Sure, I thought I might puke when I first opened my mouth, but afterward, I'd felt lighter. Freer. As if life in general had unlimited possibilities. I had a feeling the weight of responsibility would never leave my shoulders entirely, but it had lightened afterward. Noticeably.

My phone dinged and I nearly jumped out of bed to get it. Probably just work, but there was a chance it was a message from Addy. Unfortunately, it was one of my brothers, probably ready to give me shit, either for my confession about our sperm donor or my efforts to get back in Addy's good graces.

Callan: The Hell phone tree is buzzing like a hornet's nest about what you said in class last night. You sure you don't want to come with me to talk to our father? It's not for two weeks. Plenty of time to wrap your head around what you want to say.

I sighed and scrubbed a hand across my eyes. Not the message I wanted to wake up to, that was for sure.

Me: I appreciate it, but I'm taking baby steps here, bro. If I ever want to speak to him, I'll reach out, but only on my timeline.

Callan: I get it. I just feel like I need some closure. Which sounds so stupid I can't believe I just said it.

Me: Cricket's been watching too much Dr. Phil and filling your head with shit.

Callan: Leave Cricket out of this.

Me: Easy there, killer. I was just teasing.

Callan: So did Addy take your sorry ass back yet?

I really hated having brothers sometimes. They honed in on your weak spots and drilled their finger in there. I gave it right back to them, but fuck. I could use a little support.

Mom's voice filtered through my head, saying that one word. Delegate.

Me: Not yet. In fact, I could use your help. I need to think of my next move here. You and the boys free for a brainstorming session Friday night?

Callan: Are you kidding me? Ethan will do cartwheels into the Tavern if he knows he can give you wooing advice. Daxon will probably give terrible advice, but at least he'll be comic relief. I'll round 'em up. Hell, maybe we can even get Blaze to join us, though I doubt it. He's holed up at Mom's place, calling Ben every two seconds to see if he's back from his work trip.

I felt like a failure as a big brother. I hadn't even been over to see Blaze yet. The one day off I'd had since he'd been back, I'd spent it getting high with Neil and licking my wounds. I'd fix that today though. In fact, I needed a quick shower and break-fast and then I'd get my day started. After delivering breakfast to Addy, I'd head on over to see how Blaze was doing.

Me: I'll ask him to come. Maybe throw on some brotherly guilt for ghosting us when he moved away.

Callan: Good luck with that. He's gotten even more stubborn since he's been gone.

As soon as the hot water heated, I took a shower and put on jeans and Addy's favorite long-sleeve T-shirt, even though I thought it was a little too tight on my biceps. Last time I wore it, Addy's gaze had drifted over my torso like I looked good enough to eat. I hopped in my truck and hightailed it to Coffee, nodding hello to pretty much everyone I passed as I waited in line.

"What can I get you?" the young barista asked in a bored voice.

"Chai tea, bran muffin, and a coffee with cream."

I heard a snicker behind me and looked over my shoulder as I handed the barista a twenty-dollar bill. Lucy stood there with a small child on an iPad next to her and another one in her arms, poking me in the shoulder.

"Morning."

Lucy was beaming like she's already gotten started on her daily caffeine intake. As a mom of young kids, she probably had. "Didn't take you for a Chai tea drinker." Then she winked.

"Go ahead and add this to the gossip that's circulating. I'm delivering breakfast to Addy." Lucy's grin got even wider.

The barista handed me my change and I moved down the line to wait on my order. Lucy also moved down the line after ordering, her youngest drilling me in the shoulder yet again as

Lucy argued with the older daughter about turning down the volume of her device. I made a cross-eyed face at the little one that made her forget about poking me and start giggling uncontrollably.

And just that quickly, a pang hit my chest, worse than I'd ever felt before. It was so acute it nearly took me to my knees right there in the line at Coffee.

I wanted that.

I wanted that with Addy.

A lazy morning at Coffee, a kid or two or three that looked just like Addy poking me in the chest. The music of a child's laughter the soundtrack of my day.

"Ace? You okay? Your order's ready." Lucy's voice interrupted me.

I jolted out of my thoughts, a sudden urgency making me jump into motion. I pulled Lucy into a hug that had her jaw dropping open. Before she could ask what had gotten into me, I let go, snatched up my order, and turned to leave.

"Thanks, Lucy. You're the best!" I nearly ran out of Coffee, taking care not to spill the drinks as I got in my truck and blazing out of town, headed straight for Addy's house.

I kicked up a cloud of dust as I came to a stop at the end of her driveway. Hopping out, I grabbed the breakfast and hoped she was home. Thank God for Hell's gossip train. I now knew Addy was teaching two yoga classes each morning due to popularity and space issues. According to my watch, she should have just gotten done with her second yoga class of the day.

After knocking on her door, I was about to run around back to find her when the door popped open. There stood the personification of sunshine, her hair piled messily on top of her head.

"Ace?" She smiled and I just stood there staring at her, awed by the way I felt like I was home. Her smile faltered. "How come you knocked?"

I blinked, remembering I held drinks and a muffin for her. "Oh, um, I brought you breakfast."

She stepped out of the house and plucked the tea from my hands, blowing on it before taking a sip. "Chai tea, just the way I like it. But I meant, why did you knock? Normally you just march into my yard unannounced."

Jesus. I was an ass of epic proportion. No wonder she wasn't sure if she wanted to give me another chance. I handed her the little white bag that held her muffin as a peace offering.

"Yeah, sorry about that. I figured knocking might be more civilized."

Addy looked in the bag, and then back at me. "I don't know. I kind of like you uncivilized."

I groaned. "Addy." She couldn't say things like that or I'd have a serious case of blue balls that no amount of cold showers would help.

"Ace." She stepped closer, her midriff tank showing lines of sweat under her breasts. Her tie-dye stretchy pants highlighted the curve of her hips. "Thank you for breakfast."

"I told you I'd keep proving that I'm ready for a real relationship with you. One where you're my priority."

"I've actually been thinking about that a lot and I've already made up my mind."

Every metabolic process in my body screeched to a halt. Oh fuck. She'd already decided? "Wait. Please. Addy, just give me more time to prove it to you. You're right not to take me at my word. Watch what I do. I don't care how long it takes. I'll prove it to you, I promise."

Addy gave me a long hard look, then turned her back on me. This couldn't be it. No way was this the end for her and me. It couldn't be. I lifted a hand to reach for her, but she bent over at the waist and deposited her cup and the bakery bag on the ground in that super bendy way of hers. Then she turned back toward me and grabbed my shirt with both hands, dragging me down so we were eye level.

"I don't need you to prove anything more than seeing how you handled yourself last night in front of the whole town. You opened up, Ace. To me, to the town, to your family." Her eyes sparkled up at me. "Nobody's perfect and I bet that won't be the last fight we have as a couple."

My heart restarted and the birds came out to chirp.

I could barely get the words out. "We're a couple, then?"

The blinding smile she gave me was all the answer I needed. My hands swooped down to grab those luscious hips, pulling her against me and laying a kiss on her that started with a heavy dose of desperation and ended with an enduring passion for this woman.

Addy tasted like forever. The little moan from the back of her throat was added to my list of favorite sounds, right there with the giggle of children. I wanted to hear it every day for the rest of my life. I pulled back eventually, stealing quick kisses as we both caught our breath.

I stared deep into her blue eyes, giving her a promise that I'd follow up with a ring and any type of wedding she wanted. But I didn't want to scare her off, not when she'd just given me another chance. I'd save the rest of those plans for later.

"I promise you I'll always put you first. I love you, Adelia Bammingford."

Her face and neck went pink and the smile was immediate. "I love you too, Ace Hellman."

And then my lips were on hers again, right where they belonged.

"DUDE, you look in worse shape than me," Blaze said from his old bed at Mom's house. His high school sports trophies were out on the table Mom used for paying bills, back before Blaze moved in. Mom must have taken the trophies out of the boxes in the attic and put them up just to make him grumble.

I shot him the middle finger, but inside I was so happy to see him again I wasn't sure what to say. He looked like hell. Deep red scratches on his face. His arm in a sling, his leg in a full-length cast. Dark circles under his eyes and the beard that had grown out rounded out the haggard look.

"I'm fabulous. Got the girl, so all is well in my world." I dragged a chair from the corner of the bedroom and had a seat next to him.

Blaze frowned. "Then why do you look like you're in pain."

I dropped his gaze. "We're taking things slow."

Blaze boomed out a laugh, only sobering when he clutched his ribs. "Oh shit, that's great. That was worth the pain in my bruised ribs."

"Shut the fuck up," I grumbled. When he had himself under control again, I turned the conversation around to push *his* buttons. "So how come you're not at Ben's yet?"

Blaze instantly frowned. "He's not back from his trip yet and the dumbass didn't leave a key under the mat like normal people. He should be back this weekend though."

I let that sit between us for a bit while he told me about his injuries. We spent the rest of the afternoon shooting the shit like old times, neither of us straying into topics too personal. I knew my brother. If I asked the hard questions right away, he'd find a way to bust out of that bed and leave Hell again, broken bones or not. I'd have to bide my time and coax his troubles out of him. Whatever they were, we'd handle it together. As a family.

But I knew it deep in my gut. Something wasn't right here. It was more than his injuries from the fall. There was more to Blaze's return to Hell that he wasn't saying yet, I'd bet my life on it.

CHAPTER THIRTY-THREE

ce

WHEN I ASKED Addy on a date that night, I'd wanted to pull out all the stops. Fancy dinner a few towns over, then ice cream while strolling Main Street here in town to show everyone I was serious about her, and then I'd drop her back home with another one of those kisses that made me lose my mind. Instead, she begged me for a quiet picnic where it was just the two of us.

God help me. I wasn't sure if I could keep my hands—and my dick—off her if we went somewhere private. I wanted to take things slow and show her I was all in on this relationship. Previously, I'd fucked her and said it was just "scratching an itch." What a fucking asshole. I could do better. Way better.

I'd taken a cold shower, come up with the five grossest things I could think of in case I needed the mental imagery to control myself, and then lectured myself in the mirror before I left my house.

Her house was lit up in warm light when I pulled up her driveway. I killed the engine and climbed out, pulling a bouquet of wildflowers out too. As much as Shelby was amazing with the flower crowns, I'd wanted to do this one myself. Only one lady had chased me away from her rosebushes as I'd scavenged my neighborhood for flowers. I should have just gone to Mom's house. She had every flower known to man growing in her yard, but involving my mother in my date plans just didn't sit well with me. Before I knew it, she'd be taking over and telling me what to do. That was just Nikki Hellman's way.

I knocked on her door and sucked in a deep breath. I realized I'd never really given myself anything to get excited about over the years. I'd piled on responsibilities and obligations until I forgot what giddy anticipation felt like. But I was fucking giddy right now.

The door swung open and my smile faltered.

"Ace!" Addy's father bellowed with a shit-eating grin. "Those are some beautiful flowers you got there. I suppose you're here for Addy?"

I blinked in surprise. At least he got my name right finally. "Y-yes. We have a date tonight. Did you and Jackie move in?" I began envisioning a lifetime of cold showers.

"Nah." He swung his hand through the air and I ducked back. Last time I met Neil at a door, I'd needed frozen peas on my face. "I just thought that I should have done the dad thing years ago when Addy went on dates. It's, uh, come to my attention that I may have slacked on some parental duties over the years." He shifted suddenly, both hands coming up with index fingers points right at me. His frown was almost comical. I didn't know he knew how to frown. "You don't have any bad intentions toward my daughter, do you? You know I have a mean left hook."

I schooled my face into a serious expression even though I'd be laughing about this later. I could see Addy behind her dad, rolling her eyes as she grabbed a purse that she slung across her body.

"Definitely not, sir. I'm in love with the woman."

Neil's face split into a grin and he pulled me into a back-slapping hug, nearly crushing the flowers that I rescued at the last second. "Ahh, I knew you were one of the good ones." He let me go and slid out the door around me. "I'll get out of your way. Got a date of my own." He waggled his eyebrows and took off walking down the driveway.

When I turned back to the door, Addy stood there looking sheepish. "Sorry. He insisted. Ever since we made up, they've been trying to be there for me, even if they're a few years—or decades—too late. It's kind of sweet."

I held out the flowers to her, which she took and dug her nose into. "I think it is too. But is he walking all the way to the campground? I could give him a ride."

Addy waved me into the house as she went in search of a vase. "No, he parked the RV down the road. Said he didn't want it to be an eyesore on my property."

I watched her moving about her small place, her long hair as wild and crazy as it always was, several small braids and even a peacock feather peeking out as she moved back and forth. I loved how she almost always wore skirts, the temptation to slide my hand up her leg and find out what she was wearing underneath turning my brain inside out. She was fucking hot and I couldn't believe I'd ever thought she was annoying.

Shit. I had to adjust my zipper. Mental image number one: that burn Joe got two years ago that got infected. By the time Addy was done with the flowers, I'd gotten myself under control. And by the time we parked at the lookout, the crashing ocean waves our backdrop for our date, I'd had to move on to mental image number two. Addy's hand innocently resting on my thigh on the drive over had caused a situation.

"Salad for you, with extra microgreens, but no kale. Roasted chicken and sautéed veggies for me."

"Wow. You on a diet or something?" Addy smirked.

"Nah. Just figured I'd follow your lead and try to eat something a little more nutrient dense." I opened the container and couldn't meet her gaze. "Just ignore the side of french fries."

Addy threw her head back and laughed. I shook my head at being such a dumbass. Ethan had been right. First dates sucked compared to the second, third, and hopefully our hundredth. Why I'd ever been one-date Ace was a mystery to me.

"I think I'm going to try to get my nickname around town changed to one-woman Ace," I said absentmindedly when we were done eating. I tossed the carton on my dash, patting myself on the back for leaving a few of the fries behind instead of inhaling them all.

Addy crawled across the truck to squeeze in front of me and sit on my lap, her legs draped across the center console. I wrapped my arms around her and leaned in to kiss her when a loud bang made us both jump. A single, all-white seagull stared us both down from the other side of the windshield. Then he banged his beak against the glass again, a maniacal gleam in his beady eyes.

"Holy crap! I've heard how aggressive the seagulls are, but I've never seen one in action." Addy shifted on my lap and I groaned. Seagull or not, she couldn't shift like that or I'd have to call up mental image number three.

The seagull pecked again, harder this time and Addy squealed. She leaned over and picked up one of the fries. The bird's eyes tracked her as she moved it left and right along the windshield. He pecked again and Addy screamed and dropped it with a fit of nervous laughter.

"Aggressive little fuckers. Let's put the seagull out of his misery and get back to our date. On three, I want you to hit the window button and I'll throw it out. Then you immediately hit the button to roll it back up."

Addy nodded, practically vibrating with excitement. "This is all because of those fries. If you ate food that actually nourished you, he wouldn't bother us, you know."

I gave her a look that just made her shrug her shoulders. I

hated when she was right. Her fingers rested on the proper buttons and I yelled three.

The second the glass was down enough, I threw the food as far as I could. Thank God I had quick reflexes because the seagull was already too close for comfort when I made my toss. He followed the food like I hoped he would, and Addy got the window back up. We both watched as he devoured it and then took flight with one last fry in his beak.

"Dang, those things are much bigger up close," Addy sighed.

Fucking seagull was trying to highjack my date, but I had more tricks up my sleeve to woo my woman. I reached down to the floorboard and held up an amber bottle I'd stashed there. "An after-dinner digestive, madam?"

Addy did a double take. "You bought one of my tinctures?"

I nodded. "Damn right I did. Some of those guys at the station need all the digestive help they can get. They stink up the place, but this has been helping." And it was true. I'd gotten them all hooked on it and their wives had even thanked me.

Addy's face practically melted. Well, shit. I hadn't meant to make her cry on our date.

"You bought my tinctures?" she asked again, voice softer.

I shook my head and leaned over to cup her face. "Why is that so hard to believe? You're the smartest person I know with all this plant stuff. Every home in America should have a bottle. You're amazing and I'm so sorry I gave you shit about it before."

She leaned her head into my palm, her eyes gazing up at me with love and trust and affection. I made a vow to myself to always be the man she needed so she'd never lose that look.

"I love you, you know," she whispered.

"I love you too." I kissed the tip of her nose. "Come on. I brought blankets so we can lie in the back and stare at the moon." I paused. "And recharge our...something?"

Addy grinned. "Chakras."

"Yeah, that's what I meant."

It wasn't until we were snuggled in the back bed of my truck, a mountain of blankets under and over us, that I remembered the question I wanted to ask her.

"Any chance you know how a cloudy white rock got in the pocket of my turnout jacket?"

With my arm around her while she cuddled up to my side, Addy tilted her head to look up at me. "Um, that was me."

I kissed her forehead. "I figured. Mind telling me what it's for?"

Addy's fingers stroked up and down my chest, slowly turning my overactive brain off and turning my body on. "It's a moonstone. It provides protection, awareness, and focus. I figured you could use all three with your dangerous job."

Well, fuck. Now I could barely breathe. That might be one of the nicest things someone had ever done for me. "When did you do that?"

"When I was there for the photoshoot. I normally keep that crystal in my purse, but I snuck inside while you were washing the oil off your chest. Joe had to help me since I didn't know which jacket was yours."

That little shit hadn't said a damn thing to me. Joe, that is, not Addy. I rolled her to her back and held myself over her. I could see the moon reflecting in her eyes. I could also see a hesitation there, as if she wondered if I'd be mad over her interfering with her crystals. I winced, berating myself for being such a jerk all these years about her oil, tinctures, and crystals.

"No one has ever done something that nice for me," I whispered. The tension left her eyes. I lowered my head and pressed my lips to hers, hoping somehow the physical touch would give her a glimpse of just how much I loved her. Her full bottom lip was like a siren, calling me to graze my teeth across it and then soothe it with my lips. Addy made that sound in the back of her throat and lust surged through me so strongly, I forgot about my list of five mental images. I couldn't remember a damn one of them.

Addy hitched her knee up and rested her leg across my hips.

The heat of her core pressed against me and I knew it was a lost cause. Whose fucking ridiculous idea was it to take things slow? Sounded like some shit from Ethan's mouth. I pushed all thoughts of slowing down—and my brothers—from my brain and slid my hand up her thigh, over her hip, and grabbed on to her ass.

"Addy?" I whispered in between kisses. Her hands tightened in my hair.

"Don't you dare say we have to take things slow," she gasped against my lips.

"Fuck no." I pulled back and saw her eyelids drooping, her mouth wet from my kisses. "I was going to ask if you could do that thing with your boobs and your mouth and my cock."

Addy grinned. "Later, for sure. Right now, I want to feel you inside me."

"Yes, ma'am."

Somehow with the bed of my truck digging into every single bone I possessed, a mountain of blankets, and more clothing than I ever wanted to wear in Addy's presence again, I got my jeans shoved down far enough to fulfill her request. I slid my hand under her skirt and bundled the material up by her waist. Addy reached down and shifted the sliver of purple underwear to the side and let her legs fall to the sides, opening herself to me without hesitation. I was really fucking glad we weren't fighting any longer. This was way better than being enemies.

I wasted no time, notching myself at her dripping opening, the heat of her enveloping my cock one glorious inch at a time as I slowly slid home.

"Fuck, Addy. I swear next time I'll get all our clothes off first. I just need to be right here." I didn't let go of her hips until I was all the way inside, a shiver wracking my spine at the pleasure that rolled through me.

"Wait. Ace." Addy lifted her head. "Condom."

I stilled, not feeling any of the panic I thought I would. "Do you want me to wear one? Or are you just thinking I'll freak out?

Because I gotta be honest with you, Addy. I really want to see you pregnant with our baby. I want to see your boobs grow, your belly expand and know that I was the one who knocked you up."

"Ace!" Addy's jaw dropped but there was a smile in there too.

"What? It's true." I pulled out just a bit and thrust back inside, too overwhelmed with her scent all around me to stay still. Even during a conversation about making babies.

"Well, it's not the right time of the month for that," Addy huffed.

I put my hands down on the bed of the truck and pulled almost all the way out and thrust back in slowly, watching my cock disappear inside her body until my balls slapped against her ass. Fucking hell. I'd almost lost this. Almost lost this woman who turned me inside out.

Addy moaned and pulled her knees up higher. "You're right. Fuck the condom."

"That's my girl." I cupped her breast, wishing I'd taken the time to undress her properly. There'd be time for that later. Right now, I wanted to see her howl at the moon while I sent her over the edge.

I slid that hand down her torso, my hips picking up speed the more noise Addy made. My right leg shook like a damn rookie. Fuck, if I didn't get her where she needed to be, I was going to end this far too early. What the hell was mental image number five?

I found her clit, my thumb twitching out a rhythm that matched my thrusts. The blush on Addy's cheeks spread down her neck and into the tank top she still wore. Her hand tightened on my neck and then she was rolling her head back, her face pitched to the night sky.

"Ace..." she keened. I felt her tighten around my length, the pulses fluttering rapidly like the vein in her neck. I only got two more unsteady thrusts before I was spilling myself inside of her, making a mental picture of her coming undone under the moonlight. Pleasure exploded up and down my body, but all I focused on was Addy, the woman fate had brought me decades ago. The only girl who saw a sad six-year-old boy and gifted him with her precious flowers. The only woman who saw all the way through my grumpy act to the heavy baggage and helped me carry the load.

As my forehead slumped down to hers and our panting breath mingled, I envisioned a couple thousand nights just like this one, outside making love to Addy under the full moon. I was one lucky motherfucker.

EPILOGUE

*A*ddy

IT WAS our six-month anniversary from the day we got back together. Not that I was counting, or anything. It was just that it had been the best six months of my life. Ace and I had settled into a steady relationship that supported us both while also allowing us the freedom to chase after what we wanted beyond our relationship. My tincture business ramped up every single month. I'd had to hire on a high school student part-time to help me make my batches, label the bottles, and ship everything out.

Ace was thriving at the fire station. He'd learned the ropes of the new job, while also delegating what wasn't absolutely necessary that he get done himself. His family had also really stepped up to make sure Ace wasn't bearing the brunt of all the family drama, and boy, was there a lot of that since Blaze returned to Hell. Ace had dropped the local hero act and just started being open and real with everyone. The result was that everyone who'd thought highly of him simply for his good looks and bravado now loved him for being an absolute gem of a human being.

Mayor Rip better watch out or Ace could easily boot him from behind that big desk at town hall. Not that Ace wanted to be mayor. He was cut out to help people in their darkest time of need.

That's exactly what he'd been for me. Hell, that's what we'd been for each other. We both had our emotional wounds that needed healing and none of my tinctures or salves was a better balm than each other.

No matter how crazy things got, I always made time for my two morning yoga classes. The daily practice was as much for my clients as it was for me. Familiar faces were already beginning to roll out their mats and mill about my forest before class started. Forest bathing was catching on around town.

It had taken quite a bit of meditation to sort it out, but I'd finally accepted that I was weird and I didn't care who knew it. I let my tie-dye hippie flag fly and found that I attracted those who also had a bit of a hidden hippie flag. Once I was truly able to be wholly myself, I found my tribe and hadn't felt lonely since.

Ace walked out the back of our house—he'd moved in about a month after we got back together, saying he couldn't stand me living alone—and kissed me on the cheek as he walked by. His mat was under his arm and he looked like he just rolled out of bed which I knew he had. His hair was adorably smashed to one side, but I couldn't seem to take my eyes off of him. He unfurled his mat and began to do some warmup stretches. He'd just come off a long shift and would be stiffer than normal. Over the last six months he'd remarkably improved his flexibility. At first Ace could barely touch his toes, a fact that had alarmed me and irritated him. He'd taken yoga on like a challenge, getting most of his crew to also take the class once he started to see the benefits in less injuries on the job.

Ace's muscles flexed against his AHFD T-shirt as he stretched his arms. Then he lifted his hands up to the sky and I got a peek of tan skin below the hem of his shirt and a little dark trail of hair I'd traced with my tongue last night when he got home and snuck into bed with me. Heat bloomed on my cheeks just thinking about what came after.

"Are you ogling my son, Yedda, honey?" Nikki's loud voice pulled me out of my daydream about what I was going to do to Ace the second all these people got off my property.

Yedda had set up her mat right behind Ace, her mat barely a foot away from the edge of his. Ace swiveled his head and shot Yedda a wink, which did not help the situation. One did not give Yedda encouragement. She had more than enough already.

"You bet your ath, I am!" Yedda cracked a smile that showed every single inch of her gums sans dentures.

Nikki patted her hair, neatly pulled back in a ponytail that was remarkable subdued for her. "I do make 'em handsome, don't I?"

"You were the prettieth pageant queen Auburn Hill hath ever theen!" Nikki practically glowed under the praise from Yedda.

A loud belch cut the air, cutting off any further discussion of beauty queens or handsome sons. All heads swiveled in Lenny's direction. He seemed unperturbed by the bodily eruption, but one of the young moms on the mat next to him gave him the stink eye before scooting her mat a few inches away. As per usual, this class was already getting away from me and we hadn't even started yet.

"Believe me, I've heard worse in a yoga class," I said dryly. "Bodies produce all kinds of sounds when they get bendy. All perfectly natural." But I swore to the goddess, if Lenny let out a fart, I was going to sprinkle nuts under his mat next time and let the squirrels dole out my revenge.

I looked out at the rest of the class all standing on their mats and ready for class to begin. Every single one of Ace's brothers were here today—even Blaze who could still only do half the poses—along with my parents in the back, and some of Ace's firefighter buddies. A sprinkling of other townsfolk and I had myself a packed class.

"Let's put palms together at heart center and welcome the day," I began.

The rest of class went relatively smoothly, with only one more burp from Lenny and a little whoop from Yedda when we did a forward fold. She pretended to fall and caught herself with her hands squarely on Ace's ass, but he'd taken it well, helping her back to her feet. And her own mat, which Nikki had kicked back a few inches while Yedda was busy squeezing my boyfriend's backside. Nikki had muttered something about a safety violation and it made me smile seeing how alike she and her son were. All in all, a success.

"Bowing to you, thank you for being present with me today. Namaste." I dipped my head and paused to silently thank the goddess for the privilege of leading these people through their yoga practice.

When I lifted my head to instruct everyone to open their eyes and get up slowly, all eyes were already trained on me with giddy anticipation. Confusion had me frowning. And then movement to my left had me swinging my head to see Ace standing next to my mat.

"Wha—?"

Ace reached out a hand and pulled me to my feet. Everyone else in my peripheral vision stayed seated, a remarkable task when normally they darted around like drunk goats as soon as class ended.

"Addy," Ace said, looking all kinds of sweaty and shy, which was so not like him. Sure, he'd changed quite a bit over the last six months, but he still resorted to being a grump as a default personality. Just that now he felt comfortable being grumpy in front of everyone, not just me or his brothers.

"What are you—?"

My words fizzled and so did my brain when Ace didn't say a damn thing but lowered onto one knee right there in the dirt. The females all oohed in the background and then sound went fuzzy as I realized what was happening.

"I made up my mind a long time ago never to trust anyone ever again. My father had ruined love for me, showing me it wasn't to be trusted. And then the universe brought me you, Adelia Bammingford. You, with the wild blonde curls and the flower crown and the patience of a saint. I wasn't ready to accept what you had to offer me back when we were six years old. But thank the goddess, the universe brought you back to me. You gave me a second chance and now I see what you've been trying to show me all along. Life absolutely can be trusted and it can be beautiful. But nothing is more beautiful than this life with you by my side."

My eyes filled with tears before the first sentence was over. They spilled over now, even as I smiled back at Ace. The man was so brave, wearing his heart on his sleeve in front of his family, friends, and peers.

He squeezed my hand and pulled a ring from his pocket. He held it up to me, but with the tears I had going on I couldn't even see the thing. "This ring is a rose quartz, surrounded by the durability of diamonds and the preciousness of gold. Rose quartz is a symbol of love and acceptance. It brings the wearer comfort and joy, soothing all heartache, which is what I strive to be for you. I want to be your rose quartz for the rest of our lives. Will you marry me, Addy?"

I couldn't even speak. I just nodded yes with every fiber of my being. Ace jumped to his bare feet to put the ring on my finger with a smile that could have lit a forest fire. Everyone watching clapped and cheered, along with a few lewd comments from some of my soon-to-be brothers-in-law that made me grin. Ace picked me up and spun me around, my hair flying out in an arc, the tops of the pine trees spinning into a green daze.

"I fucking love you," he growled as he slowly slid me down his body to put me back on my feet.

"I love you too." I went up on my tiptoes and kissed him, earning more hoots and hollers, mostly from Yedda. Ace dipped his tongue in, demanding entrance and taking the kiss in a wildly inappropriate direction in front of half the town, but if he didn't care, I didn't care either. Not when my heart was exploding. Holy shiitake mushrooms, I was engaged. We were getting married.

"I can't believe you stole the show when I had a surprise for you," I said breathlessly when he finally quit nibbling on my lips.

"Surprise?"

I almost forgot about it in all the excitement. I had to push his arms off me, which made him growl. Under a blanket right by my mat I'd hidden his six-month anniversary surprise. Compared to the gorgeous ring on my finger, it paled in comparison. I bent to fling off the mat, standing back up and presenting him with one of my handmade flower crowns. This one was more greenery than flowers with a male recipient in mind. I'd learned my lesson the hard way in kindergarten.

I shot Ace a wink. "I made you a flower crown. It's no proposal, but—"

Ace shut me up with another kiss. "I fucking love it." He took the crown from my hands and placed it on his head, looking like Julius Caesar himself. "Now how quickly can we get these assholes off our property so I can fuck you right here in nature? I love the yogasms, but I need an Addy-gasm."

My mouth gaped open. "Shh! Your mother is over there."

But Ace wasn't joking. He turned to the crowd and used his Captain Hellman voice. "Everybody out! Party's over!"

I buried my burning face in his chest. Most everyone laughed and quickly left, but our family came up to congratulate us first.

Meadow ran over and squealed in my ear. "Told you good dick was everything!"

I shushed her, trying to pull her farther away from everyone so her inappropriate comments were muffled. "Jeez, Meadow."

She grinned impishly and snatched my hand to gaze at the ring.

"Welcome to the family, my dear. I always wanted a daughter." Nikki's eyes were filled with tears. She hugged me so hard I thought I might have a few broken ribs. When she released me, she threaded her arm through my free one and clung on.

"Never thought I'd see the day, bro." Blaze clapped Ace on the shoulder and gave me a simple head nod that was so Blaze it made me smile. He wasn't one for hugs and affection, but his nods and expressions spoke volumes.

"Well, Antonio, you've done me proud. That was an incredible speech you gave there." Dad hugged Ace and then me, kissing me on the cheek with misty eyes. "You're still my little girl though. Don't think this Abraham character changes things."

Tears clogged my throat. Our relationship had gotten so much better since I'd been honest with them about how I felt. "It's Ace, Dad."

"Sure, sure." Dad was already checking his pockets for his stash.

"You're going to make a beautiful bride, honey." Mom kept swiping at her cheeks, a blubbering mess.

"Oh! We get to plan a wedding, Jackie!" Nikki squealed in my ear, finally letting me go and latching on to Mom instead. The two mothers walked away, probably making plans Ace and I would have to veto.

"Eloping sounds pretty good. What do you think, wood nymph?" Ace muttered.

I giggled, but then got clobbered by a hug from Ethan that ripped me away from Ace.

"I have a sister!" he yelled. Then he lifted me up and twirled me around, just like Ace.

"Jesus, E. You gonna braid her hair and trade nail polish?" Blaze asked, always deadly with his deadpan humor.

Ethan put me down to glare at his brothers. Funny how you fall in love with a man and somehow get a whole new family in the process. These boys had welcomed me into their fold the last six months. I could barely remember a time when I'd felt lonely.

"I guess this means you called dibs, huh, brother?" Ethan asked Ace slyly.

"Dibs?" the word tasted like acid in my mouth.

Ace pulled me back to his side and gave his younger brothers a dirty look. "It sounds bad, but I promise we only call dibs to prevent fights. It's not meant to be derogatory, I swear."

"Mhm." I wasn't totally convinced.

"I tried telling them..." Callan agreed with me.

"Dude, shut the fuck up," Daxon barked. Ethan tilted his head back and howled with laughter. Ace just punched him in the arm.

I found myself grinning from ear to ear watching their antics, feeling like I could burst with all the joy I felt.

Ace pointed to the driveway. "Now get the hell off our property so Addy and I can celebrate our engagement properly."

More hoots and hollers and a face as red as a tomato later, we were finally alone. Ace slid his arms around my waist and I fell into his chest, right where I belonged. Who would have guessed that the grumpy boy and the hippie girl would be getting married...and actually happy about it?

STAY TUNED for details about Blaze's book, Bro Code Hell, set to release soon!! Join my mailing list here to be the first to know about new releases...

ACKNOWLEDGMENTS

Thank you so much for reading Grumpy As Hell!

Special thanks to Jennifer Olson for the incredible Cover Design and for the hours cover model searching that were so incredibly tedious. Thank you to Judy Zweifel for triple checking this manuscript and making it shine as usual.

To my Rays of Sunshine: you give me life. <3

ABOUT THE AUTHOR

Marika Ray is a USA Today bestselling author, writing small town RomCom to make your heart explode and bring a smile to your face. All her books come with a money-back guarantee that you'll laugh at least once with every book.

Marika spends her time behind a computer crafting stories, walking the beaches of southern California, and making healthy food for her kids and husband whether they like it or not. Prior to writing novels, Marika held various jobs in the finance industry, with private start-up companies, and then in health & fitness. Cats may have nine lives, but Marika believes everyone should have nine careers to keep things spicy.

If you'd like to know more about Marika or the other novels she's currently writing, please find her in her private Reader Group.

If you want to take your stalking to the next level, here are other legal-ish places you can find Marika:

Join her Newsletter -
http://bit.ly/MarikaRayNews

Amazon - https://www.amazon.com/author/marikaray

Goodreads - https://www.goodreads.com/author/show/16856659.Marika_Ray

Bookbub - https://www.bookbub.com/authors/marika-ray

TikTok - https://vm.tiktok.com/ZMJvnQ2Cv

ALSO BY MARIKA RAY

Made in the USA
Middletown, DE
29 November 2022

16455682R00156